To Do Something Beautiful

Rohini

Sheba Feminist Publishers

ACKNOWLEDGEMENTS

Sheba would like to thank Bernadette Halpin and Kasha Dalal for their voluntary editorial help.

First published in 1990 by Sheba Feminist Publishers, 10a Bradbury Street, London N16 8JN.

Typeset by Russell Press, Nottingham, England

Printed and bound by Cox & Wyman, Reading, England

British Library Cataloguing in Publication Data
Rohini
    To do something beautiful
    I. Title
    823 [F]

    ISBN 0-907179-50-9

PREFACE

I know it is not usual for a novel to have a preface, so perhaps I should begin by explaining why I think one is needed.

Anyone who writes a novel presupposes a good deal of background knowledge on the part of its readers — historical, political, geographical, and cultural. To put all this background in would mean inserting passages which sound as if they come out of a conducted tour, or else extensive footnotes — neither of which is very appropriate. On the other hand, lack of background knowledge can be a real barrier to comprehension for readers from another part of the world: words are more easily translated than daily experience. The only way to overcome this communication gap is for us to find out more about one another — which requires imagination, but also information. This preface is an attempt to fill in some of the essential background for readers who are not familiar with Bombay, or India. (Those who are, need not read any further.)

To begin with, Bombay — at least in the opinion of most of us who live there, even if, like me, we migrated there as adults — is different from any other place in India. The most industrial and only really cosmopolitan city in the country, its inhabitants come from all regions, religions and communities. Despite the efforts of the Shiv Sena (a Maharashtrian chauvinistic organisation) no single community is dominant; and while it would not be true to say that communal harmony reigns, there is less communal tension and rioting than in most other parts of India. 'Bombay Hindi', a kind of lingua franca which is somewhat different from pure Hindi, has evolved to enable people with many different mother tongues to communicate with one another. People from different communities live and work together, but some barriers remain. Food, for example: what you may or may not eat is strongly governed by religion, and this may inhibit some from sharing food with people of other castes or communities.

Another consequence of the industrial culture of Bombay is that many women work outside the home, and there is a relatively high degree of freedom for women. Under the Factories Act, facilities provided for women workers include workplace crèches wherever more than thirty women are employed, but this law is not usually implemented unless the union fights for it. Many employers have responded to the necessity to provide facilities for women by ceasing to recruit women into the large-scale sector of industry, so that women are increasingly being forced into the small-scale and informal sectors which are not regulated by the Factories Act and where they therefore have virtually no rights and are often subjected to sexual harassment. Many work as domestic servants; almost all middle-class households and a few working-class households employ part-time servants to do the washing and cleaning. Cooking and childcare are more usually done by women of the family, although sometimes servants are employed for these jobs as well. Many women work as domestics for several households in order to earn enough, since the work is very poorly paid. Live-in servants are less commonly found.

Terms indicating family relationships are not necessarily used only for actual relatives. The term for an older relative may be used to indicate respect even if the person addressed is not actually older. In most families in India, relationships are still strongly patriarchal. Some communities practice menstrual taboos, and arranged marriages are still the norm. Child marriage is illegal, but continues to take place; likewise the giving and taking of dowry was outlawed by the Prohibition of Dowry Act 1961, but the practice is spreading rather than declining. Polygamy is legal only among Muslims but a report in 1975 revealed that it is practised to an equal degree among Hindus. Owing to the government's population policy, contraception and abortion are available free of cost; the Medical Termination of Pregnancy Act 1971 provides for single mothers to have abortions and for married women to terminate pregnancies without the consent of their husbands.

The climate in Bombay is hot and very humid. There are three seasons: a very hot summer which begins in March and continues until around the second week of June; then the monsoon, with heavy rains which tail off in September; after the monsoon it briefly gets hot but then cools off for the winter in November. It never gets really cold. A heavy monsoon causes a great deal of inconvenience, yet it is welcomed because water shortages are common, especially during the summer. Only a few favoured parts of the city get running water for twenty-four hours a day, while people in other areas have to collect and store water for use during the day. If the previous monsoon has been a bad one in the lake area, from where the city gets its water supply, the cuts may be severe — for instance, thousands of households may get only fifteen minutes of running water per day, and slum households may have to fetch water from considerable distances.

Residential accommodation in Bombay is in short supply, and consequently property prices have rocketed. More than 60 per cent of the city's population lives on the streets or in bastis consisting of unauthorised structures built of anything from brick and asbestos to plastic sheets and coconut leaves. These have no sanitation apart from open drains which sometimes get blocked and overflow, especially during the monsoon. There may be public toilets near by; if not, residents have to find an open place to serve as a toilet. Each basti has a few public water taps which are shared by a large number of families. Many of these shanty towns are controlled by 'slum lords' who have their own lumpen gangs and have to be paid large sums of money for the 'right' to build huts on the land. But these structures remain illegal, and families may lose everything they possess when municipal squads come and demolish the slums because the land is wanted for some other purpose. Other working-class families live in chawls — one to four-storey tenement buildings where the separate apartments (usually one-roomed) open on to a common corridor. In old chawls there are shared toilets, but most new chawls have toilets in each apartment. The rest of the residential accommodation consists mostly of blocks of flats which increasingly are replacing the old bungalows. Some of them are very luxurious, in sharp contrast to the bastis which may be situated alongside.

Each household is entitled to a ration card (although not all succeed in getting one) with which they can buy rice, sugar, wheat, kerosene and cooking oil at controlled prices from their local ration shop. There are often shortages or delays in the delivery of rations and, almost always, long queues waiting to get them.

The overcrowding in the city is reflected in the schools; except for a few very expensive ones, these often have sixty to seventy children in a class and run two shifts a day, morning and afternoon. It is even more evident in the public transport system, which consists of buses and local trains. Travelling by these can be a nightmare, especially during peak hours, and the whole system breaks down completely at least once every monsoon due to flooding. Many companies run their own bus fleets to bring employees to work from several fixed points and take them back after work — this is popularly known as 'point-to-point transport'. Others run between the workplace and one or two points, usually stations.

The workforce of Bombay is polarised between the highly unionised workers in large-scale industry and the largely unorganised workers in the small-scale and informal sectors. There are few craft or industrial unions (except in textiles); most trade unions fall into one of these categories: (1) independent or employees' unions, run entirely by the workers themselves — these vary from being extremely militant to being 'chamcha' unions controlled by management; (2) units affiliated to central unions which are linked to political parties or to professional unions run by local leaders — here factory-level activists are usually dominated by the outside leadership; and (3) an intermediate type: employees' unions which have as an office-bearer (usually president) a leader of a central or professional union — these vary from being basically independent to being fairly dependent on the outside leader for negotiations with management and major decisions. Agreements are generally signed for a period of three years, and negotiations, on average, go on for twelve months, sometimes for much longer. However, wages do rise between settlements because of Dearness Allowance (D.A.) which is linked to the Consumer Price Index and constitutes the largest component in many Bombay wage settlements. There are different types of D.A. schemes, some of which are much more effective than others in off-setting price increases.

There is virtually no social security for most of the population, and no unemployment benefit at all. The Employees' State Insurance Scheme (E.S.I.S.) provides for sickness and maternity benefits for low-paid workers and their families and is financed by contributions from workers, employers and the government. However, E.S.I.S. hospitals and clinics frequently lack the necessary medicines and equipment, so that workers may be forced to get private medical treatment. Better-paid workforces usually negotiate their own medical and maternity benefit schemes with the companies which employ them.

What more is there to say about Bombay? If you pay it a short visit, your dominant impressions are likely to be of crowds, dirt, colour, and a desperate struggle for just about everything. But those who live there for any length of time generally find it difficult to think of settling down anywhere else in the world, and this is largely due to the warmth and vitality of the people living in it. I hope at least some sense of this comes across here.

This book is dedicated to all the women with whom I have worked.

Rohini, Bombay 1990.

CHAPTER 1

Free at last! Renu stood on the balcony gazing out vacantly and feeling that all life, all energy, all hope had been drained out of her. The large eyes which dominated her face were half hidden by heavy lids which she didn't have the will to prevent from drooping. The profusion of stray hairs escaping from a thin plait hanging down her back suggested a lack of care for appearance which was unusual in a girl of sixteen, an impression which was confirmed by the crumpled state of her blouse and ankle-length skirt.

Less than two weeks of this drudgery, and already she felt as if she couldn't bear another day. When her cousin had come and told them about this job as a full-time maidservant — with a good family, all meals provided, enough pay to be able to save something, and Sunday evenings free — they had received the news with such joy, such gratitude, that it would have been impossible for her to refuse. For some time it had been getting more and more difficult to feed and clothe everyone with their meagre income, and pressure had been building up on Renu, as the eldest, to get married and relieve them of a mouth to feed. However, when her parents began to make enquiries, they found to their dismay that all the prospective in-laws were demanding a dowry amounting to several thousands of rupees. When had all this started? At the time they themselves got married, it had not been the custom in their caste to give or take dowry. The marriage expenses had been shared between the two families and didn't come to more than a thousand rupees. What were they to do now? The only thing was to send Renu out to work — she could support herself and save up her dowry at the same time.

Renu was not at all thrilled by this prospect. At first she was able to avoid any such catastrophic change in her life by pointing out drawbacks in all the job offers which came her way, but now she knew she had no excuse for refusing. On the contrary, her brother and sisters and even her friends, once they came to know about it — showered her with envy and awe: going to Bombay, to the big city! How they wished they were in her place! And then her cousin was there, within easy reach, in case she should need any help. What was she so worried about? Renu didn't know how to account for the heaviness of heart with which she finally climbed on to the bus, hugging her small bundle of belongings as if it were her last defence against a hostile world.

She had been right, too, to dread the prospect. It was one thing to help your mother at home — even if the work was hard and boring at times, there was a comforting feeling of familiarity about everything and you could always look forward to escaping and having a good time with friends or brother and sisters. Whereas here you were at everyone's beck and call — there were twelve people altogether in this household — and you had to keep working from morning until night so that by the time you were allowed to go to bed, you were ready to cry from exhaustion and nervous strain. Even when you got those precious few hours of freedom on Sunday evening, what could you do with them? Watch the Hindi film on television, or stand on the balcony and stare out like this — that was all. There was no friend, not a single friend to listen to your complaints. A lot of good it was, having a cousin within easy reach! The only time she was free, he would have closed up his vegetable stall and gone off to enjoy himself with his friends. It was all right for him; he chatted with everyone who came to his stall, he knew everyone in the neighbourhood and everything that went on in it — that was how he had managed to find this job for Renu. Above all, he could do what he wanted, he didn't have to live in a house full of employers who were constantly telling one to do this and do that, whereas she.... Tears of bitterness filled her eyes as she thought how miserable her own life was by comparison.

Renu's employers lived on the top floor of one of the solid, old four-storey apartment blocks which were strung out monotonously as far as the eye could see along the east side of S.T. Road. The other side of the road was more varied; from the balcony she could see the shops opposite, and further north there was a basti, an industrial estate, more shops, another basti. But the furthest Renu had been was up to her cousin's vegetable stall which stood just beyond the industrial estate; most of her boring errands were confined to the nearby shops, especially the ration store where she sometimes had to stand and wait for hours in the burning sun until she got to the head of the queue.

On the next balcony a tall, rather thin woman stood, looking as tired and despondent as Renu felt. But within a few minutes came the sound of a baby's crying and she hurried inside. Renu had seen her several times before, always wearing attractive saris, had even met her once or twice on the stairs or at the shops. On those occasions she had smiled in a friendly way, but when she wasn't smiling her face looked sad. What could women like that have to feel sad about, Renu wondered? They lived in their own homes, good apartments; they had husbands who earned plenty and could support them and their children in comfort; they didn't go out to work, or if they did, had interesting jobs, not like this endless, soul-destroying drudgery. Again the tears came into her eyes. This couldn't go on, she simply wouldn't tolerate it! Already she could scarcely recognise herself as the gay, carefree girl, full of laughter and jokes, she had been only two weeks ago. A few more weeks of this and she would go insane! But what could she do? Run away home? But they would be so angry, most likely they would just beat her and send her back. Run away somewhere else? That was too dangerous — after all she was a girl, she thought bitterly, and girls don't stand a chance on their own. What then? She would catch her cousin, she thought fiercely, and force him to find a solution. He was responsible for getting her into this situation, let him find a way of making it tolerable for her. How, she couldn't imagine — but something *had* to be done — something had to be done!

CHAPTER 2

Kavita came out on to the balcony because it gave her some relief from the oppressive sense of confinement which attacked her indoors, but she saw nothing of the road, the traffic, the shops or the girl on the neighbouring balcony; her gaze remained entirely inward. It seems strange, but sometimes it is easier to concentrate on what is going on in your mind when you are out in the open. Kavita's attempt at concentration, however, was soon interrupted by a wail from the baby who should have been fast asleep, and she had to respond promptly to prevent him from waking up too soon. The baby had just quietened down and gone back to sleep when there was a knock at the door. Who could it be at this time? Kavita hoped it was not a visitor; the thought of having to entertain, to be cheerful, talkative and attentive, was too painful for words. But she had to open the door. A strange woman with a bag, short, curly hair, wearing a kurta and jeans. Not the usual sort of saleswoman, Kavita thought. If she's selling something cheap, I'll buy it and get rid of her like that. But the woman didn't offer her anything; she smiled, and suddenly she wasn't strange at all.

'Mariam! Is it really you?'

'Am I so changed?' Mariam laughed as she came in. 'You look just the same.'

The familiar voice, the laugh she loved, the manner she knew so well suddenly overwhelmed Kavita, and she couldn't understand her first reaction. 'No,' she said as she threw her arms round Mariam and kissed her, 'you haven't changed at all. It's only that you were the last person I was expecting to see. You were so determined to stay on in England when we left that I had no hope of meeting you here at all!'

They stood smiling at each other until a howl broke the silence. Mariam raised her eyebrows questioningly. 'I have another baby,' explained Kavita. 'I'd better get him.' The howls were getting louder and more desperate. Mariam followed her into the children's bedroom. Three corners of it were occupied by a cot and two beds, the fourth by a large cupboard. Beside each bed was a small desk and chair, with books on the shelves above, and the walls were covered with colourful children's paintings. The women had to pick their way through the toys which were scattered on the floor. As Kavita lifted the screaming baby and began to pacify him, Mariam glanced at the beds on which two girls of around nine and seven were still asleep, seemingly impervious to the noise.

'Is this Asha?' she asked, looking at the elder one. 'She's grown so big, I can't recognise her at all!'

'She was only a baby when you saw her,' Kavita assented. 'That,' pointing to the other little girl, 'is Shanta, and this is Sunil,' indicating the baby who had stopped crying and was surveying the stranger from the vantage point of his mother's shoulder. Mariam held out her hands to take him, but he turned his head away.

'And you?' asked Kavita. 'What about you?'

Mariam turned down the corners of her mouth a little ruefully. 'No time for babies,' she laughed. 'I was working so hard I hardly had time to sleep.'

'Tell me about it,' said Kavita. 'But first I'll get you something to drink.' She tried to put the baby down and go to the kitchen but he crawled wailing after her, and she had to carry him on her hip while she made the coffee. When she came back with it, Mariam was standing on the balcony and looking out.

'This place is very pleasant,' she remarked. 'The view is not bad and you can feel the sea breeze.'

'I know,' Kavita agreed, coming to stand beside her. She was slightly taken aback when Mariam turned round suddenly and began examining her face instead, holding it gently by the chin.

'Why are you so thin?' she asked seriously. 'And you look tired... sleepy.'

Kavita hesitated. So many people had noticed the dark rings round her eyes, and she had always lightly turned their questions away by saying, 'Isn't that usual with a baby?' But she knew that was an evasion — in fact Sunil had started sleeping through the night — and anyway, Mariam was different.

'I've been taking pills because I have trouble getting to sleep,' she started to explain slowly, then suddenly changed her mind and asked abruptly, 'You're going to stay with us, aren't you? Please?'

'I've already left all my other luggage at my aunt's place, and she's expecting me to stay there,' began Mariam a little doubtfully.

'Oh but that's so far away!' protested Kavita. 'I'll never get to see you. Please stay here, at least for some time. Your aunt can do without you, I'm sure.'

'All right,' agreed Mariam, somewhat surprised at Kavita's tone of entreaty. 'I'll tell you what: I'll go back tonight, since she's expecting me, and then I'll come here tomorrow equipped for a good long stay. But where's Ranjan? What is he doing now?'

'He teaches at the university four mornings a week. It's a good job — quite a lot of money and not much work. The rest of the time he works at home. He also runs some study circles — they discuss various theoretical texts, as well as working-class history. But he should be coming any minute now, so you can meet him yourself. You're not in a hurry to go, are you?'

'No, I'll stay for a while. Sit down and talk to me.'

'I never sit,' laughed Kavita, and sure enough, a sleepy voice called from the other room, 'Mummy, come here'. She went into the children's bedroom and emerged a few minutes later with the little girls. 'This is

Mariam,' she told them. Mariam bent down smiling to kiss them. Both girls allowed themselves to be kissed, but Shanta clung to Kavita whereas Asha immediately came to sit on Mariam's lap and talk to her. 'I won't get a chance to say anything now,' smiled Kavita, and it was true. Asha kept up a constant stream of chatter, lively and amusing, until suddenly the front door opened and Ranjan walked in.

Not even the most insensitive stranger could have missed the change in the atmosphere. Kavita tensed, Asha stopped talking, Shanta withdrew further into herself and even the baby stopped playing on the floor and crawled to his mother. Ranjan seemed to be equally tense and was visibly embarrassed by the warmth of Mariam's greeting. 'What has Kavita been telling you?' he asked, barely responding to her smile.

'She told me about the study circles and discussion groups,' replied Mariam slightly hurt. 'How are they going? And how are you?'

Ranjan relaxed and smiled more warmly. 'All right, I suppose,' he replied vaguely. 'What brings you here after so long? Holiday?'

'Ah, that's what I wanted to discuss with you. I've come back to stay, and you will have to advise me about what work I can do. I've been away for so long that I'm totally out of touch.'

Both Ranjan and Kavita were staring at her incredulously. Ranjan found his voice first. 'You must be joking! Come back to stay? What on earth made you decide to do that? I thought you had settled in England for good.'

'So did I,' Mariam shrugged. 'But I got fed up. It's so hard to accomplish anything there. You slog your guts out for years, and then suddenly everything's in ruins.'

'Aha! And you think things will be better here?' laughed Ranjan. 'I'm not so sure of that. But we'll be happy to have you join us.'

'Why don't you eat with us, Mariam?' interrupted Kavita, who had been laying the table. 'Ranjan has to go out again, we'd better eat now.' Turning to Ranjan, 'Mariam's coming to stay with us from tomorrow, so you'll have plenty of time to talk.'

Mariam hesitated a moment, glanced at her watch and gave an exclamation of dismay, 'How late it's got! No thank you Kavita, I'd better run. It'll take me over an hour to get back and my aunt made me promise to come home for dinner. I'll see you tomorrow, then.'

'Definitely?' asked Kavita anxiously as she saw Mariam to the door.

'I promise,' laughed Mariam waving goodbye. But as she started down the stairs she frowned slightly. 'Something's wrong,' she said to herself as she ran through the incidents of the past two hours in her mind. 'Something's certainly wrong. I'll have to find out what it is.'

CHAPTER 3

Looking at Sheetal Nagar from S.T. Road, you would never be able to guess at the intricate ramifications which spread out in all directions, reaching westwards almost up to the sea. At one time the shanty-town had been even bigger, but many of the construction workers who came to build the posh apartments now lining the beach had been evicted to make way for yet more high-rise buildings. The families that remained clung precariously to their unauthorised dwellings, their whole existence threatened by land prices which shot upwards in this once-remote suburb of Bombay as the city steadily expanded. They took some comfort from the fact that the municipality had recently cemented the narrow pathways and open drains between their hutments: surely this meant that they were expected to stay? But the sense of insecurity remained.

Laila's one-room hut was on a corner, and two of the rough brick walls were shared with neighbouring families. Sharing walls was an advantage in a way; without being able to share the expense and labour with the families on the other side, they would not have been able to build brick walls at all. The doorway opened on to one of the wider pathways running through the basti. Laila leaned against the rickety wooden doorpost, the large knot of hair at the back of her head seeming almost too heavy for her slight figure and small face. I wonder what all this socialism and unionism is about and whether it has anything to offer us women, she thought despondently as she watched the children playing outside. So far it had brought her nothing but trouble and worry, and she found it hard to imagine any change in the future. For the past two months even Sunday evenings, which was the only time Shaheed regularly spent with her and the children, had been swallowed up by some study circle or other. What was it all leading to? If she could at least look forward to some definite result, if she could feel that her present sacrifices were really contributing to a better future, it wouldn't be so bad. But no such goal seemed to be in sight.

Not that she had any right to complain. She had been more than lucky until now, and even then her life was a paradise compared with the lives of most women. When she had married at the age of thirteen in far-off U.P. and moved to the house of her in-laws, she had had her first glimpse of what women had to put up with. It was a large extended family of five brothers, the youngest of whom was her husband. The varying degrees of drudgery, humiliation and physical violence to which her elder sisters-in-law were subjected had made Laila dread the day when she would be grown-up enough to be treated the same way. But for the moment she was lucky. Her widowed mother-in-law, autocratic as she was towards the other women, took a fancy to Laila. Who knows, maybe the girl reminded her of her own little daughter who had died in childhood. Whatever the reason, she treated Laila with unusual indulgence. She allowed her to sleep in her own bed, and gave her the least unpleasant household tasks. In time Laila came to feel almost as much at home as she had in her parents' house. Her husband she very seldom saw, and never alone. He was much older than she was — perhaps nineteen or twenty — and didn't seem to take any interest in her. She remembered only one incident when they had even come close to talking to each other. Shaheed had come into the kitchen one day while she was helping with the cooking and asked his mother for food. She had smiled at Laila in a peculiar way and said, 'Go on child, give him some food, he is your husband after all.' In utter confusion, Laila looked at her and asked stupidly, 'What food? What shall I give him?' 'Give him whatever is cooked,' her mother-in-law replied impatiently. With trembling hands Laila served out the food and gave it to him, conscious without ever looking directly at him that he was watching her all the time with a smile on his face.

The incident reminded her that the present situation couldn't last for ever; any day she would start menstruating, her childhood would be over and she would have to become a wife in earnest. Mostly the thought filled her with panic, but mixed with the fear was more than a little curiosity. What would it be like? What was he really like? He didn't seem so very bad. She had never seen him angry or sulky; most of the time he was laughing and joking, and when he smiled at her his face always looked kind.

However, both her fear and her curiosity were to be prolonged unexpectedly, because for reasons which were never fully explained to her Shaheed suddenly went off, very far away, in search of work. It was almost a year before he returned, and his return was celebrated almost as much as a major festival. But he hadn't come to stay. He had come to take Laila back with him.

This time there could be no postponement. Laila cried almost as much at leaving her second home as she had at leaving her first. She set out on the journey with tears on her cheeks and her heart pounding with a mixture of fear and excitement. She who had never seen a train before was going to travel on one for almost two days. She who had not known anyone outside her parents' and in-laws' families was going to live among strangers, in a strange place. Most of all, she who had scarcely exchanged ten words with her husband was going to live with him, and him alone, in a new home. Her future was so much beyond her previous experience that her imagination failed even to begin to picture it. All she was left with was an intense emotional turmoil which she herself could not define.

Once the last relative who came to see them off had vanished together with the station platform, Shaheed turned his full attention to Laila, and she was astonished to find how easy it was to talk to him. He chatted with her in a totally informal way as if he had been a brother or cousin and she, in turn, soon forgot that he was her husband and described her childhood and family without reserve, laughing with him over the pranks she had got up to with her brothers and sisters. Later, he began to describe Bombay and the place where he had found a home for them. Again, the liveliness with which he spoke of everything, the amusing way in which he described his own blunders as he tried to find his way around in the strange city, added up to produce an impression not of someone remote and frightening, but of a friendly presence, open and even rather vulnerable. So that when night fell, although Laila herself couldn't sleep for a long time, she found it neither unpleasant nor strange that his head should gradually sink down onto her shoulder and rest there.

Life in Bombay was so bewilderingly different from the totally secluded life she had led so far that she remembered very little about the first few weeks and only knew that without Shaheed she would never have got through them. He had found them a small hut in a basti which seemed to house people from every conceivable religion, caste and corner of India. Their language sounded foreign, and it took her a while to figure out that what they spoke was a kind of Hindi.

This was a great discovery, because it gave her the confidence that she would be able to communicate with those around her. Occupationally, too, the slum seemed to contain all sorts. But a large number of men, like Shaheed, worked in the industrial estate nearby, and many of the women, like herself, worked at home or as domestic servants in the surrounding apartment blocks. So there were common concerns to talk about with her neighbours: high prices, shortages of water and kerosene, the malpractices of employers, and the occasional accident which for a while stirred up protests against unhealthy and dangerous working conditions. Gradually her life fell into place.

No one, looking in from outside, would have suspected that blissful happiness could lie hidden among so much dirt and poverty; yet Laila's life during those first months and years had an idyllic quality. Shaheed spent all his leisure time with her — going for walks, helping with the housework, and occasionally taking her to the local cinema. When she became pregnant he looked after her with almost feminine sensitivity, refusing to let her carry water or do any other heavy work. And when the baby arrived, he was as fascinated and delighted as she was, spending so much time with the little fellow that when he was sick or in a bad mood it was to his father that he would turn for comfort. Even the frustrations of life in the basti lost their edge because they were shared, and merely cemented the bond between them more firmly.

By the time the second baby had been born — a girl this time — they had saved up enough for Laila and the children to pay a visit to her parents. They were gone for over three months, and when they returned she found that things had changed dramatically. Far from spending all his leisure time at home, Shaheed now rarely spent more than one or two evenings a week with her, and even then he seemed preoccupied and not himself. Little Ishaq, who had missed his father badly, now clung to him fearfully when he was at home and cried intermittently all evening when he went out. Laila could think of only one explanation for the change: another woman. After a week of agony during which she cried every night after everyone else had gone to sleep, she finally plucked up the courage to ask him as he was preparing to go out one evening, 'Where are you going?'

'I have to meet someone,' he replied vaguely.

'A woman?' The question was out before she could stop herself.

Shaheed stared blankly at her for a second and then burst into a hearty laugh. 'Is that what's been worrying you all this time?' he asked, affectionately putting his arm around her. 'What an idea! No Laila, I promise you're the only woman in my life and always will be.'

Laila was enormously relieved but more baffled than ever. She was glad it was not another woman — anything was better than that — but what could it possibly be? 'Then why do you go out so much?' she insisted, although a little timidly. 'You used to be at home every evening, but now I hardly see you at all.'

Shaheed caught the plaintive note in her voice and decided it would be unwise to fob her off with some spurious excuse. He reflected a while and then began, slowly, 'Well, you see, it's like this. You know we often complain about how miserable our pay is compared with the pay in big factories, and how we have to work in such wretched conditions that most of us end up having some incurable disease or serious accident? Well, what can be done about that? We could try to form a union, but you know how difficult it is in small-scale places — workers get thrown out the moment they organise. And that's not the only problem we suffer from. Look at the conditions we have to live in — tiny overcrowded huts, no toilets, not enough water. You spend half your life waiting in queues — for water, kerosene, sugar, rice, wheat, cooking oil and I don't know what else. Things are getting worse all the time — more crowded, more expensive, more shortages — what is life going to be like for our children when they grow up? And there isn't even a trade union to fight against such things. So some of us have formed a group to discuss what can be done. Most of us are workers, but there is also someone from the university who comes to our discussions.'

'You're going to solve all those problems?' asked Laila incredulously. 'How is that possible?'

'Well of course not all at once, and not just the few of us by ourselves,' said Shaheed, slightly embarrassed. 'But,' gaining confidence, 'you musn't think that because these problems seem so huge nothing can be done about them — that they are decreed by God or something. They are caused by the capitalist system which was created by human beings, not God. Other workers have fought successfully to increase their wages and improve their working conditions; why can't we? Why can't we go even further than that? Who knows what we may be able to do if we all get together?'

Laila was not convinced, but she had no answer to Shaheed's arguments. She might have said, 'Why go chasing a dream when you could do more for our children's future by spending time with them now and helping them with their studies?' but she knew it would sound selfish. Not all children were as lucky as Ishaq and Farida; some children led unspeakably wretched lives with no likelihood of change in the foreseeable future. Somewhere in her, the thought of trying to give such children a better life struck a sympathetic chord; she might even do something about it herself, if only she knew what. That was not the problem. The problem was: what was the right thing to do? And she doubted very much that anything was to be gained by sitting in a group and discussing things. But she was too diffident to express such doubts to Shaheed who, after all, certainly knew more about the world than she did. So she quietly adapted herself to the new routine and gradually became accustomed to doing almost everything without Shaheed. She fought over every new encroachment, she fought over the loss of Sunday evenings. But she had a horror of being an unreasonable or hysterical wife, and when Shaheed replied to her protests by calm, reasoned explanations about the class struggle, which she only half understood, she had to admit defeat. She resigned herself to a monotonous, hard-working life, without any severe hardships it is true, but without anything very much to look forward to either. At times she remembered the earlier period with almost painful nostalgia, and though this was mixed with a large dose of resentment and bitterness, she could never quite bring herself to curse communism, socialism, trade unions and politics, which, it seemed, were responsible for the loss of her happiness.

CHAPTER 4

Geeta lived in a hut only a few yards away from Laila's. In size it was almost identical, but as the only doorway opened into a narrow gully almost completely filled by an open drain, she had to watch over her daughter constantly while she was little, for fear that she might fall into the dirty water. But neither this nor any of her other problems ever defeated Geeta. An attractive and cheerful sight with her round, classically symmetrical face and brightly coloured but never garish saris, she could call up a smile on the face of almost everyone she met.

When Anant started going to the study circles along with Shaheed, it made no dramatic impact on Geeta's life. She was used to expecting very little from him right from the time they got married. In fact, there had been stretches during which he did not have a steady job and she couldn't even rely on his providing for their day-to-day expenses. She had offered to find work as a domestic servant so that they would have at least a minimum income, but he advised her against it while she was pregnant, and as long as the child was small. 'Wait until she starts going to school,' he said, 'otherwise she will suffer and so will you.' It would have been different, of course, if they had been living with his parents, but Anant felt that they imposed too many restrictions on his freedom and had insisted on living separately even though conditions were much worse in Sheetal Nagar than in his family home. Geeta was not sorry about his decision; she realised that she, too, would have much more freedom in a place of their own, and this more than made up for the loss of comfort and security.

On the whole, Geeta was satisfied with her life. Anant was never violent with her, and never stopped her from doing anything she really wanted to do. There were rare, very rare occasions when he was affectionate to her at home or took her out to have a good time, but this was an unexpected bonus, not something to be counted on. Most of the time he lived his own life while she lived hers, and she found out more about what he was doing from Laila than from him. Her own activities were tied up with her home and locality; when her time was not being swallowed up in the endless struggle for survival in the slum, she took pleasure in playing with her little daughter and in her friendships with other women.

In fact one could almost say that friendship was a serious interest with her because she really tried to understand her friends: for example to work out why Laila, whose life superficially so much resembled her own, was nevertheless so different from herself. She would enquire into the past history of these women, and listen fascinated to their life stories. People had such interesting lives! For instance, there was this woman from the other slum, Patthar Basti, whom Geeta had once taken home because she had been ill at the market — Mangal, her name was. She had left her husband and children far away in Nagpur and was now living with another man. He also beat her just as her husband used to, and it was this man who had forced her to leave her two little girls behind. It made Geeta cry when Mangal described how after he had beaten her, when her whole body would be aching, she would imagine clasping her children, the comfort of their small bodies against hers. But she couldn't go back now — she was afraid her husband would kill her. How dreadful it must be to be parted from your children like that! Leaving a husband was different, he could manage on his own; and anyway, if he beat her, he didn't deserve to have her stay with him. But children. It must be heartbreaking!

Geeta often visited her after that, because Mangal told her how the women in Patthar Basti ostracised her except for an old woman called Kantabai who Geeta also had met. What Geeta could never understand was why Mangal continued to tolerate her second 'husband'. He had come in once while she was with Mangal and, well, he hadn't been rude exactly, but had made it very clear that her presence wasn't welcome. Geeta fled — she always shrank from violence. Mangal told her that she stayed with him partly because she had nowhere else to go, but also because she loved him. Loved him? This was a mystery indeed. Geeta couldn't truthfully say that she loved her husband although he never beat her. In fact she found it very hard to imagine how one could love a man at all. Children, certainly; women... that was not difficult. But a man? Especially if he wasn't your brother or someone you had known from childhood. It occurred to her that perhaps Laila loved Shaheed — yes, that was almost certainly the case. But then, Shaheed was different. He was a good man — good in every way. And when he was with children he was almost like a woman, just as gentle and tender. Ishaq used to cling to him the way other children cling to their mothers. He was someone you could talk to, make friends with; you could even assume that he felt the same way about some things as you did. And the best thing about him, what she liked most of all, was how kind he always was to Laila. So it was not difficult to understand that she might love him. But men like Mangal's — they were as remote as beings of another species. No matter how hard she tried, she would never be able to understand that kind of man, and without understanding, how could there be love?

Anant was different again. She had once gone to hear him speak at a factory gate meeting, and he sounded really good. Rather to her surprise, she found that not only could she understand everything he was saying but she also agreed with it; almost unconsciously she was nodding and thinking, yes, we must get rid of these kinds of injustices, yes, that sounds like a good way to do it. She had heard that he was clever and knew he was courageous and principled — if he believed something was right, he would do it whatever the risk to himself. You could certainly admire and respect such a man... but love? No, love presupposed a closeness which she just didn't feel. There were brief flashes sometimes when it seemed possible, but they always died out leaving him as distant as ever. It amazed her that women could be so similar and yet so different at the same time. As in Mangal's case, she could understand and share some of her feelings so well, while others left her completely baffled. That's what made friends so interesting!

CHAPTER 5

Ravindran's one-room hut in Sheetal Nagar, normally bare to the point of asceticism, was today crowded uncomfortably with borrowed chairs. Ravindran, short, sturdy and energetic, kept going to the doorway to look out for the people he was clearly expecting. Ranjan sat on one of the chairs fidgeting impatiently. Where were the other members of the study circle? Sunday was a workday for some of them, it is true, but they had fixed the meeting for eight o'clock in the evening keeping all such factors in mind. Ranjan found this irregularity and unpunctuality almost unbearably frustrating. You could never count on anyone — except Ravindran. He was a real find, someone quite exceptional. A young worker in a large electrical engineering firm, intelligent, militant, enthusiastic, you could always count on him to be foremost in any action, the first to come to any meeting. Moreover, being unmarried and having arrived on his own from Kerala, he lived alone and had no family ties to hinder his participation in any way. It was a pity there were not more like him.

Here was Shaheed, at last. A bit late, but that was not to be wondered at — Ranjan knew vaguely that he had family problems. Apart from that, he was as good as Ravindran, in some ways even better. He had an amazing ability to pick up Ranjan's arguments and reproduce them among his fellow-workers, but in a simpler, more imaginative form which instantly made sense to them. A born leader, surely. Nor did he simply accept arguments from authority, but constantly raised intelligent questions about them — often questions which Ranjan himself hadn't thought of which caught him off balance, and even, at times, embarrassed him.

When Ranjan first came to Bombay he had started several study circles: two in the university with the students and staff, and gradually, as he made the contacts, three more with groups of workers. The university circles were entirely satisfactory. Their participants instantly recognised the superiority of what Ranjan was telling them compared with the politics they were used to and some of them had taken part in. They found this freshness intellectually stimulating and voraciously read everything he recommended to them. The discussions were lively, well-attended, and soon resulted in the formation of a new university society which organised seminars, public meetings and even, once, a play. Ranjan was excited by the response. Here he was really in his element, he could communicate with the greatest of ease, and the enthusiasm with which his ideas were received encouraged him to hope that within a few years it might be possible to begin building a group along entirely different lines from anything that had been seen in India until then. Things had turned out even better than he'd hoped.

However, that sense of exhilaration was totally lacking in the workers' circles. They listened to him respectfully it is true, but their questions, when they asked any, often had nothing whatsoever to do with what he was telling them. How do you fight unions controlled by rightwing parties? How do you build a new union to replace a legally recognised one which is discredited in the eyes of the workers? How do you overcome union rivalry? How do you build working-class unity — in a factory, in an industrial area, throughout the country? Ranjan felt that not to answer these questions at all would discredit him, give them the impression that he had learned his 'lectures' by rote and that he couldn't speak about anything else. Yet when he tried to answer them, he found himself unable to get very far. Of course he knew all the stock arguments, but he was too intelligent and honest to fool himself (and it was also clear to him that he couldn't easily fool them) into believing that these arguments were in any way an adequate reply to their questions. At the same time his interest was aroused in the experience which had led to the formulation of these questions; for whenever they were raised, it was in the context of discussions as lively as any which took place in the university study circles, but of a totally different nature. So he gradually allowed these discussions, which had initially been an ad hoc addition to what he actually planned, to dominate the small meetings, and he had to admit that he learned a lot. A whole new world, unfamiliar in spite of his knowledge of working-class history, was opened up to him; much of it was not easily accommodated within the theoretical framework he was familiar with and temptingly invited fresh enquiry, fresh thought.

In all this, the initial purpose of the circles was lost; Ranjan was no longer playing a directing role, nor was anyone else, with the result that the discussions tended to repeat themselves and go round in circles. Their membership gradually dwindled, one group folded up altogether, and Ranjan decided to merge what was left of the other two. He consoled himself with the thought that what had been lost in quantity had been gained in quality, for those who remained not only took a leading part in the struggles at their various workplaces, but also showed an interest in and capacity for argument at a more abstract level which was quite rare. But the question still remained: where to go next?

Two more late-comers entered — Gopal and Anant. Gopal was a victimised worker who, after being thrown out of several small-scale engineering workshops for trying to organise the workers, had become a full-time activist in a union linked to a small left-wing political party. But unlike many others he had retained his independence, his single-minded commitment to the goal of organising the unorganised, rather than the usual fanatical attachment to one's own union and doctrinal allegiance to the party. Hence his participation in Ranjan's circle, which was shunned by the other activists of his union, and hence also his high standing among workers in the industrial estate, who commonly referred to the union he worked for as 'Gopal's union' even though he was only the local organiser and had no place in the leadership. Anant worked in the same factory as Shaheed and collaborated very closely with him. His comments during discussions revealed a sharp mind and wide experience in struggle, but he was less friendly than Shaheed, more reserved, more distant; looking at his thin face and deep-set eyes, you could never work out what he was thinking.

Ranjan thought it best to begin; the others would drift in one by one, but if he waited for all of them, there would be little time for discussion before people began to leave. Besides, although he had abandoned his very rigorous standards of punctuality, he still felt that if someone didn't arrive within half an hour of the time set for a meeting, he had no right to expect the others to wait for him. Accordingly, after greeting Anant and Gopal, he asked, 'Shall we begin? Since it's only a continuation of last time's discussion, the others won't have any trouble joining in when they come.' At the last meeting they had discussed the idea of a workers' party in the context of the Russian revolution, and had left off halfway when it got too late to continue.

'Yes, let's begin,' said Shaheed, looking at Anant and smiling. 'Anant and I have been talking over the problem between ourselves all week, and there are a lot of questions we'd like to raise.'

'Go ahead, then — you can start off the discussion today,' said Ranjan, pleased at the interest they were showing and yet slightly apprehensive.

Shaheed looked down and paused a moment to collect his thoughts. Then raising his eyes and looking straight at Ranjan he began, 'We can quite understand why the Russian revolution went wrong — you explained very clearly the circumstances which were against it. All that makes sense, and if there were a workers' revolution in India now, we can imagine the same kind of thing might happen. What we can't understand is what happened to the *party*. What went wrong with it — why didn't it remain with the workers? It struggled against repression all those years before the revolution without being wiped out — couldn't it have gone on struggling?'

Ranjan sighed inwardly. Sometimes you really felt like giving up. If it took so much effort to convince one small group of workers — and that too an exceptionally intelligent and open-minded group — how could he possibly win over enough of them to form something more solid? But Shaheed was waiting, and he had to respond. 'You must remember,' he began patiently, 'that the working-class was decimated in those years. The best, the most class-conscious workers were killed in the civil war. Thousands more went back to their villages because the factories had closed down and they would have starved in the cities. The workers were not only fewer in number, but as a social force they had become much weaker.'

'But they were still there, weren't they?' interrupted Anant with some warmth. 'However few, however weak, they were still there, and so long as they were there the party could have fought for them instead of turning against them and starting to repress them.'

'It's not true that the entire party abandoned the workers — a section did remain with them and suffered persecution, exile and death as a result.' Gopal was looking sceptical but as he said nothing Ranjan continued, 'I think we could just as well ask ourselves, why did the workers desert the section of the party which was fighting for them? Why didn't they support it more actively?'

There was a short silence and then Ravindran, who had been following every word, observed thoughtfully, 'That's what I don't understand. Why wouldn't the workers support those who were fighting for them — especially against such terrible repression? It doesn't make sense.'

Arvind, a self-employed carpenter who was Ravindran's neighbour, had come in only a few minutes earlier, but had quickly realised where the discussion was leading. 'But didn't you tell us,' he enquired, 'that almost the entire leadership of the party had earlier carried out policies which were unpopular with the workers?'

'They had to,' responded Ranjan, roused in turn. 'To give in to their wishes would have meant abandoning the revolution! The mass of workers didn't realise the consequences of what they were demanding.'

'That's the point, isn't it?' said Shaheed quietly but so intensely that everyone's attention turned to him. 'We're not denying that workers make mistakes, that they often misjudge what is best for them — *we* should know that better than anyone else. But does that mean someone else can make decisions for them? Decisions which have to be forced on them, which they feel are oppressive?'

'But what if the fate of the revolution depends on such decisions?' broke in Ranjan. 'Would it be justifiable for a leadership to knowingly let the revolution fail just because the workers are not yet politically conscious enough to take the right decisions? Wouldn't that be the height of irresponsibility?'

'There's no alternative,' replied Anant emphatically. 'It's supposed to be a workers' revolution, isn't it? At least, that's what you told us. And if it is a workers' revolution, then workers must make all the crucial decisions — in actual fact and not just in name. If they can't make the right decisions, then the revolution is already lost; someone else making the decisions on their behalf won't help. And it's surely better for the workers to be defeated with the party still on their side rather than with the party against them.'

'Wait a minute — that's really going too far!' protested Gopal. In some of the earlier discussions he had found himself at loggerheads with Ranjan, but now he was in total agreement. 'Suppose the revolution were to be lost today, and tomorrow the workers were to be ground down by the counter-revolution. Don't you think they would blame the party for not having saved them? In fact, if it can't take responsibility at such a moment, what is the point of having a party at all?'

'That's a good question,' murmured Anant, unheard by everyone except Ranjan. A few more workers had drifted in and now joined in noisily on both sides. Shaheed was trying to make his point of view heard above the din: 'We're not saying that middle-class people with more specialised knowledge can't advise the workers, suggest alternative courses of action, warn them, even criticise them. But not make decisions! Only workers can make decisions concerning their own lives! Otherwise the party is not a real workers' party and the revolution has no meaning!' And so on. Ranjan said nothing more, and as usual the argument ended inconclusively. It was difficult for his confidence to remain unshaken when a clear and simple point he was trying to make could get so completely lost, and when week after week he seemed to be getting no nearer to his goal.

Going home afterwards, Ranjan sank into one of his frequent moods of despondency. What was wrong? The group was such a good one, and yet it was getting nowhere. The longer it went on, the more frustrating it became. He had almost come to dread these meetings which he had once looked forward to so eagerly. And yet going home was something he dreaded even more. The only good thing which had happened recently was Mariam's arrival. Ranjan's relationship with Mariam had had a false start when he'd first met her in England — he had mistaken one kind of attraction for another and they had both suffered for it. But once the mistake was put right, he discovered in her an exceptional comrade; never before or since had he met anyone with whom he could work better. It had been a heavy loss to the political group they had built up together when she left to form the women's centre; in fact, looking back he could see that that was the beginning of the group's decline and ultimate dissolution. So he felt secretly pleased that the centre, too, now seemed to have collapsed, especially since it meant that he would have Mariam working with him again. Yes, maybe together they would be able to sort things out and make some headway.

CHAPTER 6

Patthar Basti was only a fifteen-minute walk northwards along S.T. Road from Sheetal Nagar; the two slums shared the same market, ration shop and even toilet ground, yet they couldn't have been more different. Sheetal Nagar was a quiet place, and in spite of a very mixed population there were seldom any fights — largely because there were no rival gangs trying to control the inhabitants. Of course, not everything was legal — there was, for example, illicit liquor-brewing — but even this was done quietly. Patthar Basti, however, was terrorised by the gang which controlled it, and a more violent place altogether. Kantabai had lived there ever since coming to Bombay. She was one of the earliest residents of the basti when it had been mainly a settlement of quarry workers. Most of her neighbours thought she was a widow, but in fact she had never been married. She started working in the quarry while she was very young because her elder brother was killed in an accident and someone had to support his wife and two small sons. Very soon they grew so economically dependent on her that they strongly opposed the idea of her getting married. Kantabai continued to work and support them, and this was fine while she was young but now her lungs were ruined and she could no longer continue working in the quarry. Her late brother's sons had now grown up and started earning and within a few years they got a new place and moved out, leaving her to fend for herself. Kantabai managed to keep alive by working as a domestic servant, but felt very bitter about what she now saw as her wasted life. She had sacrificed her chances of marriage and of having children of her own, because she loved her nephews and felt sorry for them. Not only had she treated them as her children but she actually thought of them as such; while they were with her, she never missed having a family of her own. Yet in return they had not treated her as a parent. They had taken their mother with them when they left, but hadn't so much as invited the woman who had done more for them than their mother.

Not that she would necessarily have gone with them. What Kantabai would have liked best was for them to stay with her, and if this were not possible, she would have liked them to send her some money so that she could stay in comfort where she was. Over the years she had developed a strange attachment to this unsavoury place; she knew practically everyone who lived there and everything which went on, and in her own way she was a respected figure. People came to her for help and advice, especially women and girls; she had learned something about herbs and could cure many of the ailments of those who couldn't afford the expense of going to private doctors and hadn't any faith in public hospitals; some people went so far as to say that she could calm down babies who were having convulsions. Even the slum dadas stood in awe of her, and she was one of the few women who could walk about at any time of day or night without fear of molestation.

When Kantabai really thought about it, she knew she wouldn't have gone with her brother's children if they had invited her; her identity was too tied up with Patthar Basti; outside it she would have felt lost, a nobody. Yet she felt bitter because they hadn't even asked, hadn't bothered to think how their aunt would survive after having ruined her health working for them. One visit a year and a gift at Diwali was surely not enough compensation for what she had given up — most of all she was worried about the loss of security in her old age. What would happen to her if her health worsened and she was unable to go on working at all? Who would look after her then? This was the question which troubled her whenever she was more breathless than usual. And there was no answer.

CHAPTER 7

Panic welled up in Lakshmi's throat as she stared down at the empty tin of cooking oil. She was already late. And if she went all the way to the shop, bought more oil, came back and only then started to cook, *he* would be home demanding his food well before it was ready, and she shuddered to think what the consequences would be. Cursing herself for failing to remember that she had run out of oil, she grabbed the tin and made for the nearest hut. Salma looked up in surprise when she heard the hoarse, urgent voice: 'I'm sorry, Salma-behen, can you let me have a little oil please, I forgot to get it earlier and now it's getting late.' She didn't need to go on because Salma sprung up immediately with a full sense of the seriousness of the crisis. 'Take as much as you want,' she said, offering her own tin. Lakshmi helped herself and thanked her profusely. As she was leaving Salma asked anxiously, 'Is there anything else I can give you? I've already cooked the vegetables, would you like some of that?'

'No thank you, Salma-behen, he's very fussy about his food, everything has to be cooked exactly the way he wants it, otherwise I will get into trouble. But thank you for offering, it's very kind of you,' and with a weak smile she vanished.

Poor thing, thought Salma, I give her a spoonful of oil and she thanks me as though I had saved her life! How can anyone live like that?

This was a question Lakshmi often asked herself. She had been married off to Shetty when she was quite young and *he* — Lakshmi never called her husband by his name, even in her thoughts — had lost no time in abusing her in every conceivable way. After the paralysis of her first shock had worn off, she decided she would be single for the rest of her life rather than undergo this daily torment, and ran away home. But he had followed her, and her parents had delivered her to him with no more than a mild plea that he should treat her well. This was what had really broken her. If her own parents could ignore her tears and desperation, begging and pleading, could knowingly send her to certain torture and almost certain death — then what was there left in the world to believe in any more? If they refused to help her, who could she turn to?

So she had resigned herself to a life in which one dreadful day followed another without hope or meaning. After this she never felt that she *did* anything — things simply happened to her. It soon became clear that her husband made his living by illegal means, helped by a gang of lumpens. They terrorised the other inhabitants of Patthar Basti and robbed, extorted and raped at will; but even they — even they — were afraid of Shetty. No one who ran foul of him could hope to survive. It was well known that he had murdered a man some years ago, but although there had been several witnesses not one could be found to testify against him — so great was the fear he inspired in friends and enemies alike. And this man, feared by the strongest and most violent elements in the neighbourhood, was the man Lakshmi was condemned to live with. What was the use of making plans for tomorrow when you never knew whether you would be alive to carry them out? Better to let things happen to you.

And what things happened! Shetty's 'job' though lucrative at times was not steady, and his expenses were unlimited, so he forced Lakshmi to earn as well — but not to go out to work, not to escape from her prison for a while. Whenever he wanted to indulge his associates or was in need of money he would invite them to sleep with her. But this was not to be her main job, only a side-line. The rest of the time she brought home work from one of the factories in the industrial estate while he pocketed the money and gave her only just enough to keep the household going. No paid supervisor could have driven her more relentlessly to work, work, in every moment she could spare from household tasks. There were times when Lakshmi felt she could bear it no longer, she must escape or go mad. But the memory of the beating he had given her after bringing her back the first time she ran away — a beating which had not spared any part of her helpless body and face — always deterred her. If he had killed her outright it would have been all right, but to think of having to go on living, working, after a beating like that... it was impossible. No, there was no escape from a demon like him, wherever she hid on the face of the earth he would find her, bring her back and beat her. There was no escape except one: death.

But death stubbornly refused to come. Time after time she had been on the brink of it and had somehow survived. Her first child was stillborn, probably battered to death in her womb. The second, a boy, managed to live, though weak and sickly. Then there were two miscarriages, the second of which almost killed her. As she lay in hospital watching the slow drip from the transfusion bottle into her veins she had wondered, why have they done this to me? Can't they even let me die in peace? But she hadn't died, not yet. She had lived to have a daughter who was, miraculously, beautiful and healthy and pleased all who saw her, even her father.

Through all this hell there had been no friends to help or support her. The other women, by and large, held aloof from her because of her reputation of being a prostitute and the lurid stories of what went on in her home. A few women like Salma pitied her and tried to help in small ways, but even they were prevented from doing any more by fear of Shetty.

No, if a spark of humanity remained alive in her, some grain of hope which prevented her from killing herself even while she longed for death, it came not from friends but from her children. Her son Chandran, now ten years old, had suffered with her every time she was beaten; not because his father beat him directly, which he seldom did, but because he clung to Lakshmi from the moment he felt she was in danger and so got in the way of many blows which were not intended for him. He suffered doubly because Lakshmi, inevitably hardened by years of brutality, often vented her bitterness on him, sometimes beating him unmercifully until her fury was spent, at other times abusing and insulting him in ways which, if possible, hurt him more. And yet he clung to her with stubborn devotion and his attempts to revive and restore her when she was hurt often brought on a flood of emotion which, painful though it was, somehow made her feel human again. That there was one living creature who loved her enough to stand by her and share her anguish was the only proof she had that she was something more than an object or a brute whose only value lay in its function and the money it could bring in. Despite herself, Chandran's love kept alive feelings which prevented her from becoming totally brutalised. And one of these feelings was the conviction that her death would inflict on the child a wound from which he would never recover and that nothing, not even her own suffering, could justify her abandoning him.

The little girl Sanjeevani was different. A sunny, cheerful child, at three she seemed, as yet, untouched by the horror around her which had so deeply affected Chandran. And although much younger, she was far less dependent on her mother — Lakshmi felt sure she would soon recover from the shock of losing her mother. Yet she was equally reluctant to abandon this child. Sanjeevani promised to grow up to be exceptionally good-looking. At present her father seemed to be fond of her: while he virtually ignored Chandran, neither persecuting him nor showing him any affection, he indulged and even spoilt Sanjeevani. To the extent that he was capable of expressing love at all, it was apparent only in his relationship with his little daughter. But who could tell what would happen once she grew up? She might be just as docile then, and he — Lakshmi's heart grew cold at the idea — if he was capable of prostituting his wife, mightn't he think of prostituting his daughter? Who would stop him if Lakshmi was not around? The thought of the happy child reduced to her own state of misery and degradation was more than Lakshmi could bear. No, even in death there could be no peace if she felt that one child would be shattered by it, the other destroyed by her husband. She was condemned to endure this torture, it seemed, until... until what, she couldn't say. However hard she tried, she could see no light at the end of the tunnel. Almost any suffering is tolerable if an end is in sight, but to live without hope — that is hell indeed. Only the belief that this was her fate could give Lakshmi the strength to go on.

CHAPTER 8

The noise, insistent and brutal, kept beating at Mangal's ears but she stubbornly ignored it, trying to continue reading the novel she was engrossed in. It was only when a couple of blows knocked her head sideways and sent the book flying to the other end of the hut that the noise resolved itself into a voice: 'Get up, you slut! Can't you even get me a glass of water? I've been driving non-stop for sixteen hours and you just sit there reading. What's the matter with you?'

Mangal's throat tightened and for a moment she thought she was going to scream, but with a great effort she controlled herself and replied quietly, almost calmly, 'You don't seem to be too exhausted to hit me, so why can't you get water for yourself? This is your house, you know where it is. Isn't it enough that I fill up the water at the tap every day?'

'Bitch! Good-for-nothing!' Ramesh aimed another blow at her and this time she really did start screaming: 'Leave me alone! Don' t touch me! I can't bear it, I tell you, I'll go mad if you go on like this!' But he beat her all the same, going on and on until the screaming stopped and all she could do was moan quietly. And then he went and got a glass of water. Not for himself, but for her. He made her drink it and attended to her bruises gently and carefully. He lifted her on to the bed and went to make tea for the two of them.

This was how it always was. Ramesh would ask her to bring him water. Or to dish out and bring his food. Or to attend to something or other, some trivial chore around the house. And she would refuse point-blank, unmoved by his pleading, threats or abuse. She was quite prepared to cook, to look after the house, to make tea, but anything which even distantly resembled servility she fiercely, almost fanatically, resisted. At such moments Ramesh lost all control, expressing his fury in bouts of brutality which he always felt ashamed of afterwards, though he would never admit it in so many words.

Mangal was already married and had two children, twin daughters aged five, when she first met Ramesh. Her husband was several years older than she was, a grim, authoritarian figure who treated Mangal harshly and never in all the years of their marriage showed her a trace of affection. Mangal was not timid nor compliant, yet he inspired in her such terror that she endured six years of the marriage in daily fear, without making any attempt to break out or rebel. Somehow he made her feel that he was capable of extreme, horrible cruelty, although he had never actually beaten her more than was commonly accepted as being normal. She worked outside the home from time to time, but this provided no escape because it was in his roadside tea-stall that she worked, and even when she was alone the shadow of his presence overwhelmed her so much that she dared not lose track of a single paisa, glass or teaspoon.

That was how she met Ramesh: he was a truck driver and regularly stopped at the stall for tea and snacks. It was only after he had come several times that she noticed him looking at her. Of course she was used to lecherous looks, comments, gestures, and they aroused no feeling in her at all, because these men were treating her just as her husband had. But Ramesh was different. The way he looked at her it seemed as if he were interested specifically in her, Mangal, even though he did not know her name and she did not know his. She had so completely lost all sense of identity, had become so resigned to her living death, that this frightened and disturbed her. She withdrew into herself, tried to avoid his gaze, and yet, perversely, her mind became more and more preoccupied with him, weaving intricate fantasies around him and herself. When eventually he spoke to her, these two conflicting impulses almost paralysed her: should she run away, take refuge in the dark emptiness she had got used to, or should she risk everything to find out about him and, even more, about herself? Ultimately it was her sense of adventure which won. She spoke to him, agreed to meet him, and despite all the difficulties of escaping the vigilance of those around, managed to go out with him occasionally.

It was like being born again. For so many years she had never thought about herself, certainly never felt that there was anything in her to attract anyone's interest or admiration, and now here was this man who was entranced by her mobile, expressive face, by everything she said or did, including her quick-witted verbal responses which excited nothing but criticism from her husband. She had felt ashamed of her fantasies, had thought them too extravagant, but this went well beyond them and she realised her experience had been too restricted even to fantasise properly. She felt no desire to think about the future, about what all this would lead to; it was enough that it was happening.

But for Ramesh the situation was intolerable. He really was in love with Mangal and wanted to have her completely to himself, yet he was forced to take fourth place to a husband and two children, and that too, in a hole-and-corner fashion, unable to move around openly with her. Once she had suggested jokingly that she should bring the twins with her and run away with him, and he had dismissed the idea in an offhand way. Mangal took this to mean that he was not interested in a permanent relationship and for the next few days she was extremely depressed. But that was not it at all. The idea of running away with her had occurred to him too, and by now he was convinced it was the only way out of an impossible situation. The problem was the children. He had no desire to be burdened with children, least of all another man's children; he wanted Mangal and Mangal alone, yet it was clear to him that she would never consent to run away without her daughters.

While she was depressed Ramesh was racking his brains, and the next time they met he had a plan. He suggested that they go to a studio and have their photograph taken together. Mangal was surprised and touched, as well as baffled. What could it mean? That he was so attached to her that he wanted to keep her image by him even when they were apart? Or that he was going to abandon her and wanted to keep a memento of their relationship? She puzzled over it for a whole week while she eagerly waited to see how the picture would turn out.

It was beautiful. Both of them had come out well — they certainly made a good-looking couple. Really, it almost looked like a wedding photograph. Mangal was still smilingly admiring it when Ramesh spoke to her in a hard, matter-of-fact voice she had never heard him use before: 'Now you decide what to do Mangal. Either you come away with me at once, or I show this picture to your husband.' At first she was so stunned that she failed to understand; then, slowly, the implications of what he had said began to seep into her mind. Her husband would kill her, of course — there could be no doubt about it. So if Ramesh had taken this step, it must mean he was desperate to have her. But why, why had he chosen to do it this way? Hadn't she herself suggested running away with him less than two weeks ago? At last the reason dawned on her. 'The children!' she exclaimed faintly. 'Can't I go and get them first?'

'I told you Mangal, you must choose: if you go home even once more, I'll show the picture to your husband.'

What could she do? She figured out that either way she would be lost to her daughters, if she went back her husband would kill her — it would be a useless sacrifice. So she followed Ramesh dumbly to his truck, unable even to cry. Looking into her stricken face, Ramesh felt a twinge of remorse, stroking her cheek he said in his usual affectionate way, 'Don't look so upset — they'll be all right, after some time they won't miss you so badly. You told me how much your sister-in-law loves them; do you think she will allow them to be neglected?'

Mangal said nothing, but continued to brood over the matter. What would her children think when she didn't return? That she had died? Would they be haunted for ever by a picture of their mother's dead body? Or would they think she didn't love them, had tired of them and left? If she could be quite sure they wouldn't think that — then at least she might get some peace. But she couldn't be sure. Her husband was sure to represent her behaviour in the worst possible light and her sister-in-law, who was quite sympathetic to her, would have no basis for contradicting him. Besides, her husband had used the children so effectively against her, they had become so much a part of the prison around her, that she had, at times, resented them fiercely — and they knew it. What tormented her most, now, was the thought that they would never know how much she loved them, she could never tell them or show them. She thought with bitter regret of the angry words, even blows, she had occasionally directed at them; would they always remember her as a bad-tempered, unjust woman, taking out her frustrations on them simply because they were smaller and weaker than she was?

Apart from this nagging pain, her life was quite good at first. Ramesh took her to Patthar Basti in Bombay where he had a small hut. He was often away for several days, sometimes more than a week at a stretch, and with only the house to look after she had plenty of time to herself. Her isolation from the world was almost complete: mostly she only related to it through money and the commodities she bought for consumption. With very few exceptions, her neighbours shunned her. Somehow the whole basti had learned that she had run away from her husband and children in order to live with Ramesh. How could they have found out? Mangal suspected that Ramesh himself had put the story about with the express intention of increasing his power over her by isolating her from the others. After the way he had blackmailed her into leaving her children, she could believe him capable of any kind of deviousness. It would have been easy for him to propagate rumours about her without considering what the consequences would be for her — a daily subjection to petty persecution from the other women. It was Kantabai who put an end to this. Mangal vividly remembered the first time the elderly, strongly built woman had entered her life; she smiled to herself whenever she recalled the occasion. She had been waiting in the queue at the water-tap, and a group of women had been speculating about details of her private life in just-audible undertones. Kantabai had come to join the queue and immediately launched into them, asking loudly, 'Aren't you ashamed of yourselves, saying things like that? How would *you* like it if...' and she proceeded to recount past and present gossip about each of the women in turn, still in a loud voice, until they were cringing with shame. After that they left Mangal strictly alone, and she came to regard Kantabai as a protector, an utterly dependable tower of strength.

Geeta, who lived in Sheetal Nagar, was different. Young and beautiful, at first sight she didn't appear to be the kind of woman from whom Mangal could expect any sympathy. Yet she had been the one to revive

Mangal and bring her home when she fainted in the marketplace. The fainting fit was a prelude to a week's illness during which Geeta came daily all the way from her own basti and cared for her with a degree of kindness and concern which more than once brought tears to Mangal's eyes. When you are hardened to meet persecution and indifference, it is kindness which stabs with the sharpest pain. And the sympathy continued after Mangal recovered. Even more than Kantabai, Geeta was a friend. Because Kantabai, despite looking like a typical matriarch, turned out to be childless, whereas Geeta had a child of around the same age as Mangal's daughters, and could fully share her anguish at her enforced separation from them.

Apart from these two women, there was no one she could talk to. Of course, there were plenty of men who made it clear they would have liked to get to know her but she ignored them as she had ignored the advances of the men who used to come to her tea-stall. She could have broken out of her solitude to some extent by taking up a job, but this was not financially necessary, nor did the idea appeal to her. Instead, she drugged herself into a kind of dream-world with stories and novels good or bad, classical or modern, Hindi or Marathi. She would voraciously read any book she could borrow or buy from the pavement stalls, and when she was unable to lay her hands on anything new, she would repeatedly re-read her stock of old books. It seemed as if this was what really kept her alive.

And then came the beatings. When her husband had beaten her, she had accepted it: it was part and parcel of their relationship, as she understood it. But with Ramesh it was different. She had risked everything to get to know him only because of a dream of something incomparably superior, and so any hint of the same authoritarianism in his relationship almost drove her mad. Ramesh's complaint was always the same: 'I slog my guts out so that you can live like a queen, reading your novels all day long. Don't I have the right to expect you to make me comfortable? Isn't that the least you can do for me?' To which Mangal would retort, 'A queen or a slave? If I wanted to be a slave, I wouldn't even have looked at you. You know I didn't come with you to be a slave, so why do you treat me like one?' And so it went on until he beat her, after which he would be conciliatory while she remained sullen.

Today, as she drank the tea he brought her, she voiced a thought which had often occurred to her. 'You wouldn't behave like this if I had lots of friends, would you? It's only because I'm helpless that you dare.'

'Who's stopping you from making friends?' he smiled. 'You can have as many as you like.'

'You know very well that I can't. You've told them some story about me, and their minds are too weak to work out that any vileness I'm supposed to be guilty of is equally shared by you. Who wants such friends anyway? They're too self-righteous to talk to me at the watertap, but I've seen the way they smile when they invite you in for tea. I can't stand such servility.'

'Talking about servility, your friend is the worst of all.'

'Who?' asked Mangal.

'The woman who comes here sometimes, from the other basti — what's her name?'

'You mean Geeta? That just shows you're as brainless as the rest of them. Can't you recognise kindness when you see it? Geeta's kindness is genuine because she's kind to everyone. It doesn't bother her in the least when people say she's befriending a whore or whatever they call me. You certainly can't call that servility. When I was ill while you were away, she was the only one who brought me food and looked after me — she and that old woman Kantabai. If you ask me, it's people like them who've really got guts, not all those goondas and strongarm men.'

Ramesh looked at her, still smiling. She always had some weird idea in her head — must be from all those books she read. In his own way, he valued her intelligence and independence of mind; she was really clever, not like other women, you could never get bored with her. Yes, he had made a good choice and he didn't regret it.

'Well, well,' he said coaxingly, 'you may be right. Let's not fight about it anyway. We have so little time together, we shouldn't waste it fighting.'

It was on the tip of Mangal's tongue to say, 'I'm not the one who starts the fights,' but she stopped herself and smiled instead. What was the use of carrying on? She might as well make the best of what she had, enjoy the good times and struggle through the bad.

CHAPTER 9

'Mummy, mummy, it's Mariam, and she's brought a bag *and* a guitar,' shouted Asha excitedly. She had answered the door, and was overjoyed to see her new friend again.

'Oh, that's fantastic!' exclaimed Kavita, almost as excited. 'You wouldn't believe how much I miss singing with you.'

'Really?' smiled Mariam, but then looked serious. 'What's the matter, Kavita? Something is wrong, I feel sure of it.'

Kavita hesitated. 'I'll tell you everything,' she said slowly, 'but first I'd better send Asha and Shanta out to play. Sunil's asleep, luckily. Children,' raising her voice slightly, 'why don't you go and play in the garden?'

'But I don't want to go out,' protested Asha. 'I want to hear Mariam sing.'

'Oh dear,' sighed Kavita. 'You can listen to her later, you know, there'll be plenty of time.' Asha was about to protest again so she added hastily, 'I'll tell you what we can do: if you promise to go out and play afterwards, then Mariam will play one song and we can sing — all right?'

'All right,' agreed Asha, and they sat in a group around Mariam in the large front room.

Mariam had already taken her guitar out of its case, and after a moment's thought she struck up a quiet, rather mournful tune. The girls obviously knew the song, but didn't join in. Kavita started singing with Mariam, but stopped halfway with a catch in her voice which made Mariam look at her with even more concern. At the end of the song they were all silent until Kavita broke the spell by saying abruptly, 'Right! Off you go to play!'

'Oh Mummy,' pleaded Shanta, 'can't we have it again? Just once more?'

It was the first time Mariam had heard her speak. 'Did you like it so much?' she asked gently. Shanta nodded and Kavita laughed. 'She's very musical,' she explained. 'Already she can sing better than Asha although she's two years younger. All right, I suppose we'll have it once more. But why don't you join in, darling? You know it, don't you?' Shanta nodded again, then waited eagerly. This time she accompanied them, and although she sang the wrong words from time to time, her tune never faltered but flowed pure and true from beginning to end.

'Bravo!' laughed Mariam when the last chords had died away. 'You will be a great singer when you grow up. But now you must go out and play.' She kissed them both and they ran out, Shanta still smiling happily.

At last they were alone together and Mariam turned to Kavita with a questioning smile. 'Well?'

'Well,' began Kavita, as though about to embark on a calm and rational explanation. But before she could get any further the pent-up emotion overwhelmed her and she broke into sobs which shook her whole body. 'Mariam, I'm so unhappy!'

Mariam stroked her back soothingly but said nothing until she was calmer. Then she asked softly, 'What is it? Is it Ranjan?'

Kavita nodded, but it was several minutes before she could reply. 'Yes, it's Ranjan. He's been having an affair for a month with one of the girls in his study circle. Now it has ended and he says that it won't happen again, but the more I think about it the more I feel sure it will. Why didn't he tell me until it had broken up? And he doesn't think he's done anything wrong, that's the worst of it. He says, "I still love you, so what's the matter?" He doesn't even think I have any cause to feel hurt. He says that if I cry and look depressed it will drive him away and make him more likely to do it again — that it is only self-pity and if I look at things rationally I will see there's no reason to be upset. Sometimes I think he has become completely hard and lost all his feelings, but that's not true either. There are times when he's really kind and nice, and even now he says that he told me about this affair only because he loved me and knew that if he didn't tell me he would have done it again, but now he won't. Oh, I don't know what to think.'

'Surely he loves you, Kavita. I remember when he first met you how he was obsessed with you — he would talk about you all the time, your beauty, your gentleness, the sweetness of your smile... and you haven't changed since then so why should he have stopped loving you? And as he says, he could have kept this affair from you, but obviously he's sorry about the deception and wants to restore the trust between you. Don't be so worried — I'm sure he loves you.'

'But then why did he do it? I don't believe he really thinks I'm not hurt; I actually told him long ago that I would be terribly hurt if he did something like this, and I even remember him saying he would feel the same if I did. And it's not just this, either. In fact, I don't know why I was so shocked when it happened because things have been so bad between us that I was expecting and even wanting something like this so that I would have an excuse to split up. It started with terrific fights soon after we got married — Ranjan would get so angry that he shouted at me and abused me, and even that wasn't the worst. Sometimes he would just dry up — become cold and hard, ignore me completely when I cried and said I was sorry and begged him to make up. This would go on for days until I was totally broken. And then suddenly he would change and everything would be fine again. But while it lasted it was hell. I can't describe what those quarrels did to me; they completely shattered me, left me feeling that I couldn't go on living. And when they were over, the memory remained like a scar and made me afraid of repeating the experience. And in a way, I think the experience was as bad for Ranjan, and the memory just as painful — perhaps it's worse to think of yourself as having been brutal than as having been abused — what do you think?'

'Certainly, I think if Ranjan had been brutal he would suffer for it. But isn't that rather an extreme way of putting the matter?'

'I don't think so. Physical violence is not the only form of cruelty, you know; there are others which are as bad. For instance, I used to be very involved in the circles here, and of course I am still just as interested and emotionally committed. But gradually it has become almost impossible for me to take part in anything. On the one hand, bit by bit the entire responsibility of looking after the children and doing the housework has fallen on me — to such an extent that when I'm sick he still expects me to do it and shouts at me if a meal is late or the house is dirty. That was one of the things we used to fight about, but I've given up now: it takes too much out of me. On the other hand, he doesn't tell me what's going on, he doesn't discuss anything with me, doesn't inform me about meetings, and it's really embarrassing because the others still regard me as a comrade and talk to me about these things, but when they see I know nothing they naturally assume I'm not interested, otherwise I would have taken the trouble to ask Ranjan. And I am afraid to dispel this illusion by asking them for information because it would be disloyal to Ranjan — I have never criticised him to anyone before. There are days on end when I get nothing from him but complaints and orders. He criticises and insults everything about me — *everything* — my appearance, my mind, my cooking, the way I look after the children and much more. It's as though he wanted to destroy my self-confidence, my personality, utterly and completely, to destroy me. You can't imagine what I've been through. Sometimes I wonder if it wouldn't be better to swallow all my sleeping tablets or walk under a bus or train with the children.'

'Kavita!'

'I wouldn't do it, of course,' smiled Kavita, 'but it's a real comfort to think about it sometimes... an end to everything... peace for ever.'

Mariam looked deeply disturbed. 'I can't believe it,' she murmured, 'I really can't. It just sounds incredible to me.'

For two whole minutes Kavita sat silent, thinking. Suddenly she nodded and said, 'I know why it sounds incredible. It's because I have abstracted all the bad moments and lumped them together, and of course it sounds incredible. Why would I carry on living with a man like that? I would have to be a masochist. But you know as well as I do that there's a different side to Ranjan. Some of the times we've had together have been the most wonderful in my life. I could never have imagined such happiness if I hadn't experienced it. There are times, even now, when we are so close, when he talks to me about things I know he doesn't mention to anyone else, not even his closest friends. At such times I feel totally convinced that he loves me, and the other times seem nothing more than a bad dream. And then... suddenly it snaps, and I find it's the good times which are a dream. Or are they? Don't you see, Mariam, that's what is tearing me apart. If I were convinced he didn't love me, if I could hate him whole-heartedly, everything would be all right, I could break with him and adjust. Or if I could love him straightforwardly and be sure that he loved me in the same way — that would be better still. But this ambiguity and uncertainty is driving me mad.'

There was a long, uneasy pause, then Kavita suddenly laughed and said in a more relaxed tone, 'It's wonderful being able to talk about it, and especially to you. In the last few days I have been thinking and thinking — brooding, Ranjan says — and my mind just goes round and round in circles, while all the time I have to do the same old chores, the washing and cooking and shopping. I have to talk to the children and try to pretend that nothing is wrong, when all the time I want to do something to express how unhappy I am — lie down and howl for a whole day, or get drunk and pass out, or jump out of the window and get smashed on the ground. I don't suppose you can understand any of this, can you Mariam? You're so rational and calm, you've probably never felt jealous or depressed in your life.'

'What nonsense!' laughed Mariam, amused at this description of herself. 'You know I am often depressed.'

'Yes, but only because your work is not going well,' smiled Kavita. 'You would never get into such a state over a personal problem, would you?'

'I have been upset for personal reasons, too. But it always helps if you are involved in some work — it gives you a reason to carry on even if you are unhappy.'

'Yes, I know. In a way it's good I have the children, because it forces me to go on living and working, and eventually I suppose I will get over it, though I can't imagine that now. But tell me, have you ever felt jealous? Were you jealous of me?'

'Jealous... no. I felt a little sad, maybe, that Ranjan forgot all about me once he met you — but then, I could understand why!'

'Not at all!' said Kavita warmly, taking Mariam's hand. 'You're so much better than I am, I don't know how he could have given you up. Besides, I'm sure you would have kept him in much better order.'

They both laughed at this, then Mariam said seriously, 'No, I'm sure something can be done. We can't let Ranjan go on like this — for his own sake as much as yours and the children's. If he really loves you, he's got to make the effort to change. And if he doesn't...'

They looked at each other, and Kavita firmly completed the sentence: 'I'll leave him.'

CHAPTER 10

The week that followed Renu's decision to insist her cousin should help her did nothing to weaken her resolution. On Friday, the mistress of the house, who kept finding fault with everything the servants did, slapped Renu for making a sharp retort, and it was all Renu could do to restrain herself from slapping her back. Instead she threw herself sobbing into a corner of the kitchen, and then counted the hours till Sunday evening.

Her cousin Shyam had an unpleasant shock when he saw her standing in front of his half-empty vegetable stall just as he was preparing to close it down. 'What's the matter?' he asked rather roughly. 'You haven't got yourself dismissed already, have you?'

'Not yet,' replied Renu quietly. She was seething with rage at his tone and manner, but determined to control herself. 'I haven't yet burned down the house or thrown one of the children from the balcony, but I will certainly do something of that sort in the coming week unless things change.'

'What kind of change? You can't pretend to me that those people ill-treat you — I know them, they're good people, otherwise I would never have asked you to take a job there.'

'Good people!' exclaimed Renu, her voice rising in anger — patience was not one of her virtues — 'Oh yes! They're certainly *very* good people to sell vegetables to! But have you ever tried living with them and doing their bidding day and night? I'm sure you wouldn't find them so good then! If you like them so much, why don't you let me look after your stall while you go and take my place?'

'Don't be silly, you don't know where to buy the vegetables, or the correct prices, or anything. Besides, they want a servant girl, not a boy. What's wrong with you? Hundreds of other girls seem to manage without any trouble.'

'Well I'm not hundreds of other girls, and I won't put up with it a single day longer. Or maybe I could put up with it,' she paused, and Shyam waited hopefully, '...if only I had a proper break at least once a week. I drudge all week till I'm ready to scream with the monotony and boredom of it, and then on Sunday evening I'm stuck away on that wretched balcony with no one to talk to, nowhere to go, nothing to do. Isn't that enough to drive anyone crazy? *You* got me into this, now it's your responsibility to find a way out. Otherwise I'm quitting right now and going home.'

'Calm down, Renu,' pleaded Shyam, softening in the face of her anger. 'Naturally you'll have a hard time at first when everything is new to you. But wait till you've made some friends and you will feel much better. I'll tell you what: next Sunday I'll ask one of the other girls to come and see you. You can go out for a walk together or something.'

'But that's next Sunday. What about today?'

'I'm afraid I can't do anything about today. I'm supposed to be going to a film and my friends have already come for me,' said Shyam indicating a group of three youths who were watching them with interest.

'I'm coming with you,' said Renu firmly, scarcely giving them a glance.

'Renu!'

'What's wrong?' asked one of the youths, coming up.

'My cousin-sister,' explained Shyam. 'She recently came to Bombay to work for one of the families in those apartments. Now she says she's bored and wants me to entertain her. I told her I'll fix up something for next Sunday, but she refuses to wait. What shall I do?'

'Why not take her with us?'

'Take her with us? Certainly not! What would people think?'

'Let them think! Come on Shyam, make up your mind fast, we're getting late.'

Take her with them! It was a crazy idea. Her parents would be shocked out of their wits if they came to know. But on one side were his friends, waiting impatiently, on the other was Renu, hands on her hips, glaring implacably at him. What could Shyam do? He shrugged his shoulders, and beckoning to Renu, walked away.

Renu silently walked along some distance behind. To tell the truth, she was feeling rather uncomfortable and wondering whether she hadn't gone too far. One girl going out with four boys! If anyone had told her earlier that she would find herself in such a situation, she would have laughed in disbelief. Yet here she was. Should she quietly turn round and go back home? They wouldn't even notice till later. But then what would she do? It was the thought of yet another intolerable evening followed by a dreary week of drudgery which finally made her decide to stick it out. After all, they were going to a public place; nothing could happen to her there, surely. And then, there was the glamour and excitement of a film to attract her. It was not like Renu to give up something once she had set her heart on it, and this was no exception.

By the time the interval came, she felt far more at ease. Shyam's friends were very nice to her and he too, once he had resigned himself to her presence, did his best to make her comfortable. She sat between Shyam and Sunder, the most handsome of his three friends. Sunder seemed to be fascinated by Renu, and she in her turn was considerably flattered to have the attention and interest of someone so sophisticated, witty and good-looking. Not that she was lacking in wit either; she was perceptive enough to see that he was pleasantly surprised to find a simple village girl such good company.

At the end of the film there was no more talk of finding a girl with whom Renu could spend her Sunday evening. There was an unspoken assumption that she would accompany the boys next week, and they were in fact wondering why they had never thought of taking girls along with them before. As for Renu, she went home with her thoughts full of the film, of Sunder, of the whole wonderful evening. And the thoughts remained with her throughout the entire week that followed. As Sunday approached again, she was in a fever of excitement; she carefully ironed her best blouse and skirt, and on the evening itself put her hair up and painted a teeka on her forehead. For the first time in her life she felt dissatisfied with her simple clothes, and began to plan what she would buy with her wages when she got them. Until then she had been making the best of what she had, and although she didn't know it, the brightness of her smile and the suppressed excitement in her eyes more than made up for any deficiencies in her dress.

Time no longer dragged for Renu after that. From the films she saw, from stories she had heard in childhood and from her own feelings, her mind elaborated a world as remote as could possibly be imagined from the humdrum everyday one in which she worked. Only Sunday evenings really existed for her; only then did her activity coincide with her thoughts. The rest of the time she lived on a plane which bore no relation to the people around her, performing her tasks mechanically, untouched by the scoldings she got for work badly done. How did it matter if they scolded her? This was not where she would be for much longer. Already in spirit she had left. In a way she was even glad she had been subjected to the indignity of being a full-time servant, since that had been the means of her gaining access to a world she could never have dreamed of when she was living in the village.

Gradually the routine changed; they didn't go out as a group every Sunday. There were times when she and Sunder went off together. He took her all over Bombay, showed her sights which astonished and at times also frightened or disgusted her. Or they simply spent the time together on the beach or in some tea-shop. And all the time their intimacy was growing, especially when the rains came in earnest and Sunder started taking her to his room. He was very different from the boys she had known in her village, and seemed to know everything there was to know about the world. A really wonderful person; and it seemed impossible to envisage any future without him. Although they never spoke about it, Renu was firmly convinced that he shared in her fantasies, and was equally subject to the emotions he had aroused in her. Concrete plans could wait; they might even spoil the dreamlike quality of the experience she was having. What was most important was the present — the beautiful, beautiful present.

CHAPTER 11

Arvind's hut in Sheetal Nagar was bigger than most; his family lived in one of the rooms while he used the other as his carpentry workshop where he worked on his own without any assistance. His daughter Lalita had left school a year ago at the age of fourteen and taken a job in a small workshop packing glass ampoules into cardboard boxes ready for sending to the big pharmaceutical firms. It had pained Arvind to take her out of school because he was proud of his bright daughter, but there was no help for it; her elder brother had to be supported through his higher education, and Arvind's income wasn't sufficient. The boy was intelligent and hard-working and his parents had set their hopes on seeing him get at least a technical qualification, maybe even a degree. The two younger boys were mischievous devils who never spent a moment longer on their studies than they were forced to, and if the choice had been between Lalita and one of them, she would certainly have been the one chosen. But as things were, she had to be sacrificed.

Lalita was not particularly unhappy about the situation. She was very fond of her family, especially her elder brother, and shared in the general hopes of his future advancement. Besides, she usually had something left after her contribution to the family income, and it was nice to have her own money to do whatever she liked with it. She enjoyed getting smart churidar-kameez sets for herself and buying presents for her family and friends. Of course the job was deadly boring and the boss was a swine — but there were times when she and the other workers, all girls and young women, managed to have fun in spite of that.

She walked to and from work with her friend Preeti who worked in the same place and lived in Patthar Basti. Preeti's case was very sad, even tragic. Her father had been earning a good salary until he had been involved in a horrible accident: his entire right arm had been chopped off by a machine when it was switched on by someone else while he was trying to clean it. He had sued the company for compensation but couldn't afford a good lawyer. The company somehow convinced the court that the cause of the accident had been his own negligence. All he got was twenty-five rupees. After that he was not only physically disabled but also mentally affected. Suddenly the family found itself getting less than half its former income. Preeti's father's younger brother had a job which paid around five hundred rupees a month, and her mother also earned a few hundred rupees making agarbattis at home. But that was far from being enough to support Preeti, her younger brother and sister, her sick father and his parents and an unmarried sister. Her aunt started working as a domestic servant, the children helped with the agarbattis and Preeti took the job at the workshop. Even so they barely managed — Preeti never had any money left after her contribution to family expenses, and they often had to borrow in order to make ends meet. It was on her account that the two girls walked to and from work instead of taking a bus; the money she would have had to spend on bus fare would have deprived the family of some little necessity. Lalita noted with concern that her friend's face now always looked tense and anxious, and her two or three churidar-kameez sets, alternated day after day, were growing progressively more faded and worn; but it was difficult to know how to help such a sensitive person without offending her.

Every evening at six-thirty the girls met outside the workshop and went home together. But today Preeti was late, and Lalita wondered why. She was about to go in and find out when her friend appeared, flustered and almost in tears. 'What's the matter?' asked Lalita anxiously, but instead of answering Preeti walked rapidly away, beginning to cry as she did so. Almost running to keep up with her, Lalita kept begging her to tell her what the trouble was, but they were halfway home before Preeti collected herself sufficiently to reply.

'It's the boss!' she said hesitantly, turning to look at Lalita as though wondering what her response would be. 'He wants me to... to go with him. He said I would lose my job if I don't. What shall I do, Lalita?' She burst out crying afresh, but now that she had started speaking seemed desperate to continue. 'What shall I do? This was the best job I could find in this area. If I lose it, I will have to take one with less pay... everyone at home will be so angry. If I take a job further away from home, I will have to pay for transport and, besides, it will take time finding a job. What'll we do in the meantime?'

Lalita was about to speak when she resumed, 'And yet, if I go with him, I'm finished. They'll be even more angry at home... my grandfather will beat me and throw me out, I know he will. Besides, I couldn't, I just couldn't do it! I can't stand it when he so much as touches me... it makes me feel so filthy, I feel like having a bath in disinfectant or something. But he'll throw me out for sure. What's wrong with me, Lalita? Why did he pick on me? Do I talk too much? Laugh too much? Somehow he's got the impression that I'm not respectable, that I'm a... I'm a loose woman. Lalita, I should never have let him touch me, should I? I should have screamed or slapped him or something. But I was too scared, and now I'm finished!'

'No, no,' Lalita tried to comfort her, 'it's not as bad as that, we'll think of something.'

'But what do you think? — do you think I'm a loose woman? Do I behave like a girl who will go with any man who asks her? Is that why he's picked on me?'

'It's nothing like that, you're just imagining things. He's probably got to know how dependent you are on your wages and so he thinks he can get his way with you. In any case, how do you know you're the only one? He hasn't done anything to me yet, it's true — sometimes he pinches my cheek, but nothing more — but how many girls have left this place since we joined! Couldn't that be the reason why they left? And even those who stayed on. Maybe there are some who were too scared to resist because they were poor — how do we know?'

'I do know,' said Preeti suddenly. 'At least I think I do,' she added rather guiltily. 'I'm almost sure Sarita goes with the boss sometimes. I see them talking, and some days she stays back after all of us have left. I used to look down on her so much! But really, now that I think about it, what can she do? A widow with two children to support and no one to help her — no wonder she's afraid to resist! And what about me? Soon I'll be like that and everyone will look down on me,' and she started crying again.

Lalita walked on helplessly beside her, unable to think of anything to say until they were almost home, when she suddenly stopped and grabbed her friend by the arm. 'Preeti! Listen!' she exclaimed, making Preeti stop in some surprise. 'I've got an idea. I told you that my father goes to some activists' meetings, didn't I? They discuss all sorts of problems there. I'll ask my father to mention it and see whether anyone can suggest anything...'

'Oh no!' interrupted Preeti in alarm, 'please, please don't say anything to your father about it. He's sure to think it's my fault, he'll think I'm a girl who goes around provoking men. I know that's how my father would react; even my mother will think that I must have done something to attract his attention — and my grandfather is so strict, if he gets to hear about it he'll thrash the life out of me!'

'My father's not like that — he would never think you were lying. But if you feel shy about it, I won't mention your name; I'll just say that one of my workmates is having this problem. Will that be all right?'

'I suppose so.' Preeti still sounded doubtful, and then she thought of another problem. 'But that will only be on Sunday, won't it? What shall I do in the meantime? I only got away today by saying that my family is expecting me to come home straight after work — but tomorrow he's sure to catch me. And if I don't go to work I'll miss my pay, I may even be thrown out. No Lalita, it's no good, there's no help for me.'

'Don't be so silly! You sound as if some great disaster had already happened. We'll think of something. I know what! Tomorrow tell him that your period has started — say you will go with him when it is over. That excuse will do for five or six days, and by then we'll surely work something out. Cheer up now — if you go home looking like that, your family will certainly suspect something is wrong. You don't want that to happen, do you?'

Preeti tried to smile and look normal as she dried her eyes, parted from Lalita and walked the rest of the way home along S.T. Road. But she was far from cheerful. It was true she felt as if a disaster had befallen her already and she could see her ruined life stretching out dreary and painful ahead of her. It was all right for Lalita to sound so bouncy — she was doing her best, of course, but the thing hadn't happened to her and she just couldn't imagine what it was like... worse than a death sentence hanging over your head. Preeti really felt that her old, innocent life was over. She would never be able to hold up her head again.

CHAPTER 12

Jackson Pharmaceuticals was one of the many engineering and chemical plants which was ranged along both sides of A.M. Road in northeast Bombay. Looking at it from the side road which led to the station, you would never have guessed that it was a factory; the row of trees through which you could glimpse a well-kept garden might have led you to believe that a mansion lay beyond. But this illusion was dispelled when you came to the front gate and saw JACKSON PHARMACEUTICALS in large letters on the name-plate, the white modern buildings, and the complicated arrangement of pipes in the background.

In the Liquids Department where syrups were bottled and packed, jobs were rotated on a regular basis among the workers — mainly women working on the packing lines, because some jobs were heavier than others and it was thought to be unfair that the same people should do them all the time. For example, on the line for the famous Jackson's Tonic, filling, capping and labelling the bottles were relatively light jobs because, for most of the time, you were simply watching the automatic machines do the work. Sitting on either side of the conveyor belt and manually putting the bottles into cartons was more tiring because you had to work at top speed; but packing the cartons into cases was worst of all — you were continuously on your feet, and by the lunch break would already be feeling exhausted.

Suzie was one of the youngest on the line; a slim, serious-looking girl, her face showed visible signs of strain as she tried to keep up with the stream of bottles coming towards her on the conveyor belt. Lucky it's not my turn to be on case packing today, she thought. I would certainly have collapsed by now. But this wasn't much better. Whichever way she shifted around on her chair, the pain would not ease; on the contrary it seemed to be spreading, down her thighs, down to her legs, making them weak and shaky so that she felt sure they wouldn't take her weight if she tried to stand. It was moving upwards too, pulling at her arms and hands, making her work more and more slowly as she slid the heavy bottles into cartons; there began to be a pile-up at her place, and she wondered in panic whether she would be able to clear it before the supervisor noticed. Even on ordinary days she only just managed to keep up, and by the end of the shift she was worn out. On days like this it was impossible.

Upwards the pain climbed, reaching her head now and making her feel dizzy and sick. This was awful — the worst thing that could possibly have happened. She was caught between two impossible alternatives: either to leave her place and be suspected of shirking, or to stay there and run the risk of vomiting. It was horrible, she was feeling worse and worse. There was no help for it, she would have to run to the toilet. At least the toilets would be open. There had been a time, apparently, before she joined, when management used to keep them locked except during the breaks. Madness!

She got up to go, but suddenly the world went black around her. Fortunately Teresa, who was sitting next to her, noticed her slumping and caught her in time to ease her back into the chair. 'Put your head down, Suzie,' she said urgently. 'Can you hear me? Down on your knees.' And she forced Suzie's head into that position. 'Just call Nirmala,' she told the next woman with the same urgency.

In a moment Nirmala was there, calmly taking over. 'Okay Teresa, good girl, you can get back to your place now, I'll take her to the doctor. Jyoti, please fill in for her till I come back, then I'll help. Can you walk now?' she asked gently, turning to Suzie.

Suzie nodded, still dazed, vaguely hearing someone whisper, 'Poor girl, she really has a bad time with her periods.' Supported by Nirmala she was slowly making her way to the door when the supervisor strode up asking, 'What's the problem?'

'No problem,' replied Nirmala, brisk again. 'This girl fainted, so I'm taking her to the sick room. I've asked someone to take her place on the line.' The supervisor looked suspicious but could find nothing to find fault with and walked away.

'I could just go and lie down in the ladies' rest room, couldn't I?' Suzie asked.

'No, you'll be more comfortable if you take something for it. And it'll be quieter in the sick room — not so much coming and going.'

Later, lying down, Suzie felt the pain slowly ebbing away, but there was another ache within her which wouldn't go so easily. Once, when she was small and had hurt herself she said, 'I wouldn't mind falling down if it didn't hurt so much.' And her father had said, 'But pain is very important to us, sweetheart, because it tells us something is wrong so that we can put it right. Without it we could injure ourselves and even die without realising it. No one likes it, but that is what keeps us alive!'

I wonder if that's true, she thought as she remembered his remark. If so, I must be one of the most alive people in the world! One thing at least was true: pain created an awareness of yourself which was totally absent at other times. Just as she never gave a thought to her stomach except when it was giving her hell, she had never been less conscious of herself than during those blissful childhood years which were now a paradise completely lost. When had it all begun to go wrong? It was her mother's illness which had started it; the illness which in the space of a year destroyed her looks and changed her into a plaintive, cantankerous invalid. From that time onwards, life had been one long, continuous torment. Her handsome, good-natured, pleasure-loving father couldn't stand the atmosphere at home and got himself a job abroad leaving her, a schoolgirl of fifteen, to look after her sick mother and younger brother. How could she possibly manage? He sent home money, of course, but he knew very well that that was not enough. She needed love, she needed help, and who was there to give it to her? Her brother Joe fell in with a disreputable lot of friends, he played truant from school most of the time and she knew he had started to take drugs but what could she do? He wouldn't listen to anything she said; in fact he often stayed away from home for days on end. So that when their uncle finally decided to take over, her relief at being rid of the responsibility was greater than her loneliness at being left without him. And her mother! Continuously in pain herself, she seemed only to find comfort in inflicting as much misery as possible on Suzie. If Suzie came home ten minutes later than usual, she would be accused of enjoying herself while her mother was in agony. If she slipped or stumbled while supporting her mother to or from the bathroom, she was accused of trying to break her back. On the hot summer nights her mother would refuse to have the fan on in the stuffy room which they shared, and Suzie would have to lie awake sweating. If, after her mother had fallen into a sedated sleep she put the fan on, she would be woken up next morning by vehement accusations that she was trying to kill her with pneumonia. And one phrase kept recurring, again and again: 'Wicked girl! God will punish you!'

How could her father have abandoned them like this? Didn't he love them at all? She often considered this question. And one answer was clear: in spite of all appearances there could be no doubt that he did love her. All his letters, his affectionate behaviour during his brief visits, testified to that. Even his extravagant gesture of moving them out of the old chawl into an expensive new flat could be seen as an expression of remorse for all the hardship she had to go through, although, paradoxically, it actually made her life harder by putting her out of reach of the neighbours who had known her all her life and often helped her.

Conversely, what became more and more certain as time went on was that he no longer loved his wife. This was an additional pain to Suzie, though she could understand very well that her mother had nothing left which could possibly attract him. What especially disturbed her during his last visit, more than a year ago, was a reference to an 'aunty' in terms she couldn't quite understand. Subsequently he stopped sending money home so regularly, and that, too, was ominous. What could divert him from even this minimal duty except a relationship which absorbed him completely? It is a terrible thing to suspect your own father of adultery, but just because it is terrible that doesn't mean it can't happen. This was what had forced her finally to give up her studies and look for a job.

The last disaster was the worst one of all, because she knew it had blighted her life for ever. In the beginning, however, she had dared to hope that it might be the opening to a bright new future. When they left the chawl she had to find a new doctor, and young Dr Mehta had been the obvious choice. What impressed her most of all was the way he handled her mother; he was not only infinitely patient, but actually managed to raise her spirits so much that she would be smiling or laughing by the time he left. And to Suzie's feelings he always showed a sensitivity which brought tears to her eyes.

What finally tipped the balance completely in his favour was one dreadful night when her mother, who had been ill for several days, became delirious and unmanageable. Panic-stricken, Suzie got dressed and ran out to fetch Dr Mehta from his bed. His calmness calmed her immediately; it was so marvellous to be able to shift the enormous burden of responsibility on to someone else for a while. By the time he had finished, Suzie's mother was sleeping peacefully, and only then did Suzie realise that she couldn't pay for the visit. A night visit would be expensive, and this month her father hadn't sent anything. Up to then she had never defaulted on any payment, and the necessity of doing so now made her shrink within herself with shame. Hardly knowing what she said, she stammered something about paying him as soon as she got her salary, and waited miserably for his reply. But instead of being annoyed, he sat down again and asked her to tell him the whole problem. Suzie's self-control was gone in a moment; her tears flowed unrestrained while she told him the story from beginning to end. What an unspeakable relief it was to talk about it! Although she had friends, she had never been able to speak to them like this; she had felt their experience was too remote from hers for them to be able to understand anything. But here at last was someone who would understand.

Dr Mehta heard her out, then smiled kindly. 'This is very sad,' he said. 'You're much too young to have to cope with such big problems. I wish I could help. But remember one thing: don't ever worry about money so far as I am concerned. I have enough rich patients to give me a comfortable income — I don't have to squeeze it out of people like you.'

To his kindness and sympathy she responded with a gratitude of almost painful intensity. She thought about him constantly, obsessively; the long hours of work passed unnoticed while she dreamed about him. She concluded, ultimately, that she must be in love with him. And this love spread warmth and sweetness over her desolate life. She told herself that she neither expected nor needed any response from him; it was enough to know he was there, and that he was what he was. Yet, almost without being aware of it, she began to watch out for him. He lived so close to her, surely she was bound to meet him some time?

It was a while before this happened, but, eventually, when she did meet him in the market, she had a dreadful shock. He was with a woman, and was carrying a little girl. He smiled kindly as usual and asked after her mother, she stammered something in reply and got away as soon as possible. He was married! He was with his wife, his child! Why had this possibility never occurred to her? The world shattered around her. She didn't try to account for her bitter disappointment, or try to reconcile it with the conviction that she had never hoped for anything. She simply felt crushed.

But worse was to follow. She knew now that she should push Dr Mehta right out of her mind, cease to think of him at all. Yet to her horror, her feelings obstinately refused to change, and her mind kept wandering back to him, dreaming dreams which she had absolutely forbidden herself. How could she feel like this, knowing he was a married man? She recalled one of her mother's phrases: 'wicked like your father'. Was it really true? Already she found herself thinking of her father with greater sympathy and understanding. But that could mean only one thing — that she herself was becoming depraved! The thought frightened her so much that she couldn't bring herself to talk about it to anyone at all. The burden of guilt weighing her down grew heavier every day until she felt she would sink under it. Her mother was right: God was certainly punishing her. But wasn't it partly his fault, too? How could he heap trouble upon trouble on a girl of only eighteen and expect her to pull through?

CHAPTER 13

Time and again Nirmala told herself, and others, that she was going to withdraw from trade union work. She wanted a few years of peace before she retired; a few years of freedom from the drudgery, the frustration, the crushing responsibility. What bothered her was not that she had missed all chances of promotion at Jackson's and still remained on the same grade she had been on when she first joined. Although she lacked any formal authority, it was to her that the workers in the department turned to when anything went wrong, and no manager, let alone a supervisor, would risk a confrontation with her without thinking twenty times about it. So, in reality, her standing was as high as she wished it to be. But there were other things which upset her. Every year the workers elected a committee to manage the day-to-day affairs of the union, and Nirmala was one of those who was elected again and again, not merely as a committee member but usually as one of its office-bearers. When there was a decision to be made, people said to the committee, 'Go ahead, you decide, you know best.' They refused to think, to decide for themselves, and so the responsibility became solely the committee's. Then if something went wrong — and who, after all, is infallible? — they would blame the committee as if they had never been given a chance to influence the decision. On the other side, she often found herself isolated on the committee. There were other women, but none of them were office-bearers, and for some reason she was frequently in the position of putting forward a point of view which wasn't supported by anyone else. After years of fighting she was weary now, and felt she deserved a rest. The most she had ever managed to stay out of the committee was for a few stretches of a year or two. After that there was invariably strong pressure on her to return, and so far she had never been able to resist.

This year was such a case. The settlement was due to expire, and the union had already tacitly agreed that the demand for transport between the factory gate and several key points in the city and suburbs would be included in the new charter. Travel was exhausting for everyone, but it was the women who were most interested in seeing this demand get through. Most of them, like Nirmala, used the local trains to get to work. The station near the factory was not a terminus, and getting on and off the crowded trains during the rush hours when commuters bulged out of the doors, and even clung to the outside of windows or rode on the roof, was a daily nightmare. Nirmala, who was short and not very strong, had more than once failed to get on to a train or to fight her way out at the right station. For her and others who lived in the western suburbs, the battle had to be repeated when they changed trains. And many of them also had a bus journey which involved waiting in endless queues watching buses go past with people hanging out of them, or sometimes, when the crowd was unruly, getting pushed and shoved yet again. When you got to work you were already tired, and by the time you got home you could hardly stand.

Compared to this ordeal, sitting comfortably in a company bus which would take you to work in the morning and home again in the evening seemed like heaven. It was not by any means a utopian demand; some of the women had friends in a neighbouring factory which ran a fleet of buses for their employees, and apparently one of the managers had said that the company benefited from the system too, because there was less absenteeism, workers arrived on time and relatively fresh for each shift, and there was no fear of disruption due to transport strikes. But Jackson's management had rejected this demand during the last negotiations and the union had let it drop, and the women had no confidence that the existing committee, almost entirely male, would make it a priority.

Nirmala was having a quiet moment in the large changing room equipped with toilets, washbasins and comfortable seats when a small delegation of women approached and surrounded her. They started speaking before she had a chance to say a word. 'Nirmala, you are our only hope! You've got to be on the committee to make sure that the demand for point-to-point transport gets on to our charter and stays there.'

'If we leave it to the men, they're sure to drop it. They'll accept more money instead — a transport allowance or something like that.'

'But we don't want money so much — I'm even ready to go without any cash increase so long as we don't have to suffer like this every day.'

'Management says that we don't need transport because we're near the station. But have they ever tried to get on those trains? Especially in the evening. You're lucky to be able to get on at all, forget about getting a seat!'

'And if you live on the western side, you have to go through the whole thing again at Dadar.'

'Look at my elbow — it got gashed on somebody's bangle when we were trying to get out the other day. You should have seen the blood!'

'We get home half dead, and then we have to start working again.'

'At this rate, we won't live to reach retirement age!'

'If other companies can have point-to-point transport, why can't we?'

'I know all that,' Nirmala said slowly when they paused for her to speak. 'What I can't understand is: why do you want me to be your representative? There are so many of you, you have all the arguments on the tip of your tongue. Isn't it time someone else took up the job of putting them forward? '

She was drowned out by a chorus of pleading voices.

'Just this once, Nirmala, you know how important it is.'

'If we don't get it now, that means at least three more years of hell and who knows whether we will ever get it?'

'It's not just having the arguments, you have to be able to put them forward convincingly. And it's not just a matter of being able to carry your point with management; first of all you have to carry your point with the rest of the negotiating committee and especially with Kelkar. You have the experience to do it, Nirmala. We don't.'

Nirmala was forced to think about this. Kelkar was the professional unionist who had been brought in as their president three years ago. A majority of the workers had wanted to bring him in because he had the reputation of being a tough leader, and the company was refusing to negotiate at all. The others had agreed in order to avoid splitting the union. And it is true that not only had he succeeded in bringing management to the negotiating table, but had forced them to sign quite a reasonable settlement. Only, there were two or three clauses in it which were definitely bad: one penalty clause, and two giving away rights previously held by the workers. The committee would certainly have objected to these, but they didn't have a chance: the final stages of negotiation were conducted by Kelkar alone, and he signed the agreement without consulting the rest of the committee, let alone the general body of workers.

So they knew that Kelkar was likely to go for large money increases at the expense of other objectives; and they also knew that it would require all their vigilance and persistence to be able to retain control over the bargaining process. Experience was important, Nirmala had to admit that.

'But I *can't* — I can't manage all alone!' she burst out almost despairingly. How did they expect her to do it? She was not superhuman!

'Pauline and Jayshree will be there. They'll support you.'

'Yes, we'll do our best. You won't be all alone.'

'The only thing is, you'll have to do most of the talking — we're not so good at that.'

'We'll all support you, not only Pauline and Jayshree. If you think more of us should stand for the committee, we'll do that too.'

Nirmala couldn't help smiling at the innocently blatant bribe. 'All right, on that condition I'll stand. But I can't guarantee anything, you understand that don't you? I can only do my best, and if I fail, I fail.'

There was unanimous agreement, and the lunch-time meeting in the ladies' rest room broke up. For the first time Nirmala noticed that the delegation of six which had initially cornered her had swelled into quite a crowd. 'So they are interested,' she thought. 'Only they don't want to take any responsibility — that's the problem.'

The women put up eight candidates for election, and all of them got in. Once she was on the committee again, Nirmala took up her task conscientiously, beginning by convincing the other members how important it was to make the demand for transport a priority. She found this easier than she had thought; she had the full support of the seven other women, and many of the men, too, lived far away and found the daily struggle to get to work and back home more exhausting than the work itself. The few objections were quickly over-ruled and it was agreed that the demand should be strongly worded and argued for in the charter.

So far, so good. Now there was nothing more they could do until negotiations began.

CHAPTER 14

'Now it's your turn to tell me your story,' suggested Kavita. 'You know, when you first turned up at the door I didn't recognise you for a moment, and the reason was I couldn't believe you could be here — it was so firmly fixed in my mind that you must be in England. What on earth made you leave?'

Mariam and Kavita were seated together on Asha's bed while the three children were playing on the floor. Ranjan had gone out but was expected back soon; there was an atmosphere of peace and contentment which Mariam had not noticed before. She sighed. 'Do I really have to go over all that?' she asked reluctantly.

'Well, not if you don't want to,' replied Kavita, a little hurt. 'It's just that when we last met, you were so engrossed with the centre — I thought some big disaster must have happened to make you leave.'

Mariam nodded. 'I suppose it's really better to talk it out rather than keep everything locked up inside. But I always keep away from the topic because it makes me feel so bad even to think about it.'

It already seemed a lifetime ago when five of them started the Asian Women's Centre in a dingy suburb of London. Everything had been so marvellous — in spite of all the problems, the struggle to get funds, the long hunt for a place, various mistakes, they had been such a wonderful team that Mariam had even left their political group in order to devote herself full-time to this. Kavita was right; she had been completely engrossed, to the exclusion of almost everything else, up to and beyond the time when Kavita and Ranjan returned to India. But their very success had created new problems: more people joined, the volume of work increased greatly, and it became impossible to carry on in the old way. There were suggestions that they should become more organised, there should be more accountability, perhaps even a more formal structure. Mariam welcomed this new stage as a challenge which they were certainly equipped to meet, and proposed a series of 'perspective discussions'. She opened the first by saying, 'Basically, the question facing us is how to cope with the expansion in our numbers and activities without abandoning the principles and methods of work which have attracted so many women to us.' She had no doubt at all they would go from strength to strength.

However, what followed was unbelievably hideous. There were various distinct points of view, and that was all right. Mariam herself was in favour of maximum diversity and autonomy. 'This should be a place where women can come and follow up whatever interests or needs they have. We shouldn't have to turn anyone away, whether she's a rape victim coming for counselling, someone who's interested in forming a drama group, or simply a woman wanting to meet and talk to other women.' Her view was at one extreme; at the other extreme were suggestions that the centre should have a formal structure and limited activities, that they should undertake only what they felt confident of being able to do and make sure that they did it well. Mariam's suggestion, they felt, meant chaos and anarchy which would make the group an easy prey for outsiders who might want to take it over.

Was she suffering from some kind of amnesia? Neither at the time could she follow, nor could she subsequently recall, how or by what stages the debate had degenerated into bitterness and acrimony. She had been accused not just of irresponsibility but of being 'politically motivated' — yes, those were the words which had been used! — in wanting a structure which would allow her political group to take over the centre. And it was not only the newer members who were saying this; among the accusers were members of the founding group, women who had worked with her for years and knew that she had in fact left the group because she thought the centre was more important than building a party. They couldn't possibly believe what they were saying! They might think her proposals wrong, even dangerous; Mariam was still prepared to consider that possibility, and she had certainly been willing to discuss it then. If they thought her wrong, of course they were entitled to argue against her. But not like this, not like this.

'It's totally beyond me how one woman can hurt another like this, with such calculated cruelty. That really broke something in me. I went a bit mad I think, after six nightmarish days and six nights of crying myself sick. I took out all my savings, borrowed some more money and bought a cheap ticket back here.'

The pain was still there, Kavita could almost feel it throbbing, and she wished she could say something, do something to ease it. But she remained silent and still, unable to express any of the emotion she felt. This had always been her problem, especially with Mariam: the times when she most wanted to convey love and comfort were precisely the moments when she became most inarticulate. There had been one previous occasion as bad as this, shortly after she was married. One day while she and Mariam were passing a hospital her friend had said casually, 'That's where I had my abortion.'

'When?' asked Kavita, surprised that she hadn't heard about it. Mariam mentioned a date, and for the next hour Kavita went about like an automaton, dazed and oblivious of what went on around her, concentrating completely on trying to unravel this earth-shattering revelation. The day would have been just a couple of months after she first met Ranjan and Mariam. They had been going out together at the time, and initially it was Mariam who attracted Kavita. But in pursuing this friendship she got involved with Ranjan, who gradually dropped Mariam. This troubled Kavita seriously, and when Ranjan asked her to marry him not long afterwards, she took the chance to question him about Mariam. 'Oh, that was a totally different kind of relationship,' he assured her. 'We both knew it was not permanent and it was understood that each of us was free to form others. You can ask Mariam, she's had plenty of boyfriends before me.' Kavita continued to feel uneasy, but pushed the matter to the back of her mind and allowed herself to be carried along by the strength of Ranjan's feelings. Now this new information was like an electric shock. She calculated and calculated. She could recall nothing about the specific date, but she knew that throughout those weeks she and

Ranjan had been together constantly; it was impossible that he could have gone to the hospital with Mariam without her knowing it. On the other hand, Mariam hadn't by then formed any other relationship after the one with Ranjan. (It was horrible, she told herself, making calculations like this, but she had to work it out.) So it could only have been his baby. And he hadn't even accompanied her. Was he really so callous? Or was she doing him an injustice?

What seemed like an eternity later Kavita said, 'Ranjan didn't tell me, otherwise I would have come with you.'

'What's that?' Mariam was puzzled, having totally forgotten her earlier remark.

'I mean to the hospital, when you had your abortion.'

'Oh, I see what you're talking about. No, Ranjan didn't know, he didn't even know I was pregnant. I didn't tell anyone, in fact.'

Relief flooded through Kavita, relief that Ranjan hadn't actually been as unfeeling as she thought he might have been. But she also felt acute misery at the thought of what Mariam must have gone through. Imagine having an abortion all by yourself. Not a pleasant experience at the best of times, but so much worse without any love or support from anyone! And why had she kept it a secret? Obviously because Ranjan had got involved with another woman — herself. Suppose she hadn't appeared on the scene? Mariam would certainly have told him about the pregnancy — perhaps even have decided to keep the baby. Might they have got married? It was not likely, because Mariam was opposed to the idea of marriage, but, such views could change, one couldn't tell. She badly wanted to talk to Mariam, find out exactly how she felt; but she was so matter-of-fact about everything that Kavita didn't dare. Instead, she went around with a sense of guilt hanging over her, a vague feeling of responsibility for a catastrophe in Mariam's life, a desperate desire to make up for it. But none of this did she say. When Mariam was absent she would talk to her for hours in her mind, pouring out her thoughts and feelings with amazing facility, but in her presence she was dumb.

Now there had been another catastrophe — clearly this incident at the centre was nothing less than that. Mariam had been badly wounded; but what comfort did she have to offer? There was so much she wanted to say, and was, in fact, saying in her head. But aloud it would have sounded melodramatic, sentimental, perhaps even ridiculous. So she only held

Mariam's hand between her own and said, 'It sounds dreadful — I can't imagine how it could have got to be like that. I liked the atmosphere so much whenever I visited the centre; it's sad to think all that is over. But I hope we can make you happy here. I think you'll be interested in Ranjan's work although, of course, it's very different from what you have been doing. Look, here he is, you can ask him all about it.'

CHAPTER 15

As Ranjan came in, Kavita jumped up with a suddenness which indicated some tension, but Mariam was more impressed by the difference from her response on the previous occasion. Kavita smiled warmly at him and said, 'Come and talk to Mariam while I get some coffee.'

Evidently put at ease by the relaxed atmosphere, Ranjan sat down. Immediately Asha and Shanta tried to climb on to his lap at the same time asking, 'Have you got anything for us, Daddy?'

'Oh dear! I forgot all about it,' he teased them. Shanta was disappointed but Asha refused to believe him and searched through his pockets until she found the sweets he invariably brought home. Sunil had been watching the scene with interest from the floor, and he now crawled up at great speed, held on to the chair and stood up, smiling expectantly at his father. 'I've got something for you too, you greedy boy,' laughed Ranjan stroking his cheek, and digging out another sweet from his pocket, unwrapped it and put it in Sunil's mouth. Sunil continued to stand there, smiling and dancing with pleasure, while dribbling stickily.

When Kavita came back with the coffee they embarked on a discussion of their former group, reminiscing about old times and trying to find an explanation for its degeneration. At first the children continued to play by themselves, but soon Shanta crept up to Mariam and whispered, 'Can't we have some songs?' and Asha interrupted their conversation saying, 'Stop talking, Daddy, Mariam said she was going to play her guitar and sing to us.'

'Go away, you little pest,' Ranjan said lightly, 'She can sing to you later.'

But Asha responded with a violence which completely threw him off balance. Hitting him with her hand she shouted, '*You* go away, you nasty Daddy, get out of the house and never come back again!'

'But why are you so angry with me? I was only joking.'

'We don't want you here. We're much happier without you — you always spoil everything!'

'All right, I will go away then,' retorted Ranjan, hurt and angry, and he walked out despite Kavita's efforts to stop him.

'Oh dear,' sighed Kavita, 'you shouldn't say such things, Asha, you know it upsets Daddy, and it's his house as much as yours.'

'But it's true, isn't it? He hurts you, and he's always grumpy with us.'

Kavita was silent, and didn't join in when Mariam started to sing with the two girls. She was feeling a little guilty. Ranjan's interest in the children had grown as time went on, so that with Sunil he could be perfectly spontaneous and easy. With Shanta, he was at times very close to her and she enjoyed being with him, at others she withdrew in a way which baffled him, seeming not to recognise his existence at all. His relationship with Asha was the least comfortable. It had been so from the start, because he had not been ready for her when she arrived, and had resented her intrusion into his life and her claim over Kavita. But things worsened as she grew older. She developed a clinging dependence on her mother and whenever there was a quarrel supported her in a way which Ranjan couldn't tolerate.

Now on top of all this Kavita, desperate for someone to confide in, had told Asha enough for the little girl to understand that Ranjan was responsible for her frequent outbursts of tears and fits of depression. She had taken comfort in Asha's sympathy and solidarity, but she now began to fear that she had unthinkingly strengthened an antagonism which could in the long run hurt both of them. It was, therefore, an enormous relief when Ranjan, in a good mood again, stuck his head in at the door asking, 'Who wants a story?' and the two girls rushed to him shouting, 'I do, I do!' His stories were wonderful, much more imaginative than her own, and the children never tired of listening to them. Watching him sitting there with both of them on his lap, as absorbed in his story as they were, she could hardly believe that he could be so different at times. This was the man she loved, there was no doubt of that; how, then, could he arouse such intense hatred and hostility in her?

That evening, again at Ranjan's suggestion, they made a trip to the beach. Mariam, almost as excited as the children, ran down to the water with the girls as soon as they reached the beach, while Ranjan and Kavita, absorbed in their own thoughts, sat with Sunil who was nervous of the water and preferred to play with the sand. Kavita tried to concentrate on the beauty of the sunset, the red sun sinking down towards the sea through a spectacular pink and purple sky, but her thoughts soon returned to the treadmill they seemed incapable of escaping. She remembered that night, that terrible night, when unable to sleep Ranjan had woken her up with the ominous words, 'There's something I want to talk to you about.'

'Can't it wait till the morning?' she had protested sleepily, still blissfully ignorant.

'No, please listen,' he insisted with an urgency which immediately alerted her. But now that she was wide awake he didn't know how to begin; while he hesitated, prevaricated, then assured her of his love for her, Kavita felt increasingly agitated, suspecting the worst yet unable to believe that it could have happened. Eventually she said with nervously twitching lips, 'If that's all you've got to say to me, I might as well go back to sleep.' Then he had come straight out with it. What had she felt? Impossible to recall. Anger. Shock. And a weird idea that surely there was still something they could do to *make it not have happened*? Only later, when it had sunk in that it had really happened, that it could not be undone any more than a dead person could be brought back to life, only then had she broken down and cried. 'Why did you do it, Ranjan, why? How could you do it to me? Don't lie to me — you don't love me. You would never have hurt me like this if you did.'

But Ranjan hadn't lied. He had got caught up in the affair without much reflection and that, precisely, was the joy of it. Unlike Kavita, who was constantly trying to make their relationship correspond to some utopian ideal of her own, this girl demanded nothing, promised nothing. She had a wide-eyed uncritical admiration for his intellectual capacities which Ranjan craved and Kavita stubbornly refused to give him; at the same time she made no concessions to him emotionally, insisted on retaining her independence and her freedom to contract other relationships if and when she chose, and this, too, Ranjan found attractive. Of course, at some level he knew that Kavita would be hurt, but he felt sure she would ultimately accept this as she had accepted so much else. What he had never expected was that their marriage would be threatened in any way, and he was shaken to find Kavita questioning whether it was ethical for her to continue living with a man who, according to her own terms, didn't love her. It was this aspect of her response which disturbed him most. When she was silent and thoughtful for long periods, as she was now, he worried that she was planning her escape from him. One good thing was that at the moment she didn't know any men who were likely to offer her the love and security which she kept complaining Ranjan had failed to provide. But one could never tell. Putting his arm around her and looking a little anxiously into her face he asked, 'What are you thinking about?'

'I was listening to the waves,' she replied, not entirely untruthfully. 'They sound so restful. It would be good just to lie on them and be rocked to sleep and never wake up again.'

'Oh Kavita! Why do you always have such depressing and morbid ideas these days? I know I haven't been an ideal husband, but I'm trying to change, can't you see that? I spend more time with the children now, and they are slowly warming up to me as a result. I wash my own clothes, even cook now and then. Tell me what more you want me to do and I'll do it. As for this other thing — it's over now, and I've promised it won't happen again. So why can't you relax and be happy?'

'It may be over so far as you are concerned, but for me it's only just begun. How can I be sure it won't happen again and again? You've made promises before and broken them. You've been nice to me before and then changed completely for no reason. I can't trust you any more, Ranjan.'

'You mean that I lied to you, that I'm a liar?'

'I didn't say that. You may have meant what you said, but you didn't have the persistence to hold to it, and I have no reason to believe that you will hold to it now. What makes me saddest of all is that I thought we had something special, something better than the...'

'But it *is* special, Kavita,' interrupted Ranjan, his arm tightening around her. 'What makes you think...'

'It's not,' insisted Kavita. 'It's just an ordinary marriage where you get tired of me and have to seek diversion with other women.'

'That's not true! Can't you understand that this other relationship was at a totally different level? Nothing was at stake. I feel nothing now that it's over — no regrets, nothing. Whereas if we were to break up I don't know what I would do!' and he smiled at her, wondering what her response would be.

Kavita smiled in spite of herself. 'Of course, in a way I can understand that, but I can't imagine it at all,' she began. 'I would never go in for that kind of affair — I would find it boring and a waste of time. I've got this ideal of an all-consuming, perfectly balanced, lifelong passion. I'd find it pointless to relate to anyone without that intensity, I wouldn't get anything out of it. And we were like that at first, weren't we? Or was it only an illusion?'

'It wasn't an illusion — we were like that and we still are. At least, *I* love you as much as I did then, in fact, even more. What can I say to convince you?'

'Nothing, Ranjan. There's nothing you can say now. You'll just have to show me. And I don't have much confidence that you'll be able to.'

So... that was it. There was nothing he could say to her. He would have to prove it — and that would take time. But that nagging doubt remained: what if someone else came into her life in the meantime, before he had time to convince her, and promised the kind of intense relationship she craved? He jumped up suddenly, almost violently, as if trying to shake off the thought. 'Let's go home,' he said, picking up Sunil and calling out to the others. Kavita followed, more slowly. Neither of them said very much on the way back.

CHAPTER 16

When the next Sunday meeting came round, Mariam went along with Ranjan. He had given her a summary of previous discussions, and she was anticipating the coming one with a sense of excitement. Ranjan's success in bringing together a group of workers who were interested in regular political discussions seemed to her quite extraordinary, and apparently the level of the discussions was also quite high. It would be interesting to see how they developed.

Ranjan was pleasantly surprised to find four members of the circle already present. When he introduced Mariam to them they greeted her politely and gave her the best seat, but then carried on talking without taking any notice of her. In a way Mariam was glad, because it gave her more time to assess them before she was called on to say anything; she listened intently and tried to connect what they were saying with what Ranjan had said about them. As the others came in, they looked at her in some surprise and then proceeded to ignore her, neither greeting her nor enquiring about her.

This time it was Arvind who opened the discussion. 'You remember last time,' he began, 'we were wondering if a party had any role to play at all if we agreed that it couldn't make decisions on behalf of the workers? Well, I was thinking about that, and I thought it would still be necessary. At present, workers are so fragmented, divided, it's impossible for us to do anything as a united force. Until I started coming to this group, I didn't know anything about what was going on in various industries...'

'Not only that,' interrupted Ganesh who worked in Adarsh Garments, the small-scale clothing factory where Shaheed and Anant were also employed, 'but even workers in the same industry don't know what's going on in the next factory...'

'Exactly,' continued Arvind. 'So one reason why a party is needed is to bring all these workers together somehow, and that's a necessary role, isn't it?'

'What about the unions?' suggested Ravindran. 'Wait a minute' he added, holding up his hands in a self-defensive gesture as Gopal turned on him angrily. Everyone laughed. 'I know what you're thinking, that the unions are divided and fight among themselves. Right? But that's precisely because they're attached to parties! Independent unions like mine are not like that. In them all workers can be united, they can really be a force to build up workers' unity...'

'Workers' unity indeed!' broke in Gopal hotly. 'What bullshit! Workers' unity in one plant, or in one company, maybe. But that's about all. What do workers in your company care about people like us, workers in small-scale industries? Does it bother you if we are thrown out, bashed up and black-listed simply because we try to form a union and get minimum wages? You are too preoccupied with your own affairs to think of helping us in any way. Is that what you call workers' unity?'

Ravindran had no answer to this. He knew that no one else in his factory lived in a basti like this or mixed with workers from small-scale industries. What is more, he himself had applied for a housing loan with the idea of booking a flat in one of the new housing estates coming up in the outer suburbs of Bombay. He had no intention of living here all his life and realised that once he moved out there would be little chance of participating in groups like this.

In the silence which followed, Ranjan doggedly put his word in: 'Isn't it obvious that at the level of trade union struggles there can be no workers' unity? How can a worker in, say, a modern, large-scale engineering or chemical plant fight alongside a worker in a small-scale workshop over issues like pay, hours of work and working conditions? They have nothing in common! It's only at a *political* level that they can be united, because the aspiration for workers' power can be common to all of them.'

'But what does that mean?' objected Shaheed. 'If it means putting into power some party which claims it is for the workers, I don't think most workers would be interested. And if it means something else, then you have to be more concrete. It's no use cooking up some so-called political programme and finding it has nothing to do with what workers actually want.'

Mariam's heart was pounding and she braced herself as if about to plunge into ice-cold water. She was following the discussion with keen interest and had been wanting to intervene for some time, but hesitated not only because she was the only woman in a group of men she was meeting for the first time, but also because her Hindi, never very good, had grown rusty with disuse and she was afraid she might not be able to express what she wanted to say. Now she latched on to Shaheed's last words. 'But what do workers actually want?' she began. 'Isn't that the first thing we have to find out? If we could systematically ask workers in each sector, each industry, what are their problems, what are their aspirations — then at least we would have some basis for deciding whether a common struggle is possible, and if so, over what issues.' She stopped abruptly. There was much more she wanted to say, especially to Ranjan, but she felt she had said enough for the present. Later would do.

Shaheed was impressed. 'I've been thinking along the same lines,' he agreed. 'Of course, it would be a huge task, and we would have to involve a lot more people, but we could make a start without waiting for all that.

Take up one sector, say, and formulate some kind of questionnaire. If it were small-scale, Anant and I could work on it, but we would need a bit of help.' He looked inquiringly at Ranjan.

Ranjan hesitated, and there was an expectant silence. 'I don't know anything about the small-scale sector except what you have told me,' he began. 'You will have to explain a lot to me. But I'd certainly be willing to do what I can, if you think I can help in any way.'

Shaheed nodded. 'Yes, I do think you can help. We have a good idea of the conditions and problems, but we're not so sure how to approach the questions — if there's going to be questionnaire, how to formulate it and so forth. You could help with that, couldn't you?'

'I can certainly do that,' said Ranjan, warming up to the idea.

'In the meantime Anant and I could meet other workers, we could discuss the idea with them and get their suggestions,' said Shaheed. 'Shall we meet after four or five days? Say on Friday, at my place?'

'That would be fine,' said Ranjan. 'Friday is some festival holiday, isn't it? Shall I come in the morning? Then we'll have all day if necessary. '

'Good,' said Shaheed. 'I'm looking forward to it.'

They wound up earlier than usual, and Ravindran offered to make tea while the others chatted informally. Mariam was introduced to those she had not met at the start and got to know where they worked, which unions they belonged to, and other information of that kind. She was relieved to find that she could communicate quite adequately and no one was shocked at her grammatical mistakes or liberal use of English words. By the time they got up to leave, she was feeling quite at home and almost regretted having to go.

'One minute, one minute!' exclaimed Arvind, striking his forehead with his hand as people were already beginning to drift out, 'I completely forgot.' Everyone stopped to listen. 'My daughter wanted me to ask about a problem — it's a good thing I remembered, she would have been mad at me if I hadn't. You know she works in a small-scale place — not even a factory really — there's no machinery, just ten women and the boss. Well, it seems that the boss is sexually harassing one of the women — one of them or two, I don't quite remember. Lalita was wondering if anything could be done about it.' There was no response and he was about to shrug his shoulders and dismiss the matter when an idea struck him. Turning to Mariam he said rather hesitantly, 'If you don't mind, do you think... it may be a good idea if you talk to my daughter and find out more about it.'

'Yes, I'd like to do that,' Mariam said at once.

'Oh good! Why not come to my house some time — you can meet her and then she can take you to meet her friend? Any evening will be all right.' When Mariam agreed he gave her directions to his house and went home pleased that he had managed to do something for Lalita.

Mariam, too, was pleased as she followed Ranjan closely through the dark passageway, till they reached a wider path. 'I'm so happy I came back!' she exclaimed as soon as they were out of earshot. 'Ranjan, I must congratulate you. What enormous potential!'

'Do you really think so?' asked Ranjan, slightly amused but also encouraged by her enthusiasm. 'I don't know. Sometimes I feel hopeful, but often I wonder if we'll ever get anywhere. It's good you suggested the idea of an enquiry — it's something new, and it'll prevent their interest from flagging.'

'Oh that! You know, for a minute I was afraid you would decline participating and I was very glad you didn't because that would have killed a lot of the interest. What I felt was that a group like this wouldn't be able to survive for ever on the basis of discussions alone — they need to do something together, and the traditional propaganda type of activity would be quite foreign to them. And it seems some of them had the same idea.'

'Yes, I know. Shaheed is quite a brilliant fellow, I'm sure he'll come up with something good. The only reason I hesitated is that I don't know a thing about the unorganised sector and don't feel confident or being able to contribute at all. Now that I've taken it on, I had better do some homework, otherwise I'll look like a fool.'

'You shouldn't be such a perfectionist,' laughed Mariam. 'I'm sure they're not expecting you to produce a huge thesis.'

'But if I take up a job I like to do it properly,' protested Ranjan.

'I know. You haven't changed a bit in that respect.' Mariam laughed again, then became thoughtful while they walked the last part of the way along S.T. Road. Had he changed in other respects, she was wondering? It never occurred to her to doubt the truth of what Kavita had told her, yet her imagination stubbornly refused to accept the picture of Ranjan it offered. She had known him to be hot-tempered in the past, but so oppressive and irrational? Surely not! What could he possibly gain by keeping Kavita out of his work? On the contrary, her assistance and advice would certainly be a help to him.

'Ranjan,' she asked suddenly, 'does Kavita ever come to these meetings?'

'Kavita?' he asked, surprised. 'No, of course not. What could she do there? And anyway, who would look after the children if she did?'

Mariam said nothing, but she was very troubled. What had happened to him? Kavita and Ranjan seemed to have got into a hopeless situation; Ranjan was not only hurting her but destroying himself yet he didn't seem to be aware of it at all . She must think of something to do — this mustn't be allowed to go on.

CHAPTER 17

No matter how much you keep postponing unpleasant decisions they finally catch up with you. Mariam sighed heavily as yet again she came to the problem she always put away without solving: how was she going to earn her living? In some ways it was very convenient, staying in her aunt's spacious old bungalow; she had her meals there, she could borrow money for travel, and what more did she need? But she knew this parasitic existence couldn't last long and she was glad of that because it also imposed an enormous emotional strain on her. Her aunt was a kind old woman who would have been glad to keep Mariam as long as she wanted to stay, but it was a real effort having to talk to her and adjust to her view of the world. Even that was tolerable; what was *not* tolerable was the constant interference of her mother in her life. To begin with, she was upset that Mariam had chosen to stay with her sister and not with her; to Mariam's first argument 'Mummy, she's a widow, and all alone' — she had replied indignantly, 'What about me? As though I'm not a widow, too! And just because I've got two sons, that doesn't mean my daughter should abandon me.' At moments like this it took all Mariam's self-control to prevent her from responding with the bitterness she felt. She could keep a guard on her tongue, but she couldn't prevent the retorts from going round in her head.

'Who abandoned whom? What about all those years and years when I was left alone with ayahs while you were enjoying yourself with your social life and parties? You not only deprived me of a real mother, you wouldn't even let me have a substitute mother — I remember every time I got attached to an ayah, she would be dismissed on some pretext or other. And do you think I didn't notice how everything changed when Navroze was born? Oh, I know he's a son, and a son needs special attention, he can't be left to ayahs all the time!' Only briefly had she felt anything like closeness to her mother, and that was during the year of her father's last illness. Always authoritarian, he had grown more and more despotic as his strength declined, had invented elaborate ways of torturing his wife such as writing a will in which she was left with nothing but his old clothes.

'You'll be left destitute, destitute!' he exulted. 'Unless you do everything I say, you'll be out on the streets when I die!'

Revolted, Mariam had protested, 'Mummy, don't let him destroy you like this! You know we would never let you starve and you yourself are an intelligent woman, you'll manage to survive.'

But her mother had been too terrorised to resist. She submitted to every humiliation his sick imagination could devise, and even after all that, still lived in fear that he would not change his will. It was at this point that Mariam decided to go to England — anywhere rather than live in a house where she was a daily witness to such perversions. She had been called back when her father was on his deathbed and was once again sickened to see her mother's conflict — dread that he would survive to oppress her once more and dread that he would die leaving her a beggar. Whatever pity or compassion she felt for either of them was almost drowned out by disgust that a human relationship could be so distorted. She remembered how Kavita, grief-stricken at her own mother's death, had been stunned when she said enviously, 'You don't know how lucky you are to be able to cry like this, Kavita. I would give anything to feel such grief for my parents. I know it must be painful — don't think I don't understand that. But there is something healing, too, in your mourning — it leaves you whole and clean. Whereas I feel as if I'm tied up in knots inside, and something is rotten but I can't get rid of it.'

Kavita had been incredulous and Mariam had given up trying to explain. When you belong to a happy family, when you have been loved and cherished by your parents all your life, it's impossible to understand the rage and emptiness left by an unhappy childhood; it's like someone who lacks colour vision trying to understand colour — or is it the other way round, someone with colour vision trying to imagine what the world must look like in black and white? Yes, it was she herself who was handicapped, thought Mariam. Something essential to her development in childhood had been lacking and she had suffered for it ever since.

After her father's death her mother had recovered rapidly. He hadn't of course cut her out of his will; it didn't suit him that people should say he left his wife unprovided for. No, they must acknowledge that she had been handsomely endowed: he had left the entire business to her alone. He probably expected that she would get it professionally managed, but she took over the management herself and ran the enterprise efficiently and well. It was a fairly small outfit which specialised in designing and producing fashionable clothes that sold for fabulous prices in some of the most expensive shops in Bombay. Mariam's mother was well qualified to handle the concern, having the imagination, the experience and the shrewdness to be able to appeal to the very élite market it was seeking to attract. Her two sons were already working for it, and now that Mariam had returned, her mother took it for granted that she, too, would join. Nothing could be further from Mariam's own interests, and yet, what was she to do for a living? She had found paying guest accommodation not far from Ranjan and Kavita, quite cheap and with meals provided; it was ideal for her and she would have liked to move in at once — but how could she pay for it? Even if she borrowed money for the deposit, she certainly couldn't go on incurring debts without any prospect of being able to repay them.

There was one possible solution. The thought of joining the family firm was horrible, but Mariam had done a computer course while she was in England, and she knew there were some jobs in her mother's business that she could do. She would bargain for her price and earn enough in three days to allow her to do what she liked with the rest of her time and to allow her to live on her own! But would her mother agree? On consideration, Mariam thought she would. She was perceptive enough to have realised that it would be difficult if not impossible to control Mariam through family ties, and therefore would probably be ready to consider this other way of keeping a hold over her. One couldn't be sure, but it was worth trying. Mariam smiled inwardly. To relate to her mother as an employee in order not to have to relate to her as a daughter — this was a solution which appealed to her!

CHAPTER 18

Life had improved considerably in Lakshmi's home. After weeks of single-minded wooing, Shetty had finally persuaded Vasanta, a young vendor he had met in the marketplace, to marry him and come to live with him. Her mother — she had no father — had been very much against the match, knowing that Shetty was already married she felt that Vasanta's position would be little better than that of a prostitute. But Vasanta herself, intrigued by Shetty's reputation as a desperado and flattered by his obvious infatuation with her, had run away and got married to him one day, and there was nothing her mother could do about it.

For some time after she moved in, Shetty remained completely preoccupied with Vasanta and virtually ignored Lakshmi. So long as she got the meals ready on time and kept the children out of his way, she could escape his notice altogether. Vasanta was the new bride, and all his attention was for her. As for Lakshmi, it never occurred to her to resent this state of affairs although she was now burdened with the cooking and washing for an extra person. All she could feel was gratitude that at least, temporarily, she had some respite from her husband's beatings and sexual demands. She couldn't even find it in her heart to take offence at the somewhat arrogant way in which Vasanta treated her, as though she were a servant or employee of some sort. Let the girl enjoy herself while she can, she thought; poor thing, she doesn't know what's in store for her. The present situation couldn't possibly last for more than a month, then the violence and beatings would surely resume. Lakshmi hoped that with two women to beat, Shetty's violence towards her would have to decline; at the same time she felt sorry for Vasanta. After all, hadn't Lakshmi herself once been young and goodlooking, even if not as beautiful as Vasanta? And look at her now — thin as a skeleton with all her ribs showing, half her teeth knocked out, her face haggard and marked with the scars of countless beatings — who would recognise the young girl of twelve years ago? And this girl would end up the same way. Perhaps she would try to run away to her mother and her mother would send her back saying, 'You didn't listen to my advice, so now you face the consequences.' No, there was no escape for her. She would slowly sink until she shared Lakshmi's fate. So what harm was there if she enjoyed life now, decked herself out and treated Lakshmi with disdain?

Lakshmi was right to think that the situation couldn't last, but she had misjudged Vasanta's resourcefulness. Less than three weeks after the marriage Shetty abused Vasanta while drunk — not a real beating, only a few slaps and verbal abuse — and she left while he was out. Of course he went straight to her mother's house, expecting her to be there and confident that he could persuade her to come back. But she was not there. For three days he searched, not even coming home to eat or sleep, but she had vanished it seemed; he was unable to find the slightest trace of her. He was mortally insulted and humiliated by this incident. Here he was, a man feared in the whole basti and beyond, fooled by a mere girl — how could it happen? He had really lost his head over her, and that made him look all the more foolish when she coolly walked out on him. His fury was enough to make him burst, and there was a convenient way to vent it: drink till he could scarcely control himself, thrash Lakshmi till she could barely move, and then drink some more until he passed out. It was the only way he could feel a man again — until he woke up to the same nagging, irritating thought.

It was only now that poor Lakshmi, cheated of her dreams of a quieter life, cursed Vasanta for the mischief she had caused. What right had she to come and inflict this on Lakshmi and then, on top of it all, walk away without a scratch or bruise? Every time Shetty went out in search of Vasanta, Lakshmi hoped against hope that he would find her, caring little what he would do to her if he did. Let her pay for her own mistakes, she thought, why should I have to pay for them?

But Vasanta failed to show up and Lakshmi continued to pay for it. She ultimately reached such a pitch of despair that she could not speak to anyone but went around with a wild look which frightened away even those who felt sorry for her. Sanjeevani, with her sure sense of self-preservation, kept away from her mother as much as possible and so managed to avoid getting beaten. Only Chandran still clung to her with a desperation which increased with her own, taking not only some of the blows meant for her but also the beatings she gave him. With a skill beyond his years he tended to and revived her after every battering, once persuading a kind taxi driver to help him take her to the nearest hospital. But by now Lakshmi was past appreciating his devotion. Once when he was trying to help her up from the corner of the floor where she had fallen, she pushed him roughly away saying bitterly, 'What's the matter with you, are you a girl or something, always fussing around me like this? Why did I bother to bring you into the world if you can't protect me? What's the use of having a son if he can't even fight that monster?'

These words were spoken without any thought and immediately forgotten; Lakshmi could never have dreamed what impact they would have. Chandran had never had a real childhood. His infancy had been an almost continuous struggle to remain alive, and as far back as he could remember he seemed to have been burdened with the frightful responsibility of guarding his mother's life — a responsibility which left him no chance of enjoying play, the companionship of friends or any aspect of the lighter side of childhood. Other children kept away from him, partly because of the reputation of his father and mother, partly because he was so withdrawn and strange. Even at school, which he attended irregularly, he had no real friends although the boy he sat next to, who came from a much poorer family but was very quick, often befriended him by helping him with lessons which he found difficult. He liked this boy, liked him very much and would have liked to be his friend, but how could he be friends with any normal child with the shame of his family background and the burden of his early maturity lying so heavy on his shoulders?

And yet he was a child, with a child's imagination; the horrors he witnessed became in his dreams grotesque beyond measure, driving him almost mad with fear — the strategies he had evolved to cope with his waking life simply did not work here. Scarcely a night passed when he didn't wake up shivering and sweating, his throat tense and aching with the screams he thought he had made although strangely enough he often found the others sleeping as though nothing had happened. Of course there were times when he woke up to real horrors, and then he would shut his eyes again, trying to escape both waking and sleeping nightmares by suspending himself somewhere in between.

That night after Lakshmi had taunted him with being more like a girl than a boy, Chandran dreamed that he had come running home from school to find a noisy crowd in front of his house. What was it? What could be happening? He pushed and wriggled his way through until he could see. His mother was kneeling down, her head on the ground and her hair all loose, and his father was beating her as he had never done before, with a heavy stick which would surely break all her bones! A few people were shouting out to him to stop, but most of them were just watching and no one was *doing* anything. Chandran struggled desperately to get through the crowd and reach her to prevent some of those cruel blows from falling on her. He reached her, clasped her, one, two blows fell on him, and then the third fell on her with a fateful thud. She collapsed completely, like a balloon from which the air has been released, and his father, after looking at her for a moment, walked away growling and muttering. A few people came to have a closer look at the unconscious woman, but no one would touch her. The crowd slowly melted away and Chandran was left alone to drag her in as best he could and begin to apply the remedies he always used. But this time they had no effect. She remained lifeless, and he realised in a flash that she was dead: nothing could revive her now. He knelt by her side stupefied, and slowly the thought crept into his mind that he could have prevented this. If instead of clasping her he had attacked his father, even killed him, this wouldn't have happened; his mother would still be alive, she would be clasping him, thanking him for saving her. But now it was too late. She was dead and he was utterly alone in the world.

The effect of this dreams was so powerful that when he woke up he actually had to creep over to where his mother lay sleeping to make sure that she was still breathing. And the next day the image of her lifeless body kept coming into his mind over and over again, together with words he had often heard her moan: 'He'll kill me, I know he'll kill me one day,' and 'Oh God, let me die, why don't you let me die?'

Later that evening Lakshmi had just begun to cook when her husband came in demanding his meal. He was not drunk and it was well before the time he usually ate, but the fact that the food was not ready was sufficient excuse for him to start beating her. Chandran noticed he was using a heavy stick like the one he had seen in his dream, and was seized with panic as he saw the dream starting to come true: the details were different but this was it all right! But it mustn't, it mustn't be allowed to end in the same way! Looking around wildly, his eyes fell on to the kitchen knife his mother had been using when she was interrupted. In a trance he picked it up, waited until his father's back was turned, shut his eyes tightly and stabbed him.

Shetty swore and let go of Lakshmi as the blood gushed out. Turning round he saw Chandran standing with the knife in his hands — the wound he had inflicted was in fact very slight, but the sight of blood as he opened his eyes had paralysed him. With a roar which sounded as if it came from some wild animal Shetty turned on him, knocked the knife out of his hand with a blow which seemed to shatter every finger, and started thrashing him with the stick. He went on and on until his arm was tired and then stalked out, still swearing and cursing. Chandran had long since passed out.

Lakshmi, who had not been badly hurt, watched the whole scene feeling sick and faint with horror. For a whole minute after Shetty left she remained frozen to the spot, and then she suddenly regained the power of motion. With a low groan she ran to Chandran and knelt down. Was he dead? Surely he must be! No child could survive such a beating and Chandran was weak and sickly. She put her ear to his chest. No, thank God, he was still alive. She set about dressing his wounds and trying to revive him. And all the time her thoughts were running on. What madness had got into the child to make him do that? He had never done anything like it before. Could it be? She closed her eyes as if to shut out the idea but it insisted on pushing its way in... could it be what she had said to him yesterday? The blood drained from her head at the thought that she was partly responsible for this. Yes, there was no other explanation for it. It's my fault, it's my fault, she kept saying to herself. But it was no use simply blaming herself, something had to be done. They would go away, somewhere he would never find them. Even if they had to live on a railway platform or pavement — anything would be better than this. Leaving Chandran still unconscious, she went in search of Sanjeevani who had gone out to play. When she came back with the little girl, his eyes were open but fixed immovably on the ceiling. 'Chandran!' she said urgently, 'Can you get up? Please try, darling. I'll help you. We're going away, Chandran, that's why you must get up.' Slowly, painfully, he sat up. How well she knew that feeling! With astonishing presence of mind, she gathered together her jewellery and all the money she could find and tied them in a bundle with some clothes and a sheet. Then, holding Sanjeevani with one hand and supporting Chandran with the other, she looked out cautiously.

It was night now, and the part of Patthar Basti where they lived was very dark. Normally this frightened her, but tonight she was pleased because her main fear was that they would be seen and followed by one of Shetty's goondas. Like shadows they crept out to the main road, caught a bus to the nearest station and then a train. Seeing a platform with a large number of sleeping and seated forms on it, she got out with the children. This would do for tonight. Tomorrow, perhaps, they would move on. She spread out the sheet, settled the children on it and went to buy some food from the station stall. When she came back she gave Sanjeevani her share, but before giving anything to Chandran leaned down over him, stroked his head and spoke to him in a tone he had never heard her use before: 'Chandran, my little boy, listen carefully to what I say because it's very important. I was wrong to make fun of you and say you were like a girl. I'm glad you're kind and gentle — do you understand that? I like you the way you are. And now I know you're brave as well: you took all that beating without once crying out. I'm very proud of my son!'

For the first time since his dream Chandran looked straight at her, and then his face broke into a painful but triumphant smile. Yes, he had been right about the dream. But he had managed to change the ending. He had changed the ending!

CHAPTER 19

On Friday morning when Ranjan knocked at Shaheed's door it was Laila who came out to see who it was. He greeted her and asked if Shaheed was in, adding, 'He's expecting me, I've got some work with him.' He was a little surprised when she abruptly turned away without another word, but he waited patiently for Shaheed to come out.

Laila stood inside the door with tear-filled eyes and trembling lips. They had been planning this outing for so long! Everything was ready, the picnic lunch already cooked and packed. She had sent the children out to play telling them to be near at hand as she would call them when it was time to leave. They, too, were looking forward to the holiday with great excitement — how could she possibly disappoint them? There was only one thing this could mean: Shaheed had completely lost interest in them. This was the one day he had agreed to spend with them in months — and now he was backing out of it. Did they mean nothing to him? She stared at him in dumb reproach and he stared back silently. When he had heard Ranjan's voice at the door and saw Laila turn round, he immediately realised what had happened. He had totally forgotten about this picnic when he fixed the appointment with Ranjan! He felt dreadfully guilty about it, but what could he do now? He surely couldn't send Ranjan back after having brought him all this way for nothing? And yet, as he looked at Laila, his heart ached. He couldn't bear to see her crying miserably. And to know that it was his fault — that made it so much worse. He slowly walked to the door and stepped out. What could he say to Ranjan? 'I'm a real idiot,' he began, feeling better as he reproached himself. 'Even when you mentioned that today was a holiday I didn't remember I had promised to go out with my family all day. What shall we do? They've been looking forward to it so much, and have got everything ready, the children will be terribly disappointed if it's cancelled now. It's all my fault, it was really stupid of me.'

Ranjan felt a twinge of annoyance, but rose to the occasion. 'Oh, we can do it another day,' he said at once. 'There's no hurry at all. How about Sunday?'

'Sunday suits me fine — but are you sure you don't mind? I'm so sorry, calling you all the way out here and then sending you back, I feel really bad.'

'What do you mean "all the way"? It's hardly ten minutes! And I'm sure my wife and children will be pleased to see me back so soon. In fact we could go on an outing as well!'

Laila had been listening carefully from inside. Now that she knew the dilemma had been resolved in her favour, she felt sorry for Ranjan and nudging Shaheed whispered that he should invite Ranjan in for tea. Still remorseful, Shaheed complied, and although Ranjan had no particular desire for tea just then, he accepted the invitation in case it should look as if he were angry if he refused.

Walking home later he gave vent to his frustration with vague gestures and mutterings. It was really too bad the way things got put off and delayed and postponed for the most trivial of reasons! No wonder nothing ever got done. Even Shaheed, who was so good in other ways, was always being side-tracked by something or the other. That was what he said to himself, but somehow, paradoxically, he found his admiration and respect for Shaheed increase after this incident. He could make a mistake and admit it, criticise himself — was that it? Partly, perhaps, but that was not the main thing. What attracted Ranjan most of all was Shaheed's concern and tenderness for his wife and children. This aspect of him had not been very apparent before, but now it seemed to dominate all his other qualities, illuminate them with a brighter light. When he thought about it, it wasn't only respect and admiration he felt for Shaheed but real affection. He was a man you would like to have not just as an associate or comrade but as a friend. A friend! That word made Ranjan realise how terribly lonely he was. He knew so many people, yet there was hardly anyone he could call a friend. The people who came closest to being that were Kavita and Mariam — two women. But no men. Of course in a superficial sense, yes, he had plenty of friends, people with whom he could talk perfectly freely and comfortably about everything — everything except himself that is, except what troubled and disturbed him most deeply. Why was that? These people would say that they knew him well, yet the most important dimension of him remained hidden from them. And this formed an almost tangible barrier, which headed him off into abstractions and generalities whenever the topic of conversation came too close to his inner self, or threatened to touch on what could hurt. What about Shaheed? With him would it be possible to get past that barrier to a real friendship? Ranjan doubted it. But he would certainly like to try.

CHAPTER 20

It was lunch-time in Adarsh Garments, the forty sewing machines were idle, and Verma, the boss, had gone out to have his mid-day meal at a local restaurant. The moment he disappeared, Anant and Shaheed seized the opportunity to call the others to gather round with their tiffin boxes and listen to their plans for a survey. Seated on tables and chairs and eating their food the workers listened with interest, but their first response was highly critical of the whole exercise.

'What's the use of writing all this down? We know about it anyway.'

'If we give the report to the government will they do anything about it? They ought to — considering the kind of malpractices that go on here.'

'What do you think? You think the government doesn't know? They know all right but they get their cut out of it too, so why should they stop it?'

'That's right — they're happy about the foreign exchange as well — Verma has a brother in the UK and most of the stuff we make is exported there.'

'The two of them must be minting money! You know the kind of shirts you get for twenty rupees here sell for fifty-sixty rupees there.'

'More than that! Nothing less than a hundred or two hundred. And when you think of the miserable pay we get.'

'Even the pay we're supposed to get is nothing. Who can support a family these days on a thousand rupees? In the last few years prices have doubled — even the rubbishy grain we get for our rations has gone up in price.'

'We should have a proper D.A. system so that our wages go up when the price index does. Where my brother works...'

'What D.A. system! First we should make sure that we get at least the one thousand we're supposed to get.'

'Yes yes, did I say we shouldn't? But in a few years that one thousand will be worth only five hundred — isn't that right? That's why we need proper D.A.'

'That comes afterwards. But this thing he's doing is clearly illegal getting us to sign for a thousand and giving us only seven hundred.'

'Three hundred rupees from each of us every month! That's how much he gets in the black.'

'Are you mad? That's only one way of getting black money! These people have hundreds of other ways. He probably says that he sells a shirt for fifty and then actually sells it for a hundred rupees. That way he makes fifty rupees of black money on every shirt he sells as well.'

'But why doesn't the government do something about it? You hear about all these income-tax raids — why don't they catch these fellows and put them in jail?'

'I tell you, they're not bothered — they are all just as corrupt themselves. Those raids are only for show — to make people think that something is being done about tax evaders.'

Anant and Shaheed listened, forgetting all about the enquiry. They had tried to form a union two years earlier, but the attempt had foundered due to the reluctance of the majority of workers. Their predecessors had tried too, and every single worker who joined the union had been dismissed. Those who remained had drawn their own conclusions, and not even the enthusiasm of new-comers like Shaheed and Anant could make them change their minds. At that time they had been forced to give up the whole idea, but now Anant couldn't resist saying, 'There's no point in relying on the government to improve our conditions, only we ourselves can do that. And naturally Verma will feel he can push us around if we don't even have a union to protect us.'

From some of the older workers there was an immediate negative response to this. 'Don't talk to us about unions! You know what happened when they tried to form a union here.'

'Seven hundred isn't much, but it's better than nothing.'

'How will we feed our children if we get thrown out?'

But the majority were silent, and waited to hear Anant's response.

'You mean you're ready to go on taking this nonsense for ever? No proper D.A., no benefits, fifty-four hours a week, and we get cheated out of three hundred rupees every month on top of all that! Don't think that things will improve all by themselves — nowhere in the world do employers give anything to workers of their own accord. If we want any improvement we have to fight for it.'

There were murmurs of approval. 'That's true. We got beaten once but that doesn't mean we'll always get beaten.'

'I'm ready for a fight. Even if we get thrown out, it'll be worth it if we manage to teach this fellow a lesson.'

'Now why should we get thrown out? He can't just throw us out if we form a union — that's an unfair labour practice!'

'Yes, but you have to prove that in court, and who's got money for lawyers and all that? I think you have to be mentally prepared to be thrown out, otherwise you'll be too scared to do anything.'

'No, no, don't say that, that's a very negative approach. If we fight, we fight to win.'

'Who's denying that? But you have to be realistic all the same, don't you?'

The discussion rambled on, but kept returning to the same point: the heavy odds against them and their helplessness should Verma resort to dismissals, which he almost certainly would. Finally, Shaheed turned the debate to a new channel by saying, 'I'd like to think we could take up this struggle on our own, but it doesn't seem to be possible. Try and imagine what would happen. We form a union and serve him with a charter. He dismisses half of us. We don't have the resources to fight it out in court, so we try direct action — a strike or gherao or something. He might dismiss the others and hire a whole lot of new workers. Or he may put the police on to us, serve us with criminal charges. Or hire goondas to beat us up. Whatever he does, we're not strong enough to fight back on our own. We'll have to call in an outside union.'

'Absolutely correct. We should get Kelkar.'

'Oh no! Kelkar is a goonda himself. He gets workers in other unions beaten up if they don't join him.'

'But don't you see, that's why he's the right man? Only a goonda can deal with a goonda.'

'What about Gopal's union? They have two or three units in this industrial estate.'

'They're good honest fellows... but so small! Do you think they're strong enough to handle Verma?'

'Not really. They can succeed only where the employer is a bit decent — not with someone as crooked as Verma.'

It was sad but true. Shaheed sighed. He had his disagreements with Gopal, but would have infinitely preferred to join his union rather than Kelkar's. Anant had an idea: 'Look, we can join up with Kelkar to begin with — until the union gets recognised. Once we feel strong enough and Verma has been forced to deal with us, we can leave Kelkar and either join Gopal or set up an independent union, whatever we decide. Doesn't that solve our problem?'

'But you can't leave Kelkar just like that! He'll get his goondas to beat you up!'

'Nonsense, he can't do that, not if we all decide to leave. I'm telling you, I know of unions which have done it, and nothing happened to them.'

'Ah, they must be big units, but a weak one like ours...'

'All the more reason why he won't be too bothered if we leave him. He makes lakhs of rupees out of the big units every time they sign a settlement, but what can he get out of us? We'll be more of a burden to him than anything else.'

'But then why would he take us on in the first place?'

By now most of the workers had been drawn into the discussion apart from a few sceptics who still felt that to form a union was to head straight for disaster. They were still talking when the boss walked in and they had to scatter to their workstations, so nothing was decided that day. But the issue was now a live one and wouldn't be laid to rest. Day after day a core group of workers would meet and thrash it out. When they finally decided to take the initial step of joining Kelkar's union and talked it over with the rest of the workers, only five decided to stay out of it.

CHAPTER 21

Lalita had been expecting Mariam to come round every day since the study circle, yet when she actually arrived she was flustered and confused. It was especially embarrassing having to talk about such a topic with her mother cooking in a corner of the room and her brothers wandering in. However, the urgency of the situation was such that she quickly gathered her wits and took Mariam into her father's workshop which was empty because Arvind had gone to deliver a table to one of his customers. She apologised briefly for the uncomfortable seat and the sawdust and wood-shavings which were everywhere, then got down to telling the whole story. It was now six days since Preeti had first talked to her about this problem, and the excuse that she had her period wouldn't last any longer.

Mariam was excited and full of ideas. 'You should get all the women together and do something collectively,' she began. 'I'm sure your friend can't be the only one the boss has approached in this way — if he's done it to Preeti he must have done it to others. Has he ever made advances to you?'

'Not to me,' Lalita replied rather shyly, 'but there's another woman ... and also a lot of girls have left; they keep leaving, and we think it must be because of this.'

'Exactly! Each one thinks she's the only one so she leaves, while he goes on doing it to more and more women because he knows he can get away with it. What we need to do is to confront him with it and show him that everyone knows what's going on. Suppose, for example, the day he asks Preeti to stay behind, she tells you and you *all* stay on? You could say to him, "We're waiting for her and we're not going till she comes with us." And the same if he tries it on any other woman.'

'That's a good idea,' responded Lalita rather hesitantly. 'But what if the women don't want to talk about it? Even Preeti... actually, she told me only because I've been her best friend ever since we went to school together. She made me promise not to tell anyone but my father, and even then I was not supposed to mention her name — she'll be upset if she knows that I have. You see, she's afraid that if anyone finds out about it, the story will get back to her family and they'll blame her.'

'But why should anyone blame her? He's the culprit. He should be exposed!'

'Yes, but you know how people are — if a girl's name gets mixed up in something like this they think she has a bad character and then it's very difficult for her to get married.'

'Is that what Preeti's afraid of?'

'Partly. But not only that — she's also afraid of getting a beating from her grandfather.'

'Then we could try something else. We could go in at night and put up posters denouncing the boss as a lecher and protesting against the way he harasses his employees. He won't like that to be publicised, but at the same time no one's name will get linked up with him.'

'Yes, that's a better idea,' said Lalita, relieved. She had been quite anxious about what might happen to Preeti if her name were publicly mentioned in this connection.

'Come, then, shall we go and meet her?'

'Yes.' Lalita was still hesitant. After a few steps she said, 'Preeti lives in Patthar Basti which is about ten-fifteen minutes walk along S.T. Road, but there's another woman from our workshop who lives in Sheetal Nagar. Should we meet her and talk to her first?'

'Yes, certainly, that's a good idea.'

Seema's family was at home when they got there, so they had to take her outdoors to talk to her in private. They outlined their previous discussion and finally came to the suggestion of a poster campaign. Seema was categorically opposed to it. 'All right, so he won't know which particular women are responsible for it, but that makes it all the worse, he'll assume we're *all* responsible — and then who knows what he'll do? He could dismiss every one of us.'

'But that is what is actually happening,' Mariam pointed out. 'He is picking on you one by one, and you either have to give in to his demands or you lose your job. Think of all the women who have already been dismissed — many times more than the entire workforce. It's as though he had thrown out everyone three or four times over. Isn't it better to stand together and fight it out instead of letting women get victimised individually?'

'That's a problem for those who are picked out,' replied Seema, looking meaningfully at Lalita. 'How will it help them if everyone else suffers?'

Lalita turned her back deliberately and started walking away, but Mariam made a last attempt. 'Well, what if I talk to him then? I'll threaten him with legal action — it may frighten him. I'm an outsider, he can't do anything to me.'

But Seema still shook her head. 'He'll know that we must have told you — how else would you know about it? He can't do anything to *you* but he's sure to do something to *us*.'

Mariam left her and ran to catch up with Lalita who was already quite a distance away. As she drew level, Lalita spat with disgust. 'Chah! She's trying to imply that I go with the boss but she must be the one who does. How else has she kept her job for so long? She's been there much longer than Preeti and I have. How can you do anything with women who're ready to sell themselves like that?'

'Don't say such things, Lalita,' said Mariam putting a hand on the girl's arm. 'We don't know for certain that she goes with the boss, and even if she does, it's not her fault — she probably needs the money.'

'There's another one like that — Sarita,' said Lalita. 'She's a widow with children. I don't think she would support us either. In fact, I can't think who would be likely to support us. Maybe Yasmine — maybe. And what's the use of that? He would just dismiss all three of us and carry on the same way.'

Mariam sighed. 'I can see this is not going to be easy. What shall we do now? The only thing I can think of is to talk to Preeti and maybe her family. If she were not so scared to speak out openly, we could try to do something.'

A chill wind started blowing as they walked towards Patthar Basti; the gloom cast by gathering clouds gave the place a menacing air as Lalita led the way down the approach road. But Mariam was not to meet Preeti that day. They had hardly entered the basti before they got talking to a knot of women who were obviously agitated about something. They stopped to listen and got so involved that they forgot all about what had brought them there. Apparently a woman had been raped the previous night by three men who had broken the bolt on her door and entered the hut.

'They were from Shetty's gang — not Shetty himself, he usually doesn't get involved in this kind of thing, but three others.'

'You mean someone actually saw them go in?'

'No, not when they went in, but quite a few people saw them coming out.'

'Yes, I was there. My God! I never forget those screams, they'll haunt me as long as I live. They went on and on until I was ready to scream myself.'

'What! All of you knew she was being raped and no one went to help?' Mariam was so shocked that she forgot where she was.

'Behenji, you don't know what those dadas are like. If you go to help, you'll be the next one to get raped — raped and murdered most likely.'

'Weren't there any men around?'

'Of course. It was night time, everyone was there. But they're just as scared. They would get their legs broken at the very least if they tried to interfere.'

'You see what things are like in this basti,' said an elderly woman bitterly. 'All of us are too bothered about saving our own skins to be able to help anyone else.'

'But you were there too, Kantabai.'

'I know I was there. I'm like the rest of you — too scared to do anything on my own. I would have gone in if here had been a single person ready to come with me. Didn't I say so?'

'They wouldn't have hurt you. At least they respect you a bit.'

'That's very nice of you — putting all the responsibility on me!' Mariam could hear the note of anguish in her voice and warmed to her more and more. 'But I'm a human being, just like you, don't you understand that? I can't fight against these things all by myself. Even now we can do something. We haven't been able to prevent this rape, but we can try and prevent the next one. If we get the culprits caught and punished, it's less likely to happen again.'

'Then why don't you go and tell the police? Not the local police, they won't do a thing.'

'But I couldn't see them from where I was standing! It's the people who saw them who will have to come forward to identify them.'

'And if they do that, *they* will be identified by Shetty's gang!'

'In any case, I don't think this would happen to any of us — she was that kind of a woman.'

'What do you mean, "that kind of a woman"? 'You mean it's all right if *some* women get raped?!' Kantabai and Mariam cried out together.

'What I mean is, if a woman leaves her husband and lives with another man, she's asking for trouble, isn't she?'

'And you should see how arrogant she is as well — won't so much as talk to us or look at us, she just sits at home reading all day!'

'All right, go on thinking that till you get raped,' said Kantabai with biting sarcasm. 'Just wait till they catch you alone and see if they stop to ask if you're living with your legal husband!'

It was completely dark now, and the women began to disperse one by one. Lalita touched Mariam's arm and Mariam noticed she was trembling. 'I think I'd better go home,' she said in shaking voice. 'It's too late for us to meet Preeti today.'

'Yes, of course,' said Mariam warmly, grasping her hand which was icy cold. 'This is no place for a girl like you. Will you be all right going home alone, or shall I come and drop you?'

'No, no. The road is right here and Sheetal Nagar is quite safe — not like this place,' and she ran off.

Mariam was rather glad she didn't have to take Lalita home because she wanted to speak to Kantabai who was still standing there, her face looking haggard.

'How is the poor woman now?' she asked softly.

Kantabai emerged from her abstraction. 'Do you want to see her?' she asked. Mariam nodded and followed her through the dark, dirty alleyways, now slushy with the monsoon rain. They entered a hut where a woman lay on a bed that occupied almost half the room. She turned her head when they entered but gave no sign of recognition or greeting.

'Have you taken her to a doctor?' Mariam asked.

'I attended to her myself. Those wounds will heal — I'm not worried about them. It's her poor mind that's gone. See, she used to know me so well but now she doesn't even recognise me.' Kantabai wiped her eyes with the pallu of her sari.

'It must have been the shock,' said Mariam. 'Are you looking after her now?'

'Yes, I'm sleeping here until her husband comes back,' said Kantabai, indicating a roll of bedding on the floor. 'But I can't stay with her all the time, I have to go out to work. What can I do? I'm all alone in the world and if I don't work I don't eat.'

'What work is it?'

'Oh, only domestic work in two flats. I used to work in the quarry but had to give up because of breathing problems. Even now, one of the buildings has a lift but in the other I have to climb four flights of stairs, and by the time I reach the top I'm panting so much it takes me ten minutes to recover. And after sweeping and swabbing the floor I feel quite ill.'

'Don't you have any relatives? Surely there's someone in your family who can help?'

'That's a long story, behenji. Let's put it like this: I don't have any relations who are prepared to support me.'

'You're Kantabai, aren't you? My name is Mariam. What is she called?'

'Mangala.'

'And this is her home?'

'Yes.'

'If I ask people, they'll be able to direct me here, won't they? I have to come back tomorrow to meet someone and I'd like to drop in, but I won't be able to remember the way at all.'

'Oh yes, ask anyone. Shall I take you back to S.T. Road now?'

Mariam had rarely felt so helpless in her life. Preeti, Mangala, Kantabai three women with such massive problems, and no solutions that she could see at present, but she was determined to find a way; no problem was insoluable if you really set your mind to solving it!

CHAPTER 22

It was afternoon, and Preeti's grandparents and father were sleeping. Her mother squatted in the doorway washing clothes on the pavement outside while Preeti lay on her mat, brooding. This is what she usually did during the time she spent at home, and the rest of the day she roamed around the basti, chatting to the women, exchanging confidences with the girls, playing with the children. Her mother, who had always got on well with her, was baffled and exasperated. 'All right, so you were dismissed, we're not blaming you for that, are we? Anyway it was your idea to take up the job in the first place. But now that you're at home can't you at least help me? Just do a bit of the housework and make a few agarbattis — is that too much to ask?'

Two weeks ago her boss had given her an ultimatum: either give in to him or don't come back to work the next day. 'I told you it was no use,' she said disconsolately as she walked back with Lalita. 'There's nothing anyone can do.'

'But still, it's not the end of the world,' Lalita consoled her. 'If you get dismissed, it's a problem for your whole family, it's not your problem only. That makes it easier to handle, doesn't it? Everyone has to try and figure out what to do.'

'That's true.' This was a new idea to Preeti, and when she thought about it she began to feel rather resentful that she had been suffering alone over what was actually a family difficulty. This made things very different; now she could go home and announce without any qualms, 'The boss told me not to come to work from tomorrow.'

Surprise, alarm, and questions met her announcement: 'Why?' 'What's happened?'

'How should I know? Why don't you go and ask him yourselves?' Preeti replied sullenly, knowing very well they would do nothing of the sort.

There were rapid adjustments to meet the crisis. Preeti's aunt found work at one more flat, her mother and brothers took on more agarbattis and even her grandparents joined in — but it was still obvious they couldn't manage. They were getting more and more into debt. Preeti felt guilty and useless at the same time, and this paralysed her. Their home became almost intolerable when rain prevented the old people from sitting outside and chatting with passers-by. They had not been able to afford any monsoon repairs, and in spite of efforts to mend their roof using bits of polythene with stones to hold it down it still leaked in four or five places. Damp, gloomy, cramped and tense, the atmosphere in the hut suited Preeti's own mood as long as she was left in peace to dwell on her troubles. But then came the constant quarrels with her mother, and she resolved to spend as much time as possible out of the house.

This afternoon, too, her mother's voice went on and on. 'Couldn't you at least wash your own clothes? We might as well get you married off for all the good you do at home. At least it would relieve me of the burden of looking after you and feeding you. Can't you see the situation we're in? I get up at four in the morning and don't sleep till twelve at night, I work myself to death to keep this family together, and you can't lift a finger to help me.' As usual, Preeti got up and walked out when she could stand it no more.

Words are often separated from their meanings by long stretches of time. When her mother said all this, it had no impact on Preeti except as an unpleasant nagging sound. Its meaning sank in only three days later as she watched her mother wearily preparing to chop vegetables for the evening meal and noted with a pang of remorse and pity the emaciated arms and legs, the prematurely lined face, the hair which was already going white. This time she got up, gently stroked her mother's back, then held her by the arm and guided her to the mat on the floor. 'I'll cook today,' she said. 'You lie down and rest for a while.' After all, for Preeti this was a matter of choice: she could work if she wanted to but she could also refuse to work and no one could force her to do it. Whereas for her mother there was no choice; she had to cling to this grinding routine because if she let go, even for a moment, her whole world would disintegrate.

After that day, Preeti contributed to the household chores and the tension relaxed a little — but only a little. The difference was that now they were sliding downwards at a somewhat slower rate.

CHAPTER 23

The children were fast asleep and Ranjan and Kavita were preparing to get to bed when they were startled by a knock on the door. Who coudd it be, at this time of night? They were even more surprised when Mariam strode in and flung herself on a chair with an expression of impatience and frustration which was most unusual for her.

'I'm sorry, barging in on you like this,' she apologised, 'but I've got to talk to someone, otherwise I'll go crazy.'

'You're soaking wet!' exclaimed Kavita.

'What on earth has happened?' asked Ranjan. They both stood and stared at her in alarm.

'It's all right, it's all right, nothing disastrous,' said Mariam, trying to laugh off the effect of her dramatic entry.

Kavita relaxed and smiled. 'Well, something *will* be disastrous unless you dry yourself,' she said, going to fetch a towel. 'Ranjan, why don't you get some coffee for Mariam? Make it really hot.'

When they were settled down Mariam began, 'It's wonderful having you around — at least you'll help me to keep my feet on the ground instead of vacillating wildly between euphoria and despair. In case you haven't guessed, I'm at the despair end right now. I've been going to those bastis every day for five days, and I've just about reached the limit of my patience.'

'You're trying to follow up those two cases — the girl who was being sexually harassed and the woman who was raped?'

'Hmm... well... "follow up" suggests movement but there's been absolutely no movement — that's the whole problem. I've met all the girl's workmates but one. Only two are prepared to do anything. The rest are not only reluctant to take action themselves but are even opposed to my doing anything on the grounds that they will get into trouble and may lose their jobs. Then the rape case — that's too sickening for words. If it were just a matter of people being afraid to testify in case of reprisals, I could understand that — though even then it's self-defeating. But there are all these disgusting arguments about the kind of woman she was, and so on and so forth — and it's *women* talking like this! I really can't take it any more.'

'But Mariam, what did you expect?' asked Ranjan. 'Didn't I tell you things are much harder than you first thought?'

'Poor Mariam,' sympathised Kavita, 'you've certainly been having a rough time.'

'And that's not all,' continued Mariam. 'On top of everything I have to account for myself. To begin with, they want to know what I'm doing there — am I a doctor, etcetera, etcetera. How on earth am I supposed to answer that? I ended up saying I'm a social worker because that was the only thing they could understand. Then, do I have children? Am I married? Why not? *Why not!* Imagine being asked a question like that! And, don't I ever wear a sari? Don't I ever wear bangles? Don't I ever wear earrings? Then they look at one another meaningfully and say: "Oh, but in your community you don't have to bother with what you wear, you can go out dressed in anything." Anyone would think I go there half naked or something! And that, too, after I specially take trouble to dress in a way which won't offend them, with a long kurta and everything!'

There was a silence. Neither Kavita nor Ranjan could offer her any advice. After a pause Mariam resumed, 'I feel like giving up, but I'm not going to — I refuse to admit defeat when I've hardly started. On the other hand, I can't carry on like this, without even anyone to talk to — it's driving me mad!'

'You can talk to us,' Ranjan pointed out. 'I would offer to come with you, too, but it wouldn't help — the women would probably close up if a man were around.'

'Someone to come with me — that's just what I want!' exclaimed Mariam, getting up and walking around restlessly. 'But you're right — a man wouldn't do.' She sat down again. 'How about you, Kavita?' she asked suddenly, looking directly at her friend.

The question threw Kavita into such turmoil that she couldn't utter a word. After a brief silence Mariam continued, 'You would be the ideal person. You wear a sari, you have children, you're married — they would immediately identify with you as a normal, respectable woman, someone like themselves. Even I would gain some respectability from being associated with you!' She laughed, then went on more seriously, 'But of course the main thing is how well you'll be able to communicate with them. You're the sort of gentle motherly figure they would confide in, and listen to as well. They can dismiss anything I tell them by saying, "Oh, that's how things are in your community, it's different for us", but they wouldn't be able to say that to you, would they? And you're so much more patient than I am. Half the time I feel I'm going to fly off the handle, so I keep quiet because I can't trust myself to speak politely. But you — I know the way you go on and on arguing, without shouting, without getting angry, but without giving up either — defeating your opponent by sheer persistence. Oh, I shall enjoy that spectacle!'

Kavita laughed, but was still speechless. She desperately wanted to agree to help Mariam, there were few things she had wanted more in her life; but she was also afraid — afraid of her own inexperience, afraid she would disappoint Mariam, and above all, afraid of Ranjan's reaction. That he would disapprove she never for a moment doubted, and the next minute he confirmed this by saying, 'But Kavita has never done this kind of work before — I don't think she'll be able to handle it.'

'It's not a question of having done it before — it's a question of having a feel for it,' said Mariam impatiently. Her mind was already made up and she was not going to be deterred by feeble arguments. 'I can't guarantee it, of course, but I'm pretty sure Kavita will turn out to have a feel for working with these women.'

'That remains to be seen. And it'll certainly upset the children if she keeps shuttling between home and the slum as you do.'

'Aha! It's not that she can't handle the work but that you can't handle the children. Is that it? Well, it's time you learned — it'll do you good.'

'Nonsense! Of course I can handle the children perfectly well — that's not the problem. But I don't have so much time.'

'Okay,' said Mariam mischievously, 'then I suppose I can't have her every day. But three days a week? No? Then at least two days? Surely it's not too much to expect you to look after the children and cook twice a week?'

'Look after the children *and* cook!' Ranjan exclaimed.

'No, I'm sure I can manage the cooking,' Kavita said hurriedly. 'And if it's on your days off, Mariam, we could go in the afternoon, couldn't we? Then the children will be asleep for most of the time and Ranjan can work at home.' She was anxious not to ruin her chances by appearing to make exorbitant demands, although at the same time it was quite clear to her that she was entitled to much more.

'That's a good idea,' agreed Mariam. 'It would be no problem for me, and in fact the women are most relaxed in the afternoon. Only a few like Lalita wouldn't be there, but you could meet them on their weekly day off. Oh good! Then that's settled.'

Kavita looked at her gratefully but also rather timidly. 'I hope you won't be disappointed, Mariam,' she said. 'I may not be any help to you in the end — I may turn out to be useless at this work.'

'Well, let's find out, shall we?' said Mariam. 'There's no point in speculating.' She yawned and stood up. 'I'd better be getting home before my landlady starts worrying about me. Thank you for the coffee and everything — it's really done me good talking to you. Has it actually stopped raining? Let me dash before it starts again!'

It was a long time before Ranjan could get to sleep that night. If he had been asked to explain his uneasiness he would have found it very difficult; yet there it was, no less real for all its inexplicability.

CHAPTER 24

Verma's response to the formation of a union at Adarsh Garments was swift and sure. Firstly, he refused to recognise the union or deal with it in any way; and secondly, he sacked six militants. This last action took the workers by surprise. They had expected something more heavyhanded — a lockout, perhaps, or mass dismissals — some attempt to terrorise them into submission. But Verma had shown unexpected subtlety; he had very carefully picked out the workers whom he knew to be the most articulate and influential and separated their interests from those of the others. In various ways he contrived to convey to them the message: I'm ready to discuss and consider your demands, but not as long as you are affiliated to Kelkar, not as long as you are associated with those trouble-makers. He did not succeed in breaking their solidarity, but he did succeed in continuing production, and the workers were left to make the next move. Although there was a strike for the reinstatement of the victimised workers, after three days everyone, including the six, decided they would have to fight this out some other way as they couldn't possibly outlast Verma's determination to smash the union.

It was precisely in anticipation of a situation such as this that they had gone to Kelkar in the first place, and they now went back to find out what he would do. He decided to take on the case; to go to court to obtain recognition of the union as representing 90 per cent of the workforce; the reinstatement of the victimised workers with full payment of their wage arrears; an end to the practice of illegal wage cuts; and negotiations on their charter.

The workers were satisfied, but met again to decide what to do about their colleagues who had been dismissed. As a gesture of solidarity, they agreed to contribute twenty rupees a month towards their subsistence — obviously inadequate, but better than nothing — and it was encouraging that even those who had refused to join the union agreed to contribute to the solidarity fund. 'I'm not against you in principle,' explained one. 'Clearly it would be better for us if we had a union, the boss would be forced to respect us then. It's just that I don't think we have much chance of success — the odds against us are too heavy.'

Mariam was not entirely happy with the situation. In her view the legal processes were too slow and cumbersome: 'It's like putting the whole thing into cold storage,' she complained to Ranjan when they were alone. 'At the moment they are agitated, ready for action; something could be done. But wait a few months and what will the situation be? They feel that something is happening because the case is in court; they even feel they're doing their bit so long as they contribute twenty rupees a month. So they'll sit back and relax, and everything will cool down. Meanwhile what'll happen to Shaheed and Anant and the others? They can't survive on 130 rupees or whatever it is they'll be getting. There will be a strong temptation to look for other jobs. That will be a further dispersal of their forces.'

'But what do you want, Mariam? I don't think anything can be gained by industrial action right now — I think they are absolutely right about that. In fact, I'm really impressed by the way they've planned and carried out this thing. If they don't succeed it'll be because Verma is too strong for them, not because of any mistaken strategy or lack of leadership.'

'I know, I know, I fully appreciate what an important step they have taken and how well they've thought it out. It's just that I wish there were some way of keeping the issue alive, not letting it fizzle out in endless legal complications.'

Getting the wives together is one way to do that, Mariam thought afterwards. She started organising a meeting without delay, and a few days later she and Kavita set off together to attend it.

This was the first time Kavita was accompanying Mariam, and although she was a little anxious about how Ranjan would manage with the children, her predominant feeling was one of wild, crazy excitement which made her feel ten years younger. At the bottom of the stairs she stopped and said, 'You know, I think this is the first time since Shanta was born that I've been out anywhere without the children? And I feel as if I've been let out of prison or something. I don't understand myself — I adore my children, I couldn't live without them, and yet I feel so happy to get away from them!'

'What's so difficult to understand?' demanded Mariam. 'However much you love them, you're still an independent person, there's some part of you that you can't express in your relationship with them — isn't that obvious? Anyway,' she smiled, 'you're looking marvellous, I've never seen you look so well since I came back. I think you should stick to my medicine and get off those drugs.'

'Drugs?' Kavita was shocked. 'Oh, you mean the sleeping pills! You make me sound like an addict. I know you can get addicted to them, but I'm not. In fact, I don't often take them now and I can probably give them up altogether. As you say, I've got a better medicine,' and she squeezed Mariam's arm affectionately.

They were meeting in the public garden where the workers usually met, because the gathering was too large to be accommodated in anyone's house. It was a small rectangle surrounded on all sides by busy roads, with a few trees for shade, and grass which had by now received enough rain to turn luxuriantly green. A few knots of women were sitting or squatting on the grass, many of them accompanied by children, and others kept arriving. When all six wives of the victimised workers and most of the others were there, they decided to commence.

'Since I've called this meeting, I'd better explain what it's about,' began Mariam. 'You must be aware of what's happening in Adarsh and the way the boss has thrown out six of the workers. You must also be aware of the kind of things he has been doing for years, like cutting 300 rupees from the salary of each worker.'

There was a buzz of conversation — this was clearly news to some of the women.

'What does that mean — cutting 300 hundred rupees?'

'You didn't know? He makes them sign for a thousand and gives them only 700 hundred.'

'And keeps the 300 hundred for himself.'

'What — from every worker?'

'From every worker every month.'

'What a swine! Here we are killing ourselves to make ends meet, and he's eating up all that money.'

'So you see,' Mariam continued, 'this struggle is very important, otherwise you'll never get what is due to you. And it will have a better chance of success if all of us women support it too.'

Conversation broke out again, the women began speaking to one another in little groups rather than addressing the meeting.

'What can we do?'

'We're contributing twenty rupees a month, aren't we?'

'I don't mind giving more if necessary.'

'No — not more than that, it's difficult enough to manage as it is.'

'How else can we help the struggle?'

'I'm ready to come to gate meetings if there are any…'

'… and shout slogans.'

'Sandeep Verma murdabad!'

'Murdabad, murdabad!'

Amidst general laughter Mariam resumed, 'Well, the first thing we should think about is the families of the victimised workers. After all, the struggle is for everyone — if it succeeds, everyone will benefit. So why should only some people suffer now? I know you are contributing twenty rupees, but that comes to just 130 rupees a month for each of them. How can they possibly manage with so little?' The six women, who were sitting together, kept their heads down. They had said nothing so far, but this was undoubtedly the problem which was preoccupying them.

'Let's see how many of us there are,' said Mariam, and she stood up to count, excluding the six. 'Twenty-eight, I think. If you can get two more women along, that'll make thirty. So let's say six women who need help and thirty women who can help them. My idea was like this. She hesitated, then called to one of the six, 'Shobha, come here.' Smiling shyly, Shobha got up and came to her side. 'Now, five of you,' indicating five of the women whose husbands were still employed at Adarsh, 'can take the responsibility of looking after her family. What I mean is, on Monday evening, one of you can cook for her family. On Tuesday another. And so on. Do you see what I mean? Each of you will supply her family with one meal a week. That's not too much, is it? By doing that we can be sure they won't starve.'

Confusion broke out as the women tried to clarify the scheme among themselves. A few problems were raised:

'I live too far away from Shobha. It'll be better if I cook for Geeta or Laila.'

'Supposing their families don't like the food we cook?'

'Who will take the food to them?'

'Isn't it better if they come and get it? Then they can take it in their own utensils.'

It was a while before Mariam understood the anxiety underlying many of these questions; then she suggested that they cook only vegetarian food in order to avoid any religious problems and the suggestion was immediately accepted. She could still sense some unspoken reservations about the idea but was pleased to note that no one actually opposed the plan, at least not openly. She was absorbed in watching them move around trying to work out the scheme and was therefore rather startled when Shobha touched her lightly on the arm and asked, 'What about us? Can't we do something too?' The other five women, who had been watching anxiously, came and joined them when they heard the question. A few men who had been interested spectators also drifted in — three or four of the dismissed workers, and Ravindran who was off work that day.

Mariam looked from one to the other and said, 'Well, what do you suggest? I can't think of anything.'

'You could save fuel by cooking your mid-day meal all together,' ventured Kavita who had been silent up to now.

'That's a good idea,' said Mariam encouragingly. 'It doesn't take much more fuel to cook a bhaji for twenty-five people than to cook it for five people if you cook it in one vessel. But if you do it in six different vessels it will use up six times as much fuel. And the same for rice and dal.'

'I don't understand,' said Geeta, puzzled. 'You mean one of us should cook for all the rest?'

'Not necessarily, but you could all get together and cook in one person's house — a different one each day, perhaps.'

'Will that really save money?' someone asked doubtfully.

'Not very much, but it will save some.'

'Normally we can't manage with the rationed kerosene — we have to buy more on the black market, which is very expensive. Maybe if we cook like this we won't need to do that,' remarked Laila.

'You can have my rations,' volunteered Ravindran. 'Half the time I don't use them anyway. And if you cook my meals along with yours, I'll be happy to pay for them — one meal on working days, two on days off.' He was eager to help and would gladly have given up his relatively lavish subsidised canteen meal in order to take both meals here if not for the impracticability of the suggestion, his factory being over thirty kilometres away.

'That's brilliant!' exclaimed Mariam. 'Why didn't we think of it before? Yes, of course, I'll buy my meals from you too. I'm sure my landlady won't mind if I explain the reason to her.'

'I could maybe take them for my family once or twice a week,' said Kavita a little hesitantly. 'I'm not sure — I'll find out and let you know.'

'I'll ask around too,' promised Ravindran. 'There are sure to be some fellows in this area who would like to buy their food from you.'

'Even if it's only a few, that'll mean some income for you,' remarked Mariam. 'It'll help to feed your children.'

'When should we start?' asked Shobba.

'As soon as possible! Tomorrow, if you like. Why don't you discuss it and work out how to organise yourselves?'

The six women put their heads together leaving Mariam and Kavita chatting to the men, all of whom Kavita was meeting for the first time.

'These small-scale employers are crooks,' remarked Ravindran. 'They should be wiped out, every single one of them.'

'But what about their workers?' asked Kavita. 'Wouldn't they lose their jobs then?'

'They will get absorbed into the organised sector,' replied Ravindran. 'If there's a demand for the articles, someone has to produce them; and if there's no small-scale sector, the production will automatically go large-scale. Then at least there will be equal competition. But look at the situation now — even my company is facing problems because of competition from people like your Verma.'

'But how can that be?' objected Ganesh. 'You're producing electrical components, we're producing garments.'

'I don't mean Verma himself, but others like him. They pay their workers 500 a month, make them work for ten hours a day, so naturally they can afford to sell their products cheaper. Our company makes better quality products, but people don't go for quality, they go for lower prices.'

'I don't know about that,' responded Ganesh, 'but according to me the main problem with employers like Verma is their attitude to the workers. They're ready to do anything rather than see us unionised and fighting for our rights. If that were changed, then the small-scale sector would be all right.'

'But it won't change! It won't change because the government encourages them to go on like that.'

The argument continued, but Kavita heard no more of it — it was time for her to get home. If she hadn't had to leave, she would have liked to sit down with Mariam over a cup of tea and ask her some of the questions whirling round in her head. Was it really true that the unorganised sector could compete successfully with large-scale industry? She had always thought otherwise. And how long could the six families survive like this? What was the likely outcome of the case? And, oh yes, she must ask Ranjan whether it would be all right to take two meals a week from the women. She wished she could talk all this over with him, get his help in sorting out her confusions. Should she? But she shrank from the prospect. Supposing he poured scorn on her ideas? She was ready to acknowledge that she had read very little compared to him, but was not ready to accept having her ideas dismissed outright. And he had a habit of doing that with whatever she said. No, it was better to try to manage on her own, with Mariam's help.

CHAPTER 25

Whatever sins he had committed, he surely didn't deserve *this* punishment thought Ramesh, looking in agony at Mangal's sleeping form on his bed. At first, when he had came back, she had not recognised him; she had just lain in bed staring upwards, and he prayed as he had never prayed before that she would recover. He took over from Kantabai the task of nursing her, and performed it with scarcely less skill and gentleness. She appeared to be improving, and one day he noticed joyfully that she was looking at him and trying to speak. But the words, when they came, struck terror into his heart. 'The children,' she told him urgently, 'it's time I went to collect them from school, otherwise they will think I have forgotten them and start crying.' And she tried to get up and go out. This time, fortunately, she was too weak to get very far; but as she regained her strength she would walk further each time, apparently in search of them. And he had no choice but to follow, because he was now repelled by the thought of inflicting the slightest physical violence on her, and she would listen to no arguments or pleas. Once she followed two little girls on the road, seeming not to hear him when he tried to reason with her that her own children would be much bigger by now, and her disappointment when she caught up with them was pathetic to see.

The only thing which could comfort him was that she now spoke to him, constantly and confidingly. But it was cold comfort, because what she said revealed such torment that it tore him apart. 'I know it's only a few metres to the school,' she told him. 'A lot of mothers let their children come home by themselves. But in my opinion they're bad mothers. It's an open road, and who knows what could happen? A traffic accident, a kidnapper. The inconvenience of going twice a day is worth it if you know that your children are safe.' Sometimes having failed to find them she would turn to him wailing, 'Oh where are they, where are they? Who could have taken them away? I knew I shouldn't have come so late, it's all my fault. I'm such a bad mother, I don't deserve to have children at all. Think what they must be suffering, poor little things, torn away from their mother like that. They're girls too, who knows what might be happening to them? And I can't do anything, anything! I didn't come in time, and now I may never see them again.'

In his despair, Ramesh thought of extreme solutions. Should he kidnap the children and bring them to her? He would do it, if he could be sure it would give her peace of mind. But he shrank with horror from what it would entail. They would not recognise him of course — they had seen him only once or twice, and that was years ago. They would be terrified and would scream and fight; he would have to be violent to compel them to come. And then they might not recognise Mangal as their mother. They might refuse to stay, run away. After all, they could hardly be kept locked up all the time. Or their father might inform the police, who would come and take them away. Then they would be back to the old situation or worse, because the police might jail Ramesh and maybe even Mangal. Worst of all: supposing Mangal didn't recognise them? She seemed to have a fixed image of two five-year-old girls in her mind, and her daughters wouldn't conform to this image at all. What if they recognised her, wanted to run into the arms of their long-lost mother, and she rejected them? Each possibility seemed more horrible than the last.

What would happen to her when he went away? The problem began to obsess him. At least while he was with her he could accompany her everywhere and make sure that she came to no harm. But he had already missed one job assignment, pleading that his wife was seriously ill. He could do this once more, perhaps, but after that his money would run out. For himself he didn't care, but he must have money to look after her, get her everything she needed. And if he went away on work? Who would take care of her? Should he put her in a mental hospital? He rejected the idea immediately. Somewhere in his memory was the image of mental patients being kept tied to their beds, and the thought of Mangal's free and independent spirit being subjected to this kind of restraint made him shudder. Better that both of them should starve to death! It was only as an alternative to the last possibility that he thought of turning to the women whose friendship with Mangal he had earlier resented so much. Leaving her still asleep, he made his way to Kantabai's hut feeling very apprehensive, yet resolved to go through with this because he had to, for Mangal's sake .

'I've come to ask you a big favour,' he began with unaccustomed timidity. 'You know I have to go away on work — I have to be out for several days at a time. I'm terribly worried about what will happen to my wife in that period. I would gladly look after her myself, but then I wouldn't have money to feed her, so I was hoping... hoping that you...' Kantabai was looking so grim that she unnerved him completely. Even after he trailed off she kept looking at him in the same way for several seconds before she replied.

'Hm! You men are all the same. First you help to drive a woman mad, and then you come running for help. What need was there for you to leave her children behind? You knew how much she was attached to them. Do you think it is such a small thing, to tear a woman from her children by force? And on top of that you beat her as well. Now you suffer for it!'

'I'm sorry, maoshi, I realise I was wrong, but all men make mistakes, don't they?' he pleaded. 'Now I want to put it right but I don't know how. Tell me what I should do, and whatever you say, I'll do it.'

Kantabai kept up her stern front because she felt it her duty to do so, but it was impossible for her not to be moved by his anguish. 'You want me to look after her while you're away — is that it? Well, if I do look after her, it's because she's like a daughter to me, not because you request it. I hope you understand that.'

'Yes maoshi, I understand, it's for her sake, not mine.'

'I'll do my best, but you know I too have to go out to work, I can't be with her all the time. I can sleep there at night and stay with her most of the day, but sometimes I'll have to leave her alone.'

'What about her other friend — the one who lives in Sheetal Nagar?'

'Who — Geetabai? But she stays so far away, and she's got a small child too. How can she help?'

'Just now and then. Maybe sometimes while you're out she could come and stay with Mangal?'

'Well, ask her. I can't answer on her behalf.'

But Ramesh was not satisfied. He turned away as if to go, then returned and shifted uneasily from one foot to the other. 'How can I go?' he asked uncertainly. 'I've hardly spoken two words to her in my life. Her husband may be there... it'll look so strange... they may not even believe me. Couldn't you go instead? They would never think of doubting you. Besides, I should get back to my house now. I'm afraid she'll get up and find me gone.'

'All right, all right, I'll speak to her, but I can't go right now. You're not leaving immediately, are you?'

'No, no, it won't be for some days yet. Thank you maoshi, I'll never forget this,' and he bent down and touched her feet before going. Kantabai watched him go, and now there was nothing but pity in her face.

Geeta had not been to Patthar Basti for some weeks, so she was surprised and shocked to hear the story. She came back with Kantabai at once, leaving her little girl Sindhu with Laila. Ramesh greeted her very differently this time, laying out tea and biscuits for the two guests on whom he now felt his whole life depended. When she understood what was required of her, Geeta readily agreed to help and insisted on adjusting her own schedule so that she could be with Mangal whenever Kantabai had to be out. 'It's no problem for me at all, Ramesh bhai,' she said, trying to stem his extravagant expressions of gratitude, 'I only wish I could do something more for her, poor thing.'

He had done everything he could; he had left enough money with the two women in case they might need it, and the arrangement was as foolproof as he could possibly have wished. Yet Ramesh left with a heavy sense of foreboding. Suppose something unexpected turned up and Geeta was busy at the same time as Kantabai? Or one left before the other arrived? No, they had assured him that they would take every precaution. He tried to still his anxiety; but the image of Mangal's face remained with him as the endless highways flashed past, and he could not rid himself of the ominous sense that he had seen her for the last time.

But when disaster came, it was not the result of any lack of co-ordination. It was early one dark, overcast morning and perhaps the sound of rain pounding on the tin roof drowned out the click of the bolt being drawn. When Kantabai woke up, Mangal was gone. Frantic, she ran out just as she was, searching all the places which were Mangal's usual haunts. It was almost noon, and Kantabai was drenched to the bone and cold as death, when someone came and told her that there was a crowd round a well which was almost dry for much of the year but now had a considerable depth of water. She knew then that she didn't even have to hurry there. Had Mangal dreamt that her children were calling her? Did she feel she was united with them at last? No one would know now — no one.

When they took Mangal out and brought her home, Kantabai tenderly wiped her and dressed her in dry clothes. Then, strong as she was, she broke down and wept like any bereaved mother. Why had God ever given her children only to take them away? What had she done to deserve this state of utter loneliness?

Ramesh, when he came back, seemed to take the news quite calmly. But he became very strange soon after — completely withdrawn and solitary. The only person with whom he still kept up some contact was Kantabai — and even that could hardly be called communication. He would sit in her hut once in a while, drinking a cup of tea and rarely speaking a word.

It was as if Mangal appeared to have vanished without a trace. Yet she left behind a vague sense of shame which hung like a cloud over Patthar Basti.

CHAPTER 26

When Mariam next went on one of her irregular visits to Mangal and Kantabai, she was puzzled but not unduly worried to find both the huts empty. She wandered over to Sheetal Nagar, and it was there that Geeta, weeping, told her about Mangal's death. Mariam had no impulse to react to the news in the same way. She listened, dry-eyed and hard-faced, and turned away without a word of comfort or sympathy. What comfort was there to offer anyway? Black anger, hatred and despair surged up inside her as she walked along without caring where she went. She had nothing to say and no wish to meet anyone, yet as she passed the building where Ranjan and Kavita lived, she turned in suddenly and ran up the stairs, two at a time. As the front door was open she went in without knocking and found Kavita cooking in the kitchen. It was quite a small room, lined on three sides with the paraphernalia for cooking and washing up; against the fourth wall was a small table with stools around it; it was the place where Kavita wrote letters and also usually entertained her friends. A small radio-cassette player allowed her to listen to the news or, as now, to music while she was working.

Kavita's smile froze when she saw Mariam's expression. 'What's happened?' she asked anxiously.

'Mangal is dead,' Mariam told her, and proceeded to describe the circumstances, gaining a grim satisfaction from the look of numb horror on her friend's face.

Kavita turned away in silence, and when she turned back her eyes were red. 'I was so sure she would recover,' she said. 'I don't know why, maybe it was just wishful thinking, but I never imagined it would end like this.'

'It shouldn't have ended like this!' exclaimed Mariam, clenching her fists. 'It *needn't* have.' She sat down on a stool, trying to find words for what she was trying to express. 'Don't you see, Kavita, she was murdered? And yes, it was those men who murdered her — husband, lover, rapists, the lot — but what do we say about the women who watched it happen — not only watched it but added their little bit of poison to her cup? Aren't they accomplices in the crime? To me,' bringing both fists up to her chest, 'the essence of feminism is nothing theoretical or abstract; it's a basic feeling of solidarity and sympathy with other women, identification with them. Geeta is a spontaneous feminist, so is Kantabai — that's obvious from the way they have related to Mangal all along. But what I find so horrifying, so frightening, and *sickening*, is that the majority of women identify themselves with the *man*, no matter how brutal or inhuman he is. In every single case you can think of — whether it's rape, wife-beating, sexual harassment, infidelity or whatever — they're so busy inventing excuses for the man that they don't begin to try and understand what the woman is going through. "Oh, she was that kind of woman. Sooner or later she was bound to get raped." "Oh, she kept nagging her husband all the time, how can you blame him for beating her?" "Oh, she makes eyes at all the men, naturally the supervisor can't keep his hands off her." "Oh, he's been faithful to her all those years, it's time he had a bit of variety." It's always the same pattern, isn't it? She identifies with the *man*, not with the woman. Of course, things are very different when it happens to her. Catch her saying, "I was asking to be raped, or harassed, or beaten", or, "My poor husband, he really needed to go off with that woman after all those boring years with me"!'

'But Mariam, aren't you doing the same thing, my dear?' asked Kavita gently, clearly disturbed by the angry bitterness in Mariam's speech.

'No, I'm not! Bullshit! I'm not identifying with any man, am I?'

'What I meant was, shouldn't we be trying to understand why these women are male-identified instead of condemning them so harshly?'

'That's something I'll never understand as long as I live! I'm too much of a woman to understand that! You know what really gets me?' She laughed mirthlessly and indicated her worn jeans and boyish hair. 'We feminists are derided for wanting to be like men. And why? Because we identify with women! Apparently that is a most "unfeminine" thing to do, that's why *nice* women don't want to join us. I've come across so many of them in England. The sort who wouldn't have anything to do with feminism because, after all, what is wrong with making yourself attractive for a man, what is wrong with giving him a bit of a cuddle if his wife is a cold bitch who doesn't look after him? Of course you wouldn't dream of asking, does *he* look after her, has he *ever* looked after her? And then there's the other sort, the home-loving, family-centred kind, whose whole existence revolves around her husband and children, but who wouldn't lift a finger to help her neighbour no matter what kind of hell she was going through. They're so *feminine*, aren't they? Yet you look inside, and they're masculine through and through!'

Kavita had turned off the stove and was looking at her gravely. Mariam looked back at her in silence for a moment, then burst out again, 'Is there any point in anything we do? That's what I keep asking myself. If most women are so happy to be slaves, if they love their chains and go out of their way to load more and more chains onto other women, then what the hell are we doing, trying to set them free? Believe me, Kavita, I'm ready to follow Mangal down that well if I don't find an answer to that question pretty soon. I can't go on in this hopeless way, feeling all the time that everything I do is completely useless, that it doesn't make any difference to anything.'

It was a demand which was also a desperate plea. At first Kavita could think of nothing to say in response so she went up behind Mariam, put her arms round her and leaned her cheek against hers. 'You mustn't...You shouldn't feel like that, Mariam,' she said hesitantly. 'There *are* women like Kantabai and Geeta, remember. And women *do* learn. No woman would react in the same way after going through a personal experience of isolation in her suffering, surely. So our task isn't quite impossible, though it may look like that sometimes. Things will change, eventually.' Her voice trailed off uncertainly.

Slowly, very slowly, the tension went out of Mariam's body, more in response to the physical contact and soothing voice than to the actual words. 'I suppose people who are powerless prefer to identify with people who have power,' Kavita continued, gaining confidence. 'You don't want to identify with the woman who's been bashed up, or raped, or deserted, even if — or perhaps precisely because — she's so much like you. It's terrifying and humiliating to feel so helpless, so vulnerable.'

How typical of Kavita! Always trying to explain something, as though that could in any way diminish the horror of it. 'I don't know,' Mariam sighed at last. 'I don't feel I know anything. The situation may improve, I suppose that's possible. It just seems so cruel and senseless that women like Mangal should have to get destroyed in the meantime. Why? Why?'

Kavita nodded thoughtfully as she sat down on another stool beside Mariam. 'We never got to know her, did we? At least, I didn't. I got the impression there was something very attractive about her, something unusual but... but tragic, yes, tragic.'

Mariam groaned and laid her forehead down on the table; then both of them sat silent and still as the kitchen darkened around them. The music had stopped playing, and soon all they could hear was the heavy rain beating its mournful rhythm against the window-panes.

CHAPTER 27

Thank God the monsoon's over, thought Lakshmi. Living on a railway platform through the rainy season with two children was far from pleasant; the platform was covered by a roof, but the railway tracks on either side were open to the sky, and the rain blew in during every heavy shower, especially if there was a strong wind. Although she had invested in two PVC sheets which she used to lay down under them and sometimes over them when they slept or sat, it was still impossible not to get wet, and once you were wet you just shivered and shivered, there was no way to get warm until your clothes and hair dried off again. Rather bitterly she thought that if she had been at home she would have welcomed the profusion of rain; Shetty could afford to keep the water out of their hut, and good rainfall this monsoon would mean less severe water shortages later on. But over here she had nothing to gain from the excess of water — on the contrary, it meant that Sanjeevani's nose was constantly running, Chandran usually had a cough, and she herself had suffered two bouts of fever which frightened her so much that she even considered going back. Going back not to live with Shetty but to die at home, because at least there the children would have a roof over their heads and food to fill their stomachs. But all her old horror at the thought of leaving them with their father returned; she had lived through worse situations before, why should she die now? It would be absurd to give up at this stage, when she actually had something to live for. Because, despite the unutterable bleakness of their material circumstances, a little shoot of hope was sprouting within Lakshmi, hope for a better life in future for herself and her children.

The basis for this hope was a change she had undergone. In the past she had felt nothing but revulsion for the person she was — for her lack of dignity, her lack of control over herself, her irrational alternations of self-abasement and violence. Although she had to take care of her appearance to avoid irritating Shetty, she had an image of herself as being perpetually dirty and unkempt. This was Lakshmi: a useless creature who hardly deserved to live, so why should she expect anything from life?

But here, on the station platform, she found her self-hatred slowly diminish. She discovered capacities for tenderness and humour which she had completely forgotten she ever had; and with these she was able to relate to her children in a quite different way. She still had a quick temper; that had not changed, and either of them could expect a sudden slap if they annoyed her. But the desire to hurt had gone; she would now never say things whose sting remained long after the effect of a slap had faded. If Sanjeevani, always the bolder of the two, dodged a blow and ran away laughing, Lakshmi would, after a moment, join in the laughter, her annoyance forgotten in the pleasure of seeing the child so happy. It was pleasant, too, to watch Chandran playing with his sister, to see him laugh like a child and drop the too-serious adult air he normally carried. In the nights she would recall half-remembered stories from her childhood to entertain them. Just the possibility of sitting or lying with them like this, without fear of interruption or molestation, was something miraculous. She knew that the railway police could be brutal and had, in fact, moved twice in order to avoid them, but they never seemed to come to this particular platform and here she felt safe.

If only they had a home, however small, and an income, however modest, she felt sure they could be a very happy little family. Achieving this was the problem which increasingly came to preoccupy her. It was warm now, but from November onwards it would be too uncomfortably cold to sleep out on the platform without any blankets, quilts or warm clothes. Besides, her little stock of money had finished long ago, and although she had bargained hard to sell her jewellery at the best price and had used the money with the utmost frugality, that amount too was rapidly dwindling. She must find some source of income, but what? There were plenty of women in her position who lived by begging, but her new-found dignity made that idea repellent. Her mind turned to the place where she used to pick up bags of metal hair-clips to be fitted on to metal strips and returned to the factory. What happened to the hair-clips after that she didn't know; perhaps they were covered in plastic, since the hair-clips you bought in the market were never bare metal. The rates were ridiculously low — fifty paise a kilo for the small clips and thirty paise for the large ones — but at least she could sit with the children and work, she wouldn't need to leave them alone. And she had a good chance of getting the work because her name was on the list of women who were given assignments on a priority basis because they were regulars. The only problem was Shetty. The factory was in the industrial estate not far from Patthar Basti and she had often seen his goondas hanging around there. What if one of them should see her and report her to him? The thought made her shudder and kept her undecided for the next few days. Yet, day by day her money dwindled further, and finally this anxiety got the better of her fear. Once a week on Thursdays the women used to go to be paid and get fresh supplies of work, and she decided to go on that day — not, initially, to get work, but to try and speak to Salma who had always been kind to her.

It was better to leave the children behind, she would be identified more easily if they were with her. And she draped her pallu over her head so that it almost covered her face. Only someone directly in front of her and quite close would be able to recognise her. Even so, she was trembling inwardly as she watched the queue of women waiting to get their work weighed, taking their pay and collecting fresh sacks. Was that Salma? No, another woman who looked exactly like her from behind. There she was! Lakshmi could hardly wait. It seemed hours before Salma reached the head of the queue. When at last she turned and started walking away, Lakshmi took a deep breath and stepped out to meet her.

'Salma!'

'Lakshmi-behen! Where have you been? We've been looking for you everywhere! Thank God you have come back at last. But where are the children?'

'I left them behind. I was afraid that one of his men might see them and recognise me. Then he might come and catch me.'

'Oh, you needn't be afraid of that! Haven't you heard what's happened?'

'What? What's happened?' Lakshmi was bewildered. 'I haven't heard anything.'

'Did you go to your village then? You've left your children there?'

'Oh no, he knows my village, he would have come and caught me there.'

'Yes, I think you're right. He did go somewhere soon after you disappeared; nobody knows where, but it could have been to your village. He told me to ask you to stay in case you came back while he was away. When he returned and there was still no sign of you he was terribly angry. I heard him smashing some pots or something inside the house.'

Lakshmi shuddered involuntarily. She could well imagine his murderous rage at having been successfully abandoned by both his wives.

'Yes, I was happy you were not there, Lakshmi-behen, he would have broken every bone in your body. After that he used to come back every night, but he stayed out all day. Until one day he came back with that girl.'

'What girl?'

'His second wife, that vendor-girl.'

'What! Vasanta?' Lakshmi couldn't believe what she was hearing. 'You mean he finally caught her and forced her to come back?'

'No. It was not like that. She came back smiling, just like the first time she came. He must have sweet-talked her into it, promised her all sorts of things, who knows? And she was not smart enough to understand his real intentions.'

'Meaning?'

Salma was silent for a moment, then she too shuddered. 'That night they started fighting — the door was shut but we could hear them all over the basti. At first they shouted at each other, then there were other noises, sounds of a physical fight. Then she started screaming — first, just now and again, then continuously.' She shuddered again. 'I was scared — we were all scared. As usual a crowd had gathered, but no one wanted to do anything. Only that old lady Kantabai, she was running around like a mad woman trying to persuade someone to go in with her and stop the fight. "Doesn't anyone in this place have any guts?" she kept asking. But you know what Shetty's like when he's angry; naturally no one wanted to interfere.'

Lakshmi felt inside her the familiar nausea of fear. It is true that after Vasanta disappeared and Shetty began to take out his frustration on her she had wished that he would find her and beat her instead. But once Lakshmi herself had escaped from the beatings she had no further interest in the matter, and now she genuinely felt horrified at what had been inflicted on Vasanta.

'Well,' Salma resumed, 'after a while Kantabai said, "Even if no one else is ready to come, I'm going to do something. We've already had one death because we didn't help a woman when she was being attacked, at least I'm going to try and prevent another." Oh, that's something else you don't know about. That, too, was due to Shetty's gang — three of them raped a woman. They didn't actually kill her, but Kantabai always says that she died the night she was raped because she went mad as a result and eventually drowned herself in a well. So Kantabai said this about preventing another death and then she vanished.

'Meanwhile we were getting more and more frightened because there were all sorts of horrible noises, and the screams were getting weaker. What was Shetty doing to Vasanta? Then there was silence. And just then, Kantabai came back with the police. How she got them along I don't know, she must have threatened them or something like that, otherwise they would never be ready to take action against Shetty. Anyway, she insisted that they go in and arrest Shetty. And then she insisted that we all go in and look at the body.' Salma covered her face with her hands. 'My God! If I hadn't seen Vasanta go in, I wouldn't have known who it was. We were all feeling sick, but Kantabai thought of everything. She made the three constables show us their identity cards, and made one of the men write down their names and numbers. She looked at us one by one and said, "All of you are witnesses to a murder." Then she looked at the constables and said, "If you let this man go, you are accomplices to a murder. We'll see to it that you get punished." They were scared of her, you could see that. She can't even read or write, I wonder how she knows about these things.' Salma was thoughtful for a while, then looked up suddenly. 'Oh, I forgot the most important thing. You know your house has two doors? Well, when the police entered through one door, Shetty tried to run away through the other. And you know why they could catch him? Because he couldn't run properly. She had cut his leg with the kitchen knife. Imagine a young girl fighting back like that!' Salma's admiration was all the greater because she herself never opposed her husband even when she knew he was wrong — and he was quite a mild man, not terrifying like Shetty.

'What happened after that?' Lakshmi was interested in the story as one which still seemed as remote from her as the *Ramayana*.

'I don't know all the details. But I know he's been put into jail for a long time. Ten years? Twenty years? I'm not sure, you can ask.' She broke off, startled, as Lakshmi gripped her arm tightly.

'What are you saying, Salma behen? You mean he's been put into jail?'

'That's exactly what I'm saying. And now that he's behind bars, people are becoming bold — they say they are ready to go and tell the police about his other murder — and even about the rape case.'

It was incredible. To be free of her husband — free to go back to her home! This was something Lakshmi had never even dared to dream of.

She still couldn't believe it. 'You mean... I can come back home without being afraid of anything?' she asked incredulously.

'Well, I'm not sure about that. My husband thinks Shetty's sure to escape, but if you're willing to take that risk, the house is yours now — no one else lives in it.'

Lakshmi didn't have to think long before making up her mind: it was better to solve immediate problems now, and face future difficulties whenever they came up. So one of her prayers had been answered — but what about the other? Suddenly Lakshmi remembered where she was and why she had come here. 'Forgive me, Salma-behen, for keeping you talking on the road like this, but can I ask just one more question?' When Salma smiled assent she continued, 'Do you think I can do this work again?' she asked indicating the heavy sack lying on the pavement.

The corners of Salma's mouth turned downward. 'I don't think he'll take you on now. Some weeks ago he called out your name and when you were not here he said he was going to strike you off the list. He's been doing the same with other women too — using illness or the slightest pretext to get rid of them. And no one who is not on the list gets any work these days.'

Salma was right. When Lakshmi went to the factory the following week, the man looked at her, then looked deliberately down the list and told her, 'Your name's not on the list, and we're not giving work to anyone else.' So the problem of finding an income remained and had to be solved. But for the moment they could survive by selling off various things from the house. Lakshmi didn't want to worry about the future — she was too busy enjoying the present.

CHAPTER 28

It was only when Renu started reappearing on the balcony every Sunday evening that Kavita realised it was several months since she had seen her do this. The girl looked as bored as ever and Kavita vaguely considered inviting her over; but what would she do if she accepted? They didn't even have a television for her to watch. It was a few weeks later when something in Renu's posture startled her into deciding to keep an eye on her. She looked and looked, and finally there was no doubt of it: the girl was pregnant. Kavita was horrified. She had no idea of Renu's circumstances, but it was not hard to figure out that this could only be a disaster for her. She couldn't have told her family, otherwise they would have come and taken her away. In any case they would probably disown her, afraid that no man would ever agree to marry her. Kavita had a dreadful sense of impending tragedy and the urgent need to avert it. But what should she do? In her perplexity she turned to Mariam for advice.

'You must take her and have it medically terminated at once,' said Mariam decisively. 'If she has the baby she'll be finished. Her employers will throw her out — they won't want the baby around. Her parents will probably do the same, and I dread to think what will happen to her then.'

'I'm afraid it may already be too late,' Kavita said doubtfully.

'Well, we should at least find out. I know it's not a pleasant thought, a young girl like that going through a late abortion, but I can't see any alternative.'

But still Kavita hesitated. How to raise such a delicate topic with a girl she hardly knew? She shrank from the embarrassment of it. And yet the days were slipping by, precious days which could perhaps mean the difference between life and death. She lay awake at night worrying and trying to compose sentences with which she could introduce the subject. But when she finally did so it was on the spur of the moment, because she found herself walking up the stairs with Renu, both of them carrying bags of shopping. 'Have you been to the doctor yet?' she asked, trying not to make the question sound too abrupt.

Renu stopped dead and turned to her with a mixture of fear and defiance. 'What doctor? Why should I go to a doctor?'

'It's better to have a check-up when you're expecting a baby,' said Kavita in an even more conciliatory tone.

'Oh, I didn't know that,' said Renu, both fear and defiance replaced by anxiety. 'What should I do? Where should I go?'

'I'll take you if you like,' offered Kavita, who knew the timings of the ante-natal clinic at the nearest hospital.

'But how can I go? Only if it's on Sunday evening. They won't let me off any other time.'

'It's on Monday morning, but I'll see about that,' said Kavita with more confidence than she felt. What was she getting herself into? She had very little contact with the people next door beyond the normal neighbourly services they performed for each other. Might they dismiss Renu if they discovered she was pregnant? It wasn't likely, but she didn't want to take any risks. Finally she told them that Renu was not well and had to be taken to a doctor. She waited in suspense while they discussed the proposition in some astonishment, but since it was she who was asking, not Renu, permission was granted.

On Monday they caught the bus and reached the hospital quite early, but the large waiting room was already chaotic and crowded with pregnant women, many of them accompanied by children. Both Renu and Kavita were tense and said very little while waiting; and it was understandable but also slightly intimidating to find the doctor looking harassed and tired by the time it was Renu's turn to be examined. She looked efficient all right, with her white coat over a starched cotton sari, but was obviously trying to get through the crowd as fast as possible, and didn't give the impression that she would welcome questions which might lead to delay.

According to the check-up and Renu's own calculations, she was more than five months pregnant and was perfectly healthy apart from being slightly anaemic. As they were leaving Kavita screwed up her courage and asked, 'Is it possible to have a medical termination at this stage?'

The doctor looked at her sharply, then at Renu and back at Kavita. 'It's possible,' she said, 'but I wouldn't advise it. Not unless the alternative is really serious. She doesn't seem to be at all psychologically disturbed. Why didn't you bring her earlier if you wanted an M.T.P.?'

'I didn't know,' replied Kavita helplessly, and followed Renu out. What should they do now? Go to the M.T.P. section? 'It's a pity we didn't come earlier,' she remarked to the girl. 'It's much easier to have an abortion at an early stage.'

'But I don't *want* an abortion!' Renu turned on her fiercely. 'I want the baby.'

Rather taken aback, Kavita walked on in silence. This girl was a mystery to her. Didn't she understand what problems she would have once the baby came? On the one hand she seemed so completely naïve, on the other, so sure of herself. But at least she had solved one problem in no uncertain manner. In a way Kavita could understand her response. After all, if anyone had suggested an abortion when she was expecting her first baby, she would have been just as outraged. And even with Sunil, although he had been an 'accident', she had vacillated and postponed taking any action until time made the decision for her — and basically she wanted to have the baby. So she was in no position to object to Renu's decision, worrying though it was. Yet another responsibility! She sighed and then said, 'Come, let's get the pills the doctor recommended.'

'Oh why?' Renu was anxious again. 'Why do I have to take pills? There's nothing wrong with the baby, is there?'

'No no, it's quite normal, I had to take these pills, too, when I was pregnant. They are good for you, and what's good for you is good for the baby, isn't it?'

Renu was reassured, but soon thought of another problem. 'What shall I tell my employers?' she asked. 'They'll be angry, won't they?'

'Do you want to stay on with them? Or do you want to go home?'

'Go home? What an idea! They would kill me. No, I would like to keep my job as long as I can.'

But how was that to be achieved? Kavita considered the various possibilities. One was to keep quiet and wait until they found out. But then it would be difficult for Renu to have future check-ups, and she would run the risk of being thrown out without warning. Also Kavita herself would be placed in an awkward position, because they would suspect her of having known about it and having deliberately concealed it from them. Yet to speak to them now was to risk a more premature dismissal. Either way a risk was involved. And there was no third alternative she could think of. As they got off the bus and started walking towards their building she said slowly, 'What I've been thinking is this: they'll be more angry if they think we have been hiding things from them.

And that's what they will think if we don't tell them anything and they find out later. So it may be better if I come with you now and talk to them. We won't say we knew you were pregnant — we'll say you were worried because your periods had stopped and when we went to the doctor we found out you were expecting a baby. Is that all right?'

'And then?'

'And then I'll try and persuade them to keep you on — after all, so long as you do the work they're not losing anything. But are you sure you can do the work?'

'Yes, certainly! What I'm worried about is that they will decide not to keep me. What will I do then?'

Kavita's heart sank but she said bravely, 'Then we'll just have to find you something else. I don't keep a servant myself, but...' She remembered how Mariam used to laugh at the philanthropic pretensions of rich ladies like her mother, their claims to help and rescue less fortunate women. Perhaps one of them might help?

Renu ultimately agreed to her suggestion, and together they rang the doorbell. It was the first time Kavita had been beyond the threshold of the flat — identical in layout to her own, but much more crowded with furniture. There was barely a sign of a book anywhere, apart from a few children's magazines. Kavita had anticipated a thoroughly unpleasant interview, and she was not wrong. There was no explicit rudeness — on the contrary they were all hospitality, receiving her with tea and biscuits and expressions of delight that she should, at last, have come to visit them. But when it came to discussing the reason for her visit, she needed all her self-control to be able to listen to them criticising Renu, sometimes quite abusively, and to defend Renu without losing her temper or irritating her hosts. She was profoundly grateful that all the men were out at work when she began, although two of them came home for lunch and had to be told everything. Clearly her presence as Renu's advocate was an embarrassment to them — one couldn't dismiss a lady, especially a neighbour, in a way which would seem discourteous. Finally they told her, 'Since you're taking such an interest in this girl, we'll keep her on until she delivers the baby — provided she does the work. After that of course there's no question. We can't keep a baby.'

'Thank you, that's very kind of you,' Kavita said quickly, getting up.

This was the most she had expected, and she wanted to leave before they changed their minds.

'We've solved the problem — for the moment,' she announced to Mariam, who had been looking after her children.

'What does that mean?' asked Mariam. When Kavita told her, she shook her head doubtfully, 'That's not a solution — it's simply a postponement of the problem,' she remarked. 'Still, I can't see what else we can do. If the girl wants to keep the baby...' She shrugged. 'We'll just have to look for something else after four months, that's all.'

CHAPTER 29

It was quite obvious to anyone travelling along A.M. Road that a dispute was in progress at Jackson Pharmaceuticals: red and black banners with anti-management slogans were draped from end to end of the front fence, and a most unflattering effigy of the managing director hung from one of the spikes. Nirmala always took her turn at staffing the tent which had been set up beside the main gate; the union committee consistently kept up a twenty-four hour presence here, partly to act as an informal picket, but mainly to provide information and encouragement to the workers on strike.

When negotiations had first broken down, the union initiated a moderate go-slow which was ignored by management; when they intensified it, management responded with chargesheets and suspensions, and it was then that they decided to go on strike. That decision had been unanimous; the company's first offer was ridiculously low, and the victimisations were an added insult. A strong gesture of protest was required, and Kelkar, the committee and the workers all agreed that strike action was called for. The strike had been solid since then, but after three months, with no settlement in sight, the situation began to get shaky. These were well-paid workers compared to those in medium- and small-scale industry, yet perhaps for this very reason their capacity to strike indefinitely was limited. When you could count on a relatively high level of income you got used to a certain standard of living, perhaps you took out a housing loan which required fairly large repayments. It became very difficult to cut down your expenditure. And although no one suggested a return to work, increasingly anxious questions were beginning to be asked at the tent, while attendance at the weekly gate meetings had dropped to just two or three workers.

On the other hand, the strike was beginning to hurt the company, too. They were losing the market for many of their products to competitors, and the longer this went on the more difficult it would be to regain their position. The action had taken them by surprise, coming as it did so early in the proceedings, and they were badly prepared for it. This is what accounted for the second offer which they made to the committee at this point. It was certainly an improvement on the first, although the average increase in wages was still far short of the demand. The most significant feature was that point-to-point transport was granted — no doubt because the negotiating committee, in their earlier round of discussions, had conveyed the impression that no settlement would be reached without this.

The offer threw the committee into confusion. At an emergency meeting held in Kelkar's office, the general secretary, an experienced and cautious unionist, was inclined to accept, sensing the growing demoralisation among the workforce. Kelkar, on the contrary, wouldn't hear of it and dismissed his arguments in a distinctly insulting manner. Outside his office the committee met again, completely at a loss. What should they do now?

'I don't think we can decide without having a better idea of what our members feel,' suggested Nirmala. She was unhappy that they had not been informed of the offer, and wanted at least to be able to estimate how they would respond if they were told about it.

'But how can we find out?' asked Pillai, the general secretary. 'Hardly anyone comes to our meetings any longer. We'll have to visit them in their homes.'

'Then let's do that. I know it's not easy, but our success depends on them, doesn't it? If they start drifting back, what will our position be?'

'We don't have to visit each and every one, do we? So long as we pick out a representative sample, enough to give us an idea of what the general body feels.'

'Are we going to tell them about this latest offer?'

'No, no. Not yet.'

'But why not? How can we find out how they feel about it without telling them about it?'

'We're not trying to find out what they feel about the offer as such, but about the strike in general — whether they're prepared to hold out, or whether they're getting fed up.'

'Yes, but wouldn't the offer make a difference? They may be prepared to hold out against the old offer but not against the new one.'

'No, don't tell them about it now, it'll cause confusion. Because we'll be telling some people and not others, rumours will start, before you know where you are there'll be ten different versions circulating. No, for the moment let's just find out whether they're getting desperate to go back to work.'

It was almost midnight by the time they dispersed, having decided who was to visit whom. After three days they would meet to discuss their findings and, if necessary, go once again to Kelkar's office to try and persuade him to change his mind.

On the afternoon of the third day of her opinion survey, Nirmala climbed the stairs to Suzie's flat feeling tired and despondent. Some of the women she had visited were not yet desperate — they were the ones with husbands who had well-paid jobs, those with savings — yet even they were anxious to know whether an end to the strike was in sight. Many others were clearly under pressure from their families to get back to work and start earning again. A few were demoralised enough to think about accepting the company's earlier offer although they withdrew, ashamed, in the face of Nirmala's scorn. Others suggested taking more aggressive action against management demonstrating, shouting slogans, staging a hunger strike or something like that, perhaps. In each case Nirmala asked herself: how would she react if she knew about the new offer? And in most cases the answer seemed quite clear.

There was no response when she rang the bell, and Nirmala wondered whether Suzie had gone out. But as the door was not padlocked it seemed likely that someone would be at home. She rang again, and this time heard slow footsteps coming towards the door. When it opened she stared in horror, hardly recognising the face which looked out at her. The girl had always looked fragile but now she looked positively ghastly, her cheeks sunken in, her arms like those of a skeleton. Suzie, too, stared back with dull eyes for almost a minute before recollecting herself and standing aside to let Nirmala come in. She made an attempt to smile, but the muscles wouldn't work.

Too appalled to speak, Nirmala walked around the flat as though making an inspection. There was an old woman, also gaunt, sleeping on a bed, but there were no signs of anyone else living there. What were Suzie's family circumstances — was the girl an orphan, perhaps? The woman could be her grandmother. In which case... The implications of this slowly began to dawn on Nirmala. She went back to the kitchen and began opening the cupboards. This was no way to behave in someone else's house, but she had to know. Empty. Empty. There were kitchen utensils, plates and cups, a little bit of tea, a little bit of cooking oil, but nothing else. Nothing which could be consumed. She came across a ration card and snatched it up, together with a couple of shopping bags which were hanging up.

'I would like to give you some tea,' began Suzie haltingly, 'but I don't have any milk or sugar.' Now that she had begun to speak it was easier to continue. 'I tried to make everything last as long as possible,' she explained, 'eating only a little at a time, and so on. But my father hasn't been sending money for the past two months, and my savings ran out more than a week ago. So I wasn't able to get the rations.' She sounded apologetic, Nirmala thought. It was crazy, but she actually sounded apologetic. 'Have you got gas?' she asked aloud. Suzie nodded. 'Now, where's your ration shop?' Suzie went to the window and pointed out the direction: 'You can't see it from here, but it's up the road.'

'All right. I'm dying for some tea, will you be a good girl and make some for me? I'll go and get some milk and sugar. Make enough for yourself and your grandma too — she may like some when she gets up.'

'She's my mother,' Suzie corrected her. 'I don't know if she will take it. She's very ill and just sleeps all the time. But I'll make it and try to feed her.' She set to work, and although her movements were slow and halting, the tea was ready some time before Nirmala returned.

The things we do to people without even knowing what we are doing! thought Nirmala as she hurried off. There wasn't a long queue at the ration shop but still, she would have to wait. She pleaded with a woman to keep her place, and went to buy dal and vegetables. Milk was a problem because there was no dairy in sight, but she persuaded the man at a small tea-shop to sell her a glassful at an inflated price.

'You'll have to take this glass back to the tea-shop,' she announced as Suzie opened the door and she walked in with her load. 'Come, let's have our tea,' because the girl was still staring. They drank their tea, and decided to wake up Suzie's mother. The woman stared wildly at Nirmala until she understood that she was being offered some tea, then caught hold of her hand and begged, 'Oh madam, please do something to help us, please see that my girl gets something to eat. Never mind me, I'm an old woman, it's time for me to die anyway. But she's only a child, and it's not right. Look at her! Nothing but skin and bones!'

'Don't worry about her,' Nirmala said gently, hearing Suzie sobbing behind her, 'everything will be all right now. But you must have something to drink — you need it too.' Then turning to Suzie and taking her hand, 'Can you manage now? Do you want me to cook something for you?'

'Yes...no...' Suzie stammered in confusion. 'I'll cook at once. Thank you for everything. You've been so kind. I'll pay you back as soon as I start getting my salary again.'

Nirmala made a dismissive gesture. 'You just concentrate on getting back your strength. I still don't understand how this could have happened. Don't you have any friends? Neighbours?'

'We haven't lived here long and we don't know anyone very well,' explained Suzie, thinking that things would have been quite different at the old chawl. Everyone was so inquisitive there, always poking around in your private life, but at least if you were in trouble people got to know and came to help. In these modern flats you had enough privacy, but you could starve to death without anyone being any the wiser.

'Well, it's our fault too,' remarked Nirmala, partly to herself. 'We should have done this much sooner — checking up how people were coping with the strike. Let us see, it may be over soon. Look after yourself, and I hope your mother gets better,' she said as she left, having slipped a twenty-rupee note into the ration card when she returned it.

Outside, she found herself trembling violently and was forced to sit down on the stairs till she recovered. Until then she had been sustained by the necessity to look cheerful and act decisively, but now her nerves gave way completely. Supposing I hadn't come — supposing this had gone on for another week or two, she thought. The image of two corpses came into her mind and she felt sick. Whose fault would it have been?

There were four more workers she was expected to visit before tonight's meeting, but she couldn't face the thought of it. Besides, it wasn't necessary. Her mind was made up already.

CHAPTER 30

Since the strike began, most of the Jackson Pharmaceuticals union committee meetings had been informal affairs, held in the cramped quarters of the tent or on the pavement outside. Partly this reflected a feeling that the real decisions were being made by Kelkar, and that their own deliberations had little significance. But this meeting, it was decided by general consent, was important enough to be held in the front room of Pillai's ground-floor flat. It was a large, tastefully furnished room, with a door opening on to the garden where children from the housing society were playing. Mrs Pillai greeted the committee members as they arrived, made sure that they were comfortably seated, and served them with tea and snacks. When one of them invited her to sit in on the meeting, she accepted at once, saying half jokingly, half seriously, 'Well, why not? I think I have suffered as much for this union as any of you!'

Pillai opened the proceedings by saying, 'I don't have any good news to report so I'll let someone else begin,' and that set the mood of the gathering. None of the others could claim to have good news either; the only encouraging thing was that by and large no one wanted to accept management's first offer, and to that extent the strike was still solid. But there was growing dissatisfaction at the apparent stalemate and the union's inaction. 'They feel we're just allowing management to sit back and starve us out.'

'Yes, they're angry because they think there hasn't been another offer, but at the same time they're afraid because they think this means that management is in a strong position.'

'I would say that the main question people are asking is: how long can we carry on like this? They feel they can't hold out much longer and they want us to force management to make a better offer.'

'Yes, some of them say they're ready to go on demonstrations, dharnas, anything.'

'We're playing with fire if we let this situation continue,' said Nirmala. 'You know what I thought? Suppose management sends a letter to each worker with details of their new offer. There would be chaos! I'm pretty sure that all the people I spoke to would be in favour of accepting.'

'That's true. I got that impression too.'

'Yes, it's only because they don't know about it that they're holding out.'

'But isn't that terribly dangerous?' persisted Nirmala. 'It's not that it can't happen. Other companies have done it — approached workers directly, bypassing the union. And they could make it seem that we have been keeping our members in the dark. Then we'll be finished — not only the strike but the union as well.'

'What are you suggesting, then? That we call it off?'

'That's impossible! It's a miserable offer.'

'We should wait a bit longer. Obviously they're under pressure — they're sure to go higher if we wait.'

'But what about our members? How do we convince them to stay out?'

'Why not organise some slogan-shouting? Then they will feel that we're taking action.'

'But that's crazy. Management will realise immediately that they don't know about the second offer and they'll manipulate the situation to their own advantage.'

'I can tell you that every one of the women will be ready to go back if they know that the transport demand has been granted. And that's almost half the workforce.'

'You're right. And there are quite a few men who would be ready to do the same!'

'Why don't we settle then? At least it wouldn't be a defeat — we would go back with the union intact.'

'Kelkar would never agree to sign. You know what he's like — it's a matter of prestige with him.'

The argument went on and on. All through it, Nirmala was haunted by a vision of two half-starved women, one old, one young; but she carefully avoided any mention of what had happened in the afternoon. She knew from experience that anything she said which could be discounted as 'emotional' would inevitably weaken her argument. She was on male territory now, and had to abide by their rules if she wanted to get anywhere. She must argue coolly and rationally, that was the only way to convince them. She had become good at it with years of practice and was more than a match for most men on the committee. She deserved every bit of the implicit faith that the other women had in her. Yet now and then something cried out within her at this betrayal of herself. Why couldn't she simply say, 'One of my girls is starving; we either have to arrange to feed her or we have to call off the strike?' Or, 'I don't like all this secrecy, let's call a general body meeting of the workers and take a vote on the offer?' It made her sick sometimes to have to go through all these complicated manoeuvres, but on the other hand she felt it would be self-indulgent to retain the purity of her principles at the cost of not being able to push through her point of view. But it was precisely this duplicity which put off women from joining the committee and made unionism an alien world to them, so perhaps by conforming to the accepted behaviour she was reinforcing the exclusion of other women! It was hopeless — whatever you did was wrong. If you thought about it too much, you would end up doing nothing. Better to do something and know, at least, that you were being useful to your workmates. And Nirmala had no doubts about that.

The solution they finally worked out was a compromise between those who wanted to settle at once and those who wanted to hold out. They would respond to the offer, re-start negotiations in order to indicate their willingness to agree, but they would hold out for a bit more. However, they wouldn't risk another breakdown in the talks — they would take whatever they could get.

The plan had been to convey their decision to Kelkar at once, but it was now long past office hours. They would have to wait till the next day to speak to Keltar, and then till the day after before they could approach management. Nirmala was impatient at the delay, but the hard-liners were pleased: it left one more day for management to come up with a better offer.

CHAPTER 31

The Adarsh Garments case had dragged on for months without the slightest progress. Verma didn't even appear in court; he would just send his lawyer, and on some pretext or other the hearing would be postponed. Mariam was disgusted. 'This is exactly what I was afraid of — it could go on for ever! Can't we do something to stir things up?' she asked Ranjan. The scheme for supporting the victimised workers and their families was working well, yet they could not be expected to remain indefinitely on the edge of subsistence. A new factory was being opened in a neighbouring industrial area, and Mariam strongly suspected that some of them had already made job applications there. No one could blame them either: they had their own lives to live, their own responsibilities; they couldn't let their children suffer for an abstract principle. Mariam blamed not them but Kelkar: 'Obviously Verma is bribing that judge — and with his ill-gotten gains he can go on doing it for years. It's worth it for him. What I can't understand is, why doesn't Kelkar take some action? He's supposed to be a strongarm man, isn't he? Then why doesn't he use some of his muscle-power? This is clearly a case for terror, not for legal dilly-dallying. Unless of course Verma is bribing him as well!'

'No, I don't think so,' ventured Ranjan.

'Why? You think he's above accepting money from employers? Not according to what I've heard.'

'No, it's not that I have any illusions about his integrity, but I don't believe Verma would think of doing it.'

'All right then, even if Kelkar is not taking a bribe in this case, he's clearly not competent to handle it. I think the workers should take the initiative, not leave everything to him.'

Ranjan nodded gloomily. 'I know. I was talking to Shaheed about that yesterday. The problem is now that they're out, it's much more difficult for them to act. They're afraid that if they try to start any agitation, the other workers will see them as doing it for their own benefit as individuals — do you see what I mean? The workers feel that the case is being pursued, why not let it take its course? So that's how things stand: those who are out are not in a position to start any action, and those who are in don't want to. You must admit that Verma is well equipped with a certain kind of low cunning. He couldn't have made a cleverer move than to pick out those six, cutting them off from the other workers, cutting off the workers from their leadership.'

Mariam paced up and down impatiently. 'No, we can't let Kelkar off like this!' she burst out. 'It's *his* responsibility to see that the case doesn't get prolonged indefinitely.' And with her usual persistence, she spent hours talking to the most responsive of the activists and finally persuaded Shaheed, Anant and Ganesh to go and pressurise Kelkar to take a more direct form of action. She decided to accompany them that evening so that she would know the outcome without delay.

As usual there was a crowd in Kelkar's office, and they had to wait for their turn to see the union leader in his little cabin. While they were waiting, another union delegation came in, and Mariam was interested to see that one of its members was a small, plump, rather elderly-looking woman — the only other woman in the entire office apart from herself.

When it was their turn, the three men went in while Mariam stayed outside straining to hear what was going on. It was impossible to follow what they were saying, but Kelkar's voice came through loud and clear. So she heard a one-sided conversation: first an indistinct murmur of voices, then Kelkar saying impatiently, 'Yes, yes, I know all that, do you think I'm not aware that judges accept bribes? The question is, what do you expect me to do about it?' The murmuring again, then Kelkar: 'Look, you can see how busy I am, you've seen the crowd waiting to see me. My people have their hands full — just following up a single case like yours is almost a full-time job for one of them. It's not possible for me to do anything more.' Then an inaudible question and Kelkar's response, 'What's the matter with you people — can't you do anything for yourselves? You expect me to do everything for you from start to finish: have I ever told you not to start an agitation? If you're so eager to do it, go and do it. But don't come here wasting my time.' Then the three men came out and the next delegation — the one with the woman — went in.

'It's useless — he's not prepared to help us!' said Ganesh bitterly as soon as the door was shut.

'But did you notice,' remarked Anant, 'he didn't tell us not to take action?'

'Yes,' agreed Shaheed. 'I was surprised at that. I thought he might say something like: "I'm running this struggle *my* way, you just keep out of it".'

'So the picture is not so bad. At least we're free to start something ourselves.'

'But what's the use of that?' objected Ganesh. 'We could have done that anyway. We didn't need to call in Kelkar if we were going to take action on our own.'

'It helps to have the case in court as well,' Anant pointed out. 'That way we're fighting on two fronts at the same time.'

'I don't see how that helps if the case isn't making any progress.'

'At least it keeps Verma busy, doesn't it?'

'How does it keep him busy? He doesn't even turn up in court.'

'Well, he has to keep paying — paying the lawyer, bribing the judge. And if at the same time we put pressure on him at the factory end, after a while it'll pinch, you'll see.'

'By that time we'll all be dead!'

Shaheed had been watching Ganesh throughout this interchange and now put an arm round his shoulders. 'We know you've got a job at the new factory, Ganesh-bhai,' he said kindly. 'Ashok told us. Don't feel bad about it — we understand what problems you must have feeding three children as well as your old parents.'

Ganesh seemed to collapse inwardly under the weight of the arm. 'It's not that,' he said miserably. 'We're managing to eat, thanks to the contributions and some scheme the women have worked out. It's my mother. She's got a terrible stomach problem. She keeps having loose motions, she's wasting away in front of our eyes, and I'm frightened. I took her to the E.S.I.S. hospital but they don't have the proper medicines — they told me to buy them on the open market. They cost thirty-four rupees for a strip of ten tablets. It's just impossible for me to buy them. That's why I went with the others to apply for this job.' He was silent for a while, then looked up at Shaheed and said, 'They've asked us to join tomorrow, but I won't go — I'll wait for some time and see what happens, shall I?'

'Don't do anything of the sort,' Shaheed said decisively. 'There must be hundreds of applications, if you don't turn up, you'll lose the job. Besides, you should start earning as soon as possible so that you can buy the medicines for your mother.'

'I feel so bad, abandoning the two of you like this. Anant bhai, you won't hold this against me, will you?' he asked pleadingly.

Anant smiled and took his hand. 'We can surely win this struggle without the sacrifice of your mother,' he said. 'Don't worry, you're not abandoning us, you're only doing what you have to do. You can continue coming to meetings and helping in other ways, can't you?'

'Yes, of course. I was thinking,' said Ganesh, still rather apologetically, 'if Kelkar refuses to help us, why not call Gopal? I'm sure he'll agree to come and give a speech at least — maybe even organise a demonstration or solidarity action by his units. And the workers respect him, they know he's honest and straightforward. If he calls on them to do something, they would take take him seriously.'

'You're right,' agreed Shaheed. 'Yes, absolutely. Gopal's the man for us — let's go and talk to him now, he should be in his union office.'

Mariam had been following this conversation with only half her attention because she was equally interested to hear what was happening inside the cabin. When she saw them waiting for her she said rather hurriedly, 'Yes, that's a good idea, you go ahead to Gopal's office, I'll come after a while,' and concentrated fully on trying to piece together the other conversation. As before, there had been a long period of quiet talking, and Kelkar's response: 'I don't understand what you're trying to say. Please be clearer.' Some explanation, then, 'Certainly not! Under no circumstances will I accept this offer. It's an insult even to suggest it. That's my final decision, and there's no point in discussing it any further.' There was an attempt at remonstrance cut short by, 'No, there's no question of my reopening negotiations until management has made a better offer. How many times do I have to tell you that? Now kindly get out of my office and let someone else come in.' Mariam was expecting them to emerge, but instead she heard the woman's voice, now loud enough for the words to be distinguished: 'It's all right for you to take that stand, Mr Kelkar, you've got nothing to lose. If our union gets smashed, you'll still have all your other units; if our people go back crawling, you'll still have your reputation for militancy. But our union is all we've got — and we're not going to let it be destroyed just for the sake of your prestige!' Then she walked out followed by her colleagues. They came and stood close to where Mariam was seated and a white-haired man with an anxious expression asked, 'Well, what shall we do now?'

The woman who was still looking heated and angry said at once, 'Our first duty is to our members, not to *him*. Whatever we do, we mustn't let them down.'

'I agree with you, Nirmala, but what does that mean?' the man asked. 'What would best serve their interests?'

'Can't they decide that for themselves? They're adult human beings, after all. I don't understand this policy of treating them like children.'

'Yes, why should we take decisions on their behalf?' someone agreed. 'Let's call a G.B.M., tell them about the new offer and put it to the vote.'

'But we still have to make our recommendations, don't we? We can't just say this is the offer, take it or leave it. Naturally they'll want to know what our opinion is.'

'So we'll tell them what we decided at our last committee meeting that we'll hold out for a bit more of an increase, but wherever they stick, we'll settle.'

'And Kelkar?'

'To hell with Kelkar!'

'How can you say that? You know that we asked him to be our president only because the majority of workers wanted him.'

'Fine, so we'll tell them what he recommends too, and let them decide. And if we come to an agreement which is approved by the general body, we'll ask him to sign and let him decide. If he wants to sign, let him sign; if not, we'll sign. If he wants to remain as our president, let him remain; otherwise, let him resign.'

'Are you sure that's all right? It sounds very irregular to me signing an agreement without the approval of the president.'

'We may not have any choice in the matter. And you needn't worry that management will object — they'll be happy to settle with or without Kelkar.'

'All right, all right. Does everyone agree with that? Then tomorrow we'll send out notices for the meeting, shall we?'

They took leave of one another and started moving away, and Mariam roused herself to follow. On her way out she touched the woman's arm and said, 'I'm glad you told Kelkar what you thought of him. He thinks he's the greatest unionist in the world but he really has no idea how to conduct a struggle.'

Nirmala remembered seeing her in the office and smiled warmly. 'That man always makes me lose my temper,' she laughed. 'Did you hear how he spoke to our general secretary? Someone who has more unionism in his little finger than Kelkar has in his whole body!'

'But why don't you get rid of him then?'

'Ah, that's what I would like to do, but it's not so easy. There are still some of our members who are his fanatical supporters, and if we were to propose leaving him now, it might split the union. We don't want that — whatever we do, we should stay together. Let's see what happens, maybe they'll get disillusioned with him ultimately. Are you also working at a pharma plant? There's a Parsi girl in our department who looks just like you — she's not your sister by any chance, is she?'

'No, I don't have any sisters, only two brothers,' said Mariam with some amusement. 'I'm not actually working at any factory — I was just accompanying those workers who were coming out when you went in. They've been thrown out for forming a union and Kelkar isn't really doing anything about it.'

Nirmala wanted to know more, so Mariam told her the whole story. She was especially interested in the part played by the women. 'That's marvellous,' she said, 'so much solidarity! It must be nice working with slum women. Our girls are better paid, but they're also much more isolated. You wouldn't believe it, but I found one of them and her mother almost starving to death because of our strike.' It was now Mariam's turn to ask for details, after having made sure that she and Nirmala could go home on the same bus for part of the way. For once Mariam didn't mind the long, slow-moving queue — it gave them enough time to exchange information and addresses, and for Mariam to suggest that Nirmala should come to the next meeting of the women. 'They meet once a week — partly to sort out any practical or personal problems, but mainly because it makes them feel better especially the wives of the victimised workers. Why don't you come along some time? You may be able to make some suggestions we haven't thought of so far.'

'That's what I was thinking. There are at least four or five of our girls living in that area. One of them stays in a working women's hostel, and I seem to remember they had some problem getting meals. And the other problem is that we don't have a crèche; we decided to leave that for the next charter because transport was a demand which got more support. We'll definitely get it some time, the company has to provide one for us, but in the meantime women with small children suffer. I'll talk to them about it.'

'Oh wonderful! Yes, you certainly must come — it'll add new life to the whole effort. We need fresh ideas. Shall I meet you at the bus stop? Then we can walk there together.'

When Nirmala got off the bus, Mariam sat back feeling satisfied with the evening's work. It was too late to go to Gopal's office, but she felt sure he would agree to help. And now this unexpected find. It was almost too good to be true!

CHAPTER 32

The atmosphere of tension was almost palpable as Mariam, Kavita and Nirmala entered the public garden which had become a regular meeting place for the women affected by the dispute at Adarsh Garments.

Nirmala had been delayed by the buses so they were a little late and the meeting had already assembled, but there was an uneasy quiet rather than the customary chatter, and there was dead silence at the sight of the stranger. Mariam felt like asking, 'What's wrong?' but instead started by introducing Nirmala to them. 'She works in a big pharmaceutical factory with a lot of women workers,' she explained. 'I brought her along because she has some very good ideas about how those of you whose husbands have been dismissed can make more money with your meals service.'

'Yes, I was very interested and impressed to hear how you have organised yourselves,' began Nirmala. 'We've just been through a strike, too, but we never thought of anything like this. It's a wonderful idea. But so far you're not making much extra money out of it, so I was trying to think of ways in which you could earn something more. One idea was this: some ladies working in our factory have small children, and since there is no crèche, this is a problem for them. There are three of them in this area, one child is not going to school at all, his mother has to keep an ayah for him, and the other two go to school in the morning but they come home by twelve and then someone has to look after them until their mothers come home at five-thirty or six. I've spoken to the ladies and they would be very happy if you look after their children for them and feed them their afternoon meal. They could pay 100 to 200 rupees per month — and I thought that if you started a crèche, you would surely find more women like that who are willing to pay quite a lot to keep their children in it.

'The other thing is that one of our women is staying in a hostel — do you know the one? If you go to the end of this road and turn left, it's very close.' There were nods of assent. 'Well, they've been having problems with their meals for a long time. At first they had a canteen run by a contractor, but there was a lot of trouble with him — he used to keep dismissing his workers, never paid them properly, bought inferior provisions, and so forth. They finally got rid of him, but since then they have had to cook for themselves and most of them are not happy with that arrangement either. When I suggested that you might be ready to supply them with meals, my friend jumped at the idea. She was sure the other women would also agree. There are twenty-five of them, so even if you supply just one meal a day for five or six days a week, you could earn quite a lot.'

Nirmala had stopped talking, but there was no response. It was unnerving, this strange silence. 'Well, what do you think of the idea?' Mariam asked impatiently. But the silence closed again behind her words. She looked in bewilderment from one to the other.

Suddenly Shobha spoke up. 'We have something to tell you,' she said, speaking rapidly. 'Actually, we should have told you earlier, before this lady took the trouble to come, but we didn't know, we thought it would be better to wait for the meeting. Four of us will be... are...' She stopped, at a loss for words.

'Our husbands have got jobs,' explained another woman, 'so we decided not to...'

'Of course we'll make our contributions like everyone else,' interrupted Shobha hurriedly. 'Food as well as money.'

'Then who is left?' asked Mariam slowly, only now recalling what she had half-heard Ganesh say in Kelkar's office. 'Only Laila and Geeta?'

'They'll have more work, they'll be able to make more money,' began one woman apologetically, but she trailed off seeing the downcast faces of the two women. Clearly, the loss of companionship was more important to them than a higher income. And it might have been even higher if the others had stayed on, since the two of them alone would not be able to take up Nirmala's suggestions.

The silence was becoming unbearable when Kavita had an idea. She leaned forward and whispered to Mariam, and Mariam in turn called out to Geeta who listened carefully and then hurried away. To the rest of the women Mariam said, 'Well, what more is there to say? At least the food and money contributions should continue, and we'll try to think of something else for Laila and Geeta. Shall we wind up the meeting?' This seemed to relieve the tension, and the women started talking as they got up and moved around. A few came up and spoke to Laila who remained seated on the grass.

'We know how you must be feeling, Laila, but you understand our problem, don't you?'

'My mother-in-law is so ill she's almost dying, and we couldn't get her the medicines.'

'The rates the money-lender is charging us, we won't be able to pay him back for the rest of our lives. '

'You know we'll still help you any way we can.'

Laila nodded and agreed with each of them, but between them hung an unspoken regret at the passing away of the closeness which had grown within the little group.

Another group was discussing the reallocation of the food contributions; someone suggested that it would now be possible to supply Geeta's and Laila's families with two meals a day, seven days a week. Hardly anyone had moved away when Geeta returned, smiling triumphantly, with three women.

Mariam smiled too as Kantabai came straight towards her. 'This is Lakshmi,' she said, introducing one of her companions. 'She has two children, no husband and no job, so I brought her along.' The other was Preeti.

'These women are from a neighbouring basti,' explained Mariam to Nirmala. 'They all desperately need employment and it was Kavita's idea that they could take the place of the women who have dropped out.'

'Geeta told me something about looking after children and cooking for a canteen — is that right?' asked Kantabai.

Nirmala described both ideas again for the benefit of the newcomers.

'What I'd really like to do is become a carpenter like Lalita's father,' said Preeti suddenly, surprising even herself since she had never expressed this desire in words before. 'From the time I was a little girl I used to love watching how cleverly he shaped the wood into all kinds of beautiful things. But,' she added in some embarrassment, 'I don't mind cooking and looking after children — at least it's better than packing those ampoules, getting your fingers cut on the broken glass.'

'We won't be able to cook such large quantities of food in our own utensils,' pointed out Laila, who had come and joined the group.

'Ah, wait a minute,' said Nirmala, 'I think there are one or two big vessels at the hostel canteen already; you could use them.'

'You mean we should go there and cook?'

'No, no, we shouldn't do that.'

'What about the crèche, then?'

'Are we going to look after the children as well?'

'Why not? One person can look after them while the other four look after the food.'

'We can take it in turns.'

'But where?'

'Will they allow us to bring the vessels here?'

'I think so,' replied Nirmala. 'But even if they don't, or if there are not enough utensils, I'll see about that. I'll collect donations from my friends and buy whatever equipment you need.'

'But we'll need a place, won't we? We can't do all that in our own houses, can we?'

A crowd of interested women and a few men had gathered around to listen. One of them now said, 'You want a place? Our neighbours are moving to Goregaon in about two months — they've got a house there now, and they want to rent out their place here. It's big enough to keep the children as well as cook.'

'But they'll ask for a lot of rent!'

'Not necessarily — if you explain your situation to them. They don't really need much money — he's got a good job in the Municipal Corporation.'

'We'll leave that to you,' interjected Mariam. 'If we come to talk to them, they'll think the group has a lot of money.'

'We can handle that, but what shall we do until they move?'

'You can use my place,' offered Ravindran who had just joined the crowd. 'I'm out all day and no one else is there.'

'Is it big enough?'

'It's quite small, but it's better than nothing.'

'Perhaps we can start with the cooking and leave the crèche until we have the other place.'

The discussion continued, with the women who had not previously met getting to know each other in the intervals between the discussion of practical details. Kantabai insisted on recounting her own story as well as Lakshmi's and Preeti's, responding to Preeti's attempts to prevent her from doing so by saying indignantly, 'Why shouldn't I tell them? How will we ever stop such things from happening if we don't talk about them openly?'

'That's right,' agreed Nirmala, who had been listening with great interest. 'We have to expose them and fight against them, otherwise everyone thinks the girl is to blame. Nothing like that has happened in our factory for a long, long time, but I remember once, when I was young, a supervisor said something to one of the girls — something obscene, you know — and the next thing we knew she was standing there with her chappal in her hand, threatening to beat him up if he ever came near her or spoke another word to her.' She laughed at the recollection. 'The supervisor looked ready to die of shame — I don't think he would ever try that again! Now, of course, they wouldn't dare; after the union was formed, no supervisor or even manager would have the nerve. But it's different in these small-scale places, isn't it? You can't even form a union without getting thrown out, that's what I've heard. So everyone keeps quiet and girls go on getting harassed.'

It was growing dark; some of the women left, but the others wrapped their saris around their shoulders against the January evening chill and carried on talking. Mariam closed her eyes and relaxed, then opened them and smiled at Kavita. 'You really saved the day,' she said. 'I thought it was all over. But this is actually better than it was before; maybe later on we can think of setting up something permanent. Not now, though — I'm so tired I can't think of anything except getting to bed.'

CHAPTER 33

Gopal readily agreed to come and talk to the Adarsh workers. A few days later a crowd congregated outside the factory in the lunch-break and waited expectantly. Gopal needed no introduction: he arrived and started speaking.

'Brothers! You may be wondering why I am talking to you since you are affiliated to Kelkar's union and I belong to another union. But that is not important. What is important is that we belong to the same class; our struggle is the same. If you win your struggle, then that is a victory for me. If you are beaten, that is a defeat for me. It is because I see you slowly losing ground that I have come here today. It will weaken us all if you are defeated. I don't want that to happen.

'I have been a small-scale worker like you. I've worked in Pune, I've worked in Thane, and I've worked here before I joined this union as a full-timer. And everywhere I have come across employers like Verma. So I know them inside out. I know just how they feel and think. The one thing they love more than anything else is money; they will do anything, legal or illegal, to get it. But the one thing they hate more than anything else is to see workers fighting for their rights, fighting to be treated like human beings. This they cannot tolerate. And so if workers make the slightest move to organise themselves, they will do anything to stop them. Yes, they will even part with their precious money! They will bribe judges, bribe the police, pay goondas. They will lock us out for months and months, even years; they will lose lakhs of rupees of production just to break one small union. For them, this is a matter of self-respect. They feel that their self-respect is damaged if they have to deal with workers as equals. Never mind that they themselves are lower than the lowest worms crawling on the earth! If they can curse a worker when they feel like it, cut his pay when they feel like it, throw him out when they feel like it — that is what makes them feel like *men*.

'I also have plenty of experience of labour and industrial courts. Out of a hundred judges, you may find one who is honest, one who gives justice to the workers. All the other ninety-nine will regularly give anti-worker judgements. Or if it is too obvious that the workers are in the right, they will drag out the case for years and years. I know of a case where a worker fighting for reinstatement died before the judgement came. Some judges do this because they are interested in money, they accept bribes — and naturally it is always the employers who can afford to give bribes. Others do it because that is how they think and feel. They too, don't like to see workers holding up their heads. Remember, this whole system of industrial courts, and so forth, was not set up to protect your rights. They may tell you that, but don't believe it! It's biased against you from start to finish, and only a very, very few lucky ones manage to get justice out of it.

'You have got caught between an anti-worker employer and a corrupt judge — that's how I see the matter. The judge has no interest in settling the case — he's making money out of it. And Verma has no interest in settling it either. He's paying money, it's true; but he's also *making* money — out of you! So he's happy — he'll drag out the case as long as he can. Meanwhile, you will get demoralised because time is going on and there is no progress. It's already... how long? Three months? Four months? And already four of the victimised workers have found other jobs. If this goes on indefinitely, it will be a defeat. Whatever Kelkar might say, in real terms it will be a defeat. Don't let that happen!

'By now you must be thinking that I'm going to ask you to go out on strike. But there's a very big danger involved in that. A man like Verma won't think twice about dismissing the whole lot of you and recruiting an entirely new workforce. And if you're out, you won't be able to do a thing about it. He'll get police protection and you'll be without jobs. So I don't think you should go out on strike; I think you should stage a sit-*in* strike. Stay in the factory but don't do any work! Don't let him take out a single shirt or a single sewing machine! You are the main source of his money — block up that source! Then let's see how long he can keep bribing the judge to postpone the case!'

The workers had listened in silence while Gopal was speaking, but as soon as he stopped, pandemonium broke out. There was mostly applause and shouts of approval, but also questions and objections.

Shaheed took charge of the meeting, insisting that they should speak one at a time and give everyone a hearing. There followed a fairly heated discussion, because although Gopal's suggestion had majority support, those who opposed it did so passionately and vociferously. But it was finally Anant who said what Shaheed himself was thinking: 'Now that we've come so far, I don't think we can go back. There is no way we can prevent Verma from finding out what we have been discussing; and he'll know that even if we don't sit-in today, tomorrow we may change our minds. So naturally he'll try to forestall us. If we go home today, it's ninety-nine per cent sure that tomorrow we'll find a padlock on the door. We have to choose between a sit-in and a lockout.'

Exactly, thought Shaheed. Gopal was clever all right. Without appearing to do more than make a suggestion, he had in fact practically ensured that the workers would adopt a militant course of action, one which would, moreover, enable Shaheed and Anant to take the lead again. That was certainly clever, but was it quite ethical? Better not start thinking about such complicated questions now, when it was necessary to concentrate on what was going on! Anant's words had sunk in, and the workers were busy making the decision which had already been made for them. No, that was not fair, not at all fair! Most of them had been in favour of action anyway: all Gopal had done was to disarm the few objectors. Shaheed brought himself back to the business at hand. If they were going to start a sit-in immediately, they had to make careful plans. It meant ensuring a constant presence in the factory — not so easy in a place which normally worked only one shift. They would have to work out a rota, inform families, organise a food supply... and, yes, keep in touch with Kelkar. Let him not say later that they had taken action without consulting him!

CHAPTER 34

'I'm really getting too old for this work,' Nirmala told herself for the hundredth time as she put her hand to her back and tried to ease the pain. After an hour or more at the belt, her back always began to ache like this; she had been to the doctor but he hadn't been able to help so she concluded it was just age. 'Time I retired,' she said to the woman sitting next to her, who smiled and said, 'You retire? The day you do that the company will fold up. How do you expect us to carry on without you?'

That was how her plans for early retirement always ended. Financially there was no problem — she could easily afford it. Her husband who worked for another company had recently been promoted to a managerial position, and their only son, a doctor, had finally succeeded in setting up a flourishing practice; her own salary was quite unnecessary to maintain the comfortable but quiet style of life they were accustomed to. And she had to admit with some reluctance that she was not as young as she had once been. The last few weeks had been utterly exhausting. The first general body meeting had authorised the committee to go ahead with negotiations, and from then on it was a matter of alternating meetings with management and meetings with workers, because this time they decided to keep their members fully informed of day-to-day developments. Nirmala came home late night after night, and even then she couldn't sleep but lay awake going over the day's events and planning for the next.

It was at such times that she most appreciated her husband. Her friends never ceased to be amazed at what he put up with, one of them once said, 'Nirmala, God must have meant you to be a trade unionist, that's why he gave you a father and a husband like that.' And it was true, Nirmala thought, she had been incredibly lucky. Her father had not merely tolerated her trade union involvement but had actively encouraged it, telling his anxious wife, 'Don't worry, the girl knows what she's doing, she can look after herself. Never mind what other people say; we know there's no harm in it, so why should we listen to them?' She had not actually refused to marry, but had laid down the condition that her husband-to-be must totally accept her union activities; and with such a stipulation it was not surprising that she remained unmarried until a relatively mature age. But then came this man who promised that if she married him she would have the freedom to do exactly as she wished — and he had faithfully kept his word throughout all the years of their marriage. A home-loving person, if he ever felt unhappy about Nirmala's frequent absences he kept his disappointment to himself, and later found compensation in the companionship of their little son. 'A husband in a million, no, ten million!' said Nirmala's friends, and she agreed. She sometimes felt guilty about neglecting her home and family, all the more so since her husband was not in the least interested in her activities and preferred her to talk about other things when she was with him. This was a preference she willingly complied with, so that the time she did spend at home was pleasant and satisfying to both of them.

Nirmala often congratulated herself on her wisdom in having helped their son to buy a house and dispensary close by, even though it had cost them a large chunk of their savings. It meant that on evenings when she was out, her husband could go and have dinner there or spend hours chatting to their daughter-in-law who enjoyed his company as much as he enjoyed hers. And now there was the added excitement of a baby on the way — without all this to keep him occupied, Nirmala's conscience would have had a much harder time. And although from time to time she would ask, 'When will I ever have time to enjoy my family?' she knew in her heart that she was too involved in her union work to give it up until she was forced to retire. In spite of all the strain, it gave her something — what was it? excitement? mental stimulation? — which her life otherwise lacked. Look at this last struggle, for example. It was like a war, a battle of wits, in which every move had to be perfectly timed. If they had gone back to work earlier, their strike would have failed. If they had stayed out longer, it would also have failed. As it was, they had managed to get as much as they possibly could under the circumstances. Yes, in order to know when to call a strike, when to withdraw it, what negotiating strategy to use, you had to have experience but something else as well, intuition perhaps. Most of the time you tread a thin line between success and disaster, sometimes you had to bluff or gamble, nothing was ever certain. If you lost you tried again, if you won you went on to something else. There was always something else; everything you did was only a small step towards an ultimate goal you never reached, 'at least not in my lifetime,' sighed Nirmala.

Yet even that small step gave you such a deep sense of satisfaction. Nirmala sometimes stole a look out of the factory windows to admire the row of buses neatly lined up in the parking area until they were needed to take the workers home. They looked so good, and it was so thrilling to watch them leaving one by one! And it was pleasant to get up in the morning knowing you wouldn't have to struggle to get to work and back by a roundabout route. Was it worthwhile having gone through all that trouble in order to make life less irksome for so many people? Surely it was! This was something which Kelkar would never understand. He had refused to sign the agreement and made his disapproval very clear, yet he made no move to resign. What did he gain by having a unit like this? Money and prestige, no doubt, and that would help him to get more money and more prestige. But he missed out on the real excitement of the fight, the triumph of the victory. One could almost pity him!

CHAPTER 35

Can a problem become less important without losing any of its importance? Yes it can, thought Kavita; if you become preoccupied with other problems, even if they remain subsidiary, your obsession with the original one diminishes. Not that she felt herself to be in any way happier — she would have denied that vehemently. Although she managed at times to forget her pain, it came rushing back and she felt miserably that at the centre of her life was an aching void which nothing could fill.

And yet it was good to have something in her life other than that void. At first she had had her children, and that had helped. Now she had much more. She had Mariam — that was a warm and comforting thought. She had several lesser but rapidly developing friendships. And she had a multitude of problems which, while they were not hers alone, were nonetheless hers to the extent that she was part of the collective which faced them. And what problems! You really had to rack your brains to sort them out. For example, the old scheme had worked without much accounting because it was simply a matter of buying as much food as possible with the limited amount of money they had, and distributing it to the six families concerned plus their few regular customers. But now they had to budget very carefully and keep an up-to-date account so that the hostel women could inspect it if they wished. They also decided to assign a cash value to the food they themselves consumed and to deduct it from their income — 'It wouldn't be fair otherwise,' Laila pointed out. 'There are four people in my family whereas Kantabai lives alone — why should she pay as much as we do?' This solved a problem for Preeti who had hesitated to take food for her large family. If she could pay and take it, her mother need not cook every day, and although it would wipe out most of her income, she would have the satisfaction of feeding the entire family on some days. 'Yes,' agreed Geeta, 'and then if we have guests we can always take extra food without feeling bad, because we'll be paying for it.'

But who would keep the accounts? Preeti was the unanimous choice being the most educated, while Kavita and Mariam would take it in turn to check for mistakes. 'But don't think we're going to do this for ever,' warned Mariam. 'You will have to take over some time, so you had better start learning now. In any case it's not good to load one person with the entire responsibility for accounting — that, too, is something which ought to be shared.' It was easy to agree with this in principle, but not as easy to put it into practice when none of the others was properly literate. Laila knew the alphabet, Lakshmi knew a few Tamil letters, and that was all. And although most of them were quite quick at mental calculations, they found it much more difficult to work with written figures. 'We'll hold classes for them,' said Mariam with determination. 'There's no alternative.'

'It's all a matter of politics,' commented Ravindran, who had been following these developments with interest.

'It seems more like a matter of mathematics to me,' laughed Kavita. 'I don't think I've ever done so much boring arithmetic in my life! If we could afford it, I would suggest investing in a calculator.'

Mariam bought notebooks and pencils for the four women and one afternoon, after the cooking utensils had been cleared away, she sat down with them on the floor of Ravindran's home with Preeti acting as an assistant teacher. At the end of the first lesson Kantabai stared at the two pages covered with unrecognisable squiggles, then slammed down her pencil with finality. 'This is absurd!' she exclaimed. 'Whoever heard of a woman of my age going to school? It's not right. I'm not coming to these classes again.'

'Don't give up so soon,' pleaded Mariam. 'Just try once more.'

'You don't understand,' explained Kantabai. 'Your hand is used to doing these things from the time it was small. My hand has grown old without ever touching a pencil. It won't move in the same way as yours.'

'But you must take your share of responsibility for checking the accounts!'

'Look... is there anyone here who is going to cheat me?' demanded Kantabai, looking around as if challenging someone to a fight. There were smiles but no answers. 'Good!' she resumed. 'Then I can trust you to check the accounts for me, can't I?' And that was the end of the matter as far as she was concerned. Even Mariam failed to persuade her to change her mind, and had to be contented with the halting progress made by the others.

No sooner had they begun to settle down than the sit-in came upon them like an earthquake. Now the places were neatly reversed: the only families who were getting an income were the six who previously had to be supported. Mariam argued in every way she could against any disruption of the present scheme; previous experience had made her cautious about changes which would introduce greater instability. Let the other women divide themselves into seven teams, she suggested, each of which would cook for the entire workforce and their families one day a week; let them use the same utensils on a shift basis; let the other women make contributions in cash, in kind, however they could; but let the two schemes be kept separate! Her secret hope, expressed to no one but Kavita, was that Geeta and Laila would stay on after the strike ended so that this group of five would become a permanent workteam. Her arguments prevailed, and the schemes were run side by side.

Ravindran's hut was now constantly besieged by hordes of women, and he was virtually rendered homeless until late at night. But far from resenting this he was ecstatic about the new situation, and whenever he was not at work would hover around benevolently, waiting for a chance to help. 'It's a privilege to be allowed to participate in your struggle,' he told Anant. 'You people are the real heroes of our time!' The opportunity to talk to him was not the least of Kavita's new pleasures. Talk, or more often argue, because she frequently found herself disagreeing with his views, especially on women. But this was very different from arguing with Ranjan. It was quite usual for Ravindran, after arguing passionately for something, to stop suddenly and say, 'Of course, of course, you're absolutely right, I never thought of it like that before.' Nor did it cost her anything to admit she was wrong; she didn't feel in any way diminished by the admission, so there was no tension, no caution, no lack of spontaneity on either side. She was able to learn a lot from him about areas of experience which were foreign to her, beginning with the question of competition between small-scale and large-scale industry which had been nagging her for months; but it was also pleasant to feel that she could tell him things which were new and useful to him. Above all, she appreciated being able to test her ideas against those of someone who was intelligent but made no claims to infallibility, and she felt reasonably sure that she performed the same role for him. She noted with some amusement that Ravindran was apparently too overawed by Ranjan and 'Mariamma' ever to disagree with them, but didn't seem to find Kavita herself similarly awe-inspiring. This perfect reciprocity was satisfying in itself, apart from anything else she might be gaining. And surely he felt the same, because on more than one occasion he walked with her all the way home up to her gate and stood there talking until she laughed and said, 'We'd better continue our conversation next time. If I wait any longer my children won't let me go out again!'

Yes, it was worth having survived the first few difficult weeks when she had gone home to cook with the tired and hungry children hanging round her instead of doing it at leisure while they slept. Now life was much easier because she brought the evening meal with her. She smiled to herself when she recalled how she had represented the innovation to Ranjan as 'a contribution to the Adarsh workers' struggle' (which, after all, it was — she hadn't been lying!) so that he wouldn't be able to object. Some women might think she was not being sufficiently assertive, but her own assessment was that in ten years of married life she had made considerable progress in the art of getting what she wanted without provoking a confrontation. It was an art she had never thought she would need when she first got married, but when something is necessary for your survival you have to pick it up — you don't have much choice in the matter.

CHAPTER 36

'Oh no! That's the end of our poster-making!' exclaimed Kavita as a familiar wail from the children's bedroom made her get up. Her front room was chaotic, with sheets of card paper, dozens of felt-tipped pens, pots of paste, scissors and magazines strewn all over the floor. As it was a special occasion, Asha and Shanta had been allowed to miss their afternoon sleep after coming home from school, and help Mariam and Kavita make the posters instead. These were to be used for what was really a double celebration, because the women had been given a new place in Sheetal Nagar on the first of March, and after some cleaning and improvements were planning to hold an International Women's Day poster exhibition there before shifting in the cooking equipment and opening the crèche.

Mariam found these sessions with Kavita and the children soothing and yet disturbing — or, rather, when she reflected there was only one disturbing element: Asha. The little girl had become deeply attached to her, so much so that she had once referred to Kavita and Mariam as her 'two mothers'. Kavita had immediately seized on the idea — it had so many dimensions which pleased her. In the first place it filled a gap in Asha's life; with unbending stubbornness she had until now rejected Ranjan as a parent, and although Kavita did her best to be both father and mother to her, she often felt inadequate to the task. She also liked to think that Asha could replace the little girl Mariam never had — she was sure it would have been a girl — and thus in some way compensate for the loss which Kavita had been connected with, though not actually responsible for. And last of all, it was nice to think that she and Mariam shared a child as well as so much else.

Mariam's feelings on the matter were more mixed. It was not that she had completely rejected the responsibility of being a parent; she knew that if, for example, anything happened to Ranjan and Kavita, she wouldn't think twice about taking over all three children. What was being asked of her now was something much less in terms of responsibility, and yet she hesitated — why? She liked the child, felt happy at their closeness — there was nothing there to make her withdraw. She knew she had to sort out this question for herself because otherwise there was a danger that she might hurt Asha, which was the last thing she wanted to do.

From her childhood she had been forced to be emotionally independent, and had got into the habit of keeping a distance between herself and others. She had never thought of getting married or having children, and yet when she found herself pregnant she had briefly considered the possibility of allowing at least that one tie to develop. Her decision to end the pregnancy had consciously cut off a direction her life could have taken and confirmed her earlier security in solitude. So that now, to be confronted with a child only two years younger than her own child would have been and claiming, moreover, to be her daughter, was extremely disconcerting. Without even knowing it, Asha with her simple devotion was demanding that she abandon a stronghold which had been painfully constructed over the years. Should she comply? And if not, how could she extricate herself without hurting Asha? She had to decide.

'One thing you can be sure of is that a child won't betray you,' said Kavita, and Mariam looked up sharply, wondering if she could have read her thoughts. But Kavita was evidently following her own train of thought, with her arms around Sunil who was now lying quiet but wide awake, his head on her shoulder. She gave him his milk and put him down on the floor but as she had anticipated, they would have problems continuing with their work while he was awake. Shanta had to give up drawing in order to head him off from anything which he might spoil. At first this was an exciting game, but it soon became frustrating never to be able to lay his hands on any of the interesting objects around, and he was about to start complaining when he caught sight of his father at the door and ran over to him with a joyful smile. Ranjan took in the situation at a glance. 'Aha!' he said as he swung Sunil up into his arms, 'you're getting bored, are you? Let's go for a nice walk in the park and leave these women to their scribbling, shall we?'

'That's a good idea. You men will only get in our way here,' responded Asha, amused at being called a woman and even more amused at having called Sunil a man.

Ranjan was about to leave with his son when he noticed Shanta looking up longingly, obviously tired of this work yet unwilling to leave it halfway. He waited a moment, then asked, 'But isn't anyone going to help me to look after Sunil in the park?'

'I'll go, Mummy, shall I?' asked Shanta, jumping up eagerly but looking anxious at the same time.

'Yes darling, the fresh air will do you good,' smiled Kavita reassuringly.

When the three of them had been working in silence for some time, Mariam suddenly said, 'You know, something keeps haunting me — it's the memory of that girl Preeti saying, "What I'd really like to do is be a carpenter". Imagine how strongly she must have felt to come out with it like that in front of all those strangers!'

'I know, that impressed me too,' agreed Kavita. 'It's such a pity she's stuck with cooking and childcare and nothing else. But what can we do about it?'

'I don't know, but I wish we could do something. It's sad to think of Preeti and other girls like her desperately wanting to do things and never getting a chance to do them.'

'Yes. A lot of these handicrafts involve not only skill but artistic talent, and so much of that must be going waste because girls are never taught the skills.'

'Oh yes, I remember when I was a child my mother used to take me with her when she went to the Chor Bazar market, all those chaotic alleyways crammed with everything from big shops to tiny stalls, and the posh handicraft emporia where her rich friends and foreign tourists did their shopping. I always used to be open-mouthed at the beauty of the things there. I still go there sometimes to have a look, even though I can't afford to buy anything. In leather, wood, stone, metal, wool, in cotton and silk — it's just amazing the number and variety of beautiful things that are made.'

'But I wonder, don't these handicrafts survive only because of our technological backwardness? What will happen to all those craftsmen when mass production takes over? Won't their talents also be wasted then?'

Asha had stopped working and was listening intently, looking from one woman to the other as they spoke. Now she asked, 'Mummy, why does Preeti want to be a carpenter?'

'Well, she said she had seen her friend's father at work, and I suppose she admired his cleverness and the beautiful things he was making, and she wanted to do the same herself.'

'And will she become a carpenter when she grows up?'

'We don't think she will get a chance. You've seen a carpenter at work, haven't you? You've seen the tools he uses? Well, it's not easy to use them properly. If someone doesn't teach Preeti how to use those tools and let her practise using them, how can she become a carpenter?'

'But why won't someone teach her?'

'Your turn, Mariam,' laughed Kavita.

'Hm! Well, a lot of people think that girls can't do some things which boys can do, like carpentry. It's like looking at Sunil and saying, "Oh! That boy can't read and write". Of course if you don't teach him, if you never let him touch a pencil or a book, he never will learn to read or write, will he? It's like that with girls and carpentry. I think some girls would be good at it if they were trained — maybe Preeti would be. But she isn't allowed to try.'

'But she doesn't want to do anything bad, does she? You said she wants to do something beautiful, doesn't she?'

'Yes, of course.'

'Then why don't people let her try? It won't hurt anyone, will it?'

'But most people in the world are not as sensible as you are, my dear,' replied Mariam, dreading the next question. To her relief, Asha turned to Kavita.

'But looking after children is beautiful, too, isn't it, Mummy?'

'Of course,' said Kavita. 'I think having my children is the only beautiful thing I've ever done,' she added rather sadly.

'Nonsense, Kavita!' said Mariam warmly. 'Perhaps the most beautiful thing, but certainly not the only one.'

Kavita shook her head. 'Being a mother is the only thing I do well,' she said. 'I'm not even a good housewife. Look at the mess this place is always in. No matter how hard I try, it never seems to stay tidy. I feel so ashamed when people come over unexpectedly.'

'You have small children and no servant,' pointed out Mariam.

'Even then, it looks bad. And I *feel* bad because I can't even look after a house properly. I haven't made such a great success of my marriage either, although I was so sure I would, at first.'

'I think you've made quite a big contribution to the collective kitchen. And what about those pamphlets and leaflets you used to write? It was marvellous, the way you could explain the most complicated ideas so that even a child could understand them.'

'Oh yes!' exclaimed Kavita, her face brightening. 'I enjoyed writing those. I'd quite like to try my hand at writing for children too — I'm sure I wouldn't have any problems communicating with them.'

Asha, who had been following this interchange carefully, now came and kissed her mother. 'Mummy, can I leave these posters now?' she asked. 'I want to draw something else.'

'Yes darling. Take some card paper, we've got plenty.'

Asha took a sheet and sat in a corner with her felt-tipped pens. They heard no more from her all evening — in fact the two women cleared away the posters and went to cook, Ranjan returned with the other children, and still she sat drawing.

'Asha, aren't you going to eat with us?' Kavita asked finally.

'Oh Mummy!' she exclaimed. 'Can't I have just a few minutes more? I've nearly finished.'

'All right. I'll start Sunil off in the meantime. Can we come and see what you've done?'

'No! Not yet. Wait till I call you.'

But it was quite a while later. Sunil had finished his meal and the others were already seated round the table when Asha called out, 'Mummy! Now you can come and see.'

From a distance Kavita got the impression of an intricate design of brilliant colours. But when she came closer she saw that it consisted of countless women and girls engaged in all manner of activities. They were dancing and singing and playing the guitar; working in factories, fields, hospitals and kitchens; writing, drawing and teaching; two women were playing with three small children; there was Preeti perhaps, a little larger than some of the others, with something which looked like a carved panel, and another woman with some tremendously complicated-looking equipment; girls playing cricket and football and two of them simply holding hands; and many, many more. Above the picture was written in an arc: 'IF IT'S SOMETHING BEAUTIFUL — ' and below, in bigger letters, 'LET HER DO IT!' Kavita took some minutes to take it in, then she exclaimed, 'It's lovely. Our posters are quite dull compared with it. Come and look at this, Mariam.'

As Mariam looked on she felt her eyes filling with tears. At last she bent down to kiss Asha and said softly, 'We'll make it the centrepiece of our exhibition. You've certainly done something beautiful today, haven't you?'

When it came to the point, she didn't have any trouble making her decision after all: it was more or less made for her.

CHAPTER 37

When Laila opened her door in response to the urgent knocking, she was surprised to see Ashok and Ganesh outside, so breathless that they could hardly speak. 'Come quickly, bhabi,' panted Ashok, 'Shaheed needs you badly.'

'But the children?' Laila asked, bewildered. 'What shall I do with the children?'

'Don't worry about them,' said Ganesh a little more calmly. 'I'll ask Geeta to keep them for the night, and tell her about Anant at the same time. But please hurry.'

'But why? What has happened?'

'Just come with me, I'll explain on the way,' said Ashok, and she began to hurry along with him, growing more and more fearful as his silence lengthened.

'What is it?' she asked again at last.

'Well, it's like this,' he began awkwardly. 'We were coming out of the union office after meeting Kelkar, and Shaheed and Anant were walking behind the rest of us. A couple of goondas armed with weapons jumped on them and started stabbing them. We heard the noise and turned back, but by the time we reached them Shaheed was down and Anant was running like the wind with one of them after him.' He paused and then continued, 'Shaheed was badly injured. It's obvious they were aiming to kill.' Again a pause. 'He was unconscious when we took him to the hospital. He is now conscious but in a very serious condition. He keeps asking for you, so we thought we had better fetch you. I'm sorry, bhabi, we're doing everything we can for him.'

So that was it. Somehow Laila always had a premonition that evil would come on Shaheed's involvement in this business, or so it seemed to her. But now that it had, strangely enough, she remained deadly calm, neither uttering a word nor shedding a tear. Ashok was rather relieved. He had been expecting her to react more strongly when he broke the news to her, hence his hesitation in doing so. What a strange woman!

At the hospital there were a few workers outside the entrance. On the way Laila had learned from Ashok that the others were searching for

Anant, because if the goondas caught up with him he too would desperately need help.

She walked along the corridors, up the stairs and along more corridors in a kind of trance. At the entrance to a ward lined with two long rows of beds, Ashok spoke to the nurse in charge who motioned him in. It was not visiting time, but the wife of the dying man would be allowed to sit with her husband provided she didn't make a fuss and disturb the other patients, most of whom were already asleep. Ashok led her to a bed which was partly screened from the others by a white curtain, pulled up a stool for her and discreetly retired.

Laila looked at Shaheed a little uncertainly. His breathing was laboured and there was an ugly gash above one eye, but he didn't seem to be in such bad shape — she had expected worse. Then she recalled what Ashok had said: it was not his head they were aiming for, they had stabbed him several times in the stomach, the chest. His eyes were closed. Was he sleeping? Very softly, almost inaudibly she said, 'Shaheed'. Immediately his eyes opened and his face came to life.

'Laila! I was so frightened you wouldn't get here in time.'

'Oh Shaheed! Why did this have to happen to you? Why you?'

'They must have been told to finish us off. They made a pretty good job of it, too. But luckily it's taken some time. I would never have been able to die in peace without seeing you.'

'Die! Don't say that. It won't come to that. Nowadays doctors can do almost anything — even bring people back to life after their hearts have stopped beating, I heard about it on the radio. Everyone is behind you. We'll make a collection and send you to the best hospital, get you the best doctors. You won't die.'

Shaheed smiled faintly. 'You must believe me Laila, the doctor who could save me just doesn't exist.' He spoke faintly and slowly, but perfectly lucidly, and his words pierced her as if she herself had been stabbed. Was there really no hope then?

'There's no hope for me,' Shaheed continued, as if answering her thought. 'That's why I was so desperate to see you. Laila...' His hand groped for hers, but as he was too weak to get it out from under the covering sheet Laila helped him, noticing with horror as she did so that the undersheet was soaked in blood. She held his hand and waited for him to continue. His eyes had closed again and she wondered in panic if he were already dying. But he opened them in a moment and smiled. 'I'm sorry,' he said, 'they've drugged me so much that I can hardly keep my eyes open. But I must, at least until I've finished talking to you. Listen Laila, I want you to forgive me for everything you've had to put up with because of me...'

'Forgive you?' Often enough Laila had felt bitter, resentful, but now all of this was swept away as though it had never existed. 'What do I have to forgive you for? I know that whatever you did was not for yourself but for your fellow-workers, for all working people.'

Shaheed shook his head almost imperceptibly. 'I know that's what I told you — that's what I told myself too. But it's not good enough. You had to take on the burden of looking after the children and the home — and me as well. And in return... in return I didn't even show you how much I loved you, didn't give you any moral support when you needed it. I didn't bother to involve you in my work so that we could be close together at times when we were physically separated. I was such a fool. I thought there was plenty of time, that we had a whole lifetime together ahead of us. And now I am well and truly punished for my foolishness.' He finished with a kind of sob, and two tears trickled from his eyes down the sides of his face. Laila was maintaining her self-control by an almost superhuman effort, but she couldn't have held out long confronted with those tears, so she laid her cheek down on his hand in order to blot out the sight without withdrawing from him. What could she say? In a way everything he said was true yet she couldn't bear to see him torturing himself like this.

After a pause Shaheed went on, his voice perceptibly weaker and his breathing more laboured. 'The other thing I wanted to tell you was... well, if we really had years more together I wouldn't need to say it, I could show you how much I love you, but now you must believe me, although I can't prove it, believe that in spite of the way I've neglected you, failed you in so many ways... you must believe that I love you... so much. That's the only thing, apart from the children, which makes me regret having to die now. Laila, please tell me, say it in so many words, say you forgive me?'

His voice was so earnest, imploring, that Laila looked up and repeated with equal earnestness, 'I forgive you.'

'And you believe that I love you?'

'I believe that you love me.'

A change came over his face — you could hardly call it a smile but that was the sense it conveyed — and his whole body relaxed. 'Now I can really die in peace,' he said. 'Don't worry about your future or the children's, Laila. My friends will look after you... they'll look after Geeta and her children, too, if anything happens to Anant. They have promised that they will, and they won't let me down.'

'But you're not going to die, you're not! You'll live a long time, even if you can't get around as easily as before. We'll all look after you when you come home from hospital — you'll see, we're going to have plenty of good times together!'

It was as if, having got over the serious business, Shaheed felt he could afford to relax and dream. 'Do you really think so?' he asked affectionately. 'Well, maybe you're right. Tell the children I'll have a lot more time for playing with them, now that I can't go out. And in the evenings we can sit and tell stories... in the dark.' His voice trailed off and his eyes closed as if sleep had finally overcome him. Laila laid her cheek down on his hand again and closed her eyes too, wisps of memory, of fantasy, drifting through her mind incoherently. She sat there until dawn broke and the ward began to stir, never noticing that the hand under her cheek was growing cold. The nurse on her morning rounds came to take Shaheed's pulse and told her, matter-of-factly but not brutally, that he was dead. His face looked peaceful and satisfied, even a hint of a smile seemed to linger on it; he often looked like that when he was asleep. Laila went to the door of the ward although in a trance, guided by the nurse's hand on her arm, and then back home, guided by Ashok. Geeta, who had hardly slept and was watching for them, came running to Laila's hut with the children, who were full of questions: 'Where's Papa?' 'How is he?' Laila smiled at them and replied dreamily, 'Papa said we will have good times together when he comes home. He will have lots of time to play with you, and we can all tell stories in the evening.' But Ishaq had already noticed Geeta's mute, anxious enquiry and Ashok's hopeless reply, 'It's all over,' and grasped at once what had happened. Bursting into wild sobs, he ran into a corner and stood there with his face to the wall, while Farida followed with a loud wail. Laila looked at them as if thoroughly bewildered; the memory of that calm, peaceful face flashed into her mind, and suddenly she was hit by the realisation that she would never see it beside her on the pillow again. All her self-control was swept away instantly — what was the good of it now? — and she threw herself face-downwards on the bed, crying loudly and beating her fists, her head, on whatever came within reach. Geeta ran to comfort her while Ashok tried to calm the children.

The sound of weeping soon brought a crowd to the door; most people had guessed what had happened because news of the attack had already spread.

CHAPTER 38

'Congratulations! It's a beautiful boy.'

Renu said nothing, but inwardly she groaned. Even in this, it seemed, she had no luck. How desperately she had hoped it would be a girl, a daughter who would be a companion and confidante! A boy could never be that. And now it was almost impossible that she would ever get another chance to have a baby. Of course, no one would understand her feelings; everyone would think her lucky to have a son to look after her in her old age.

'Want to see him before I take him to be cleaned up?' asked the attendant who was holding the baby.

In spite of herself, Renu smiled unconsciously as she looked at the funny little creature. He had stopped crying now, and was gazing straight at her. 'His eyes are open!' she exclaimed in astonishment. 'He's looking at me!'

'Well, why not?' joked the attendant. 'Don't you think he wants to know what kind of a mother he's landed up with?'

That was a new thought. Was it possible that the baby would be as disappointed with her as she was with him? That would be unbearable! Besides, was she really disappointed? He was so sweet, just as soft and helpless as a girl would have been. Maybe it didn't make such a difference after all. Why couldn't a son be as gentle and understanding as a daughter? He would certainly feel as hurt as any girl if he knew his mother had rejected him at birth. A wave of remorse brought tears to her eyes. 'Don't worry,' she whispered as she gently stroked the tiny cheek, 'I'll be a good mother to you, I promise I will.'

Half an hour later she was lying in the maternity ward with the baby beside her when she caught sight of Kavita's anxious face at the door. Renu waved to attract her attention and eventually Kavita spotted her. 'There you are!' she said as she came and sat down on the bed. 'How are you? How was the delivery? Any problems?'

'Not at all. It was very easy, though there were times when it hurt quite a lot. But now I'm feeling fine. Only a little tired.'

'What a sweet baby! Boy or girl?'

'It's a boy. The doctor said he's fine and healthy. I gave him a little milk just now, and he sucked really nicely. You should see him when he's awake — he looks even sweeter with his eyes open.'

Kavita smiled with satisfaction. She had been a little anxious about Renu's reaction in case the baby should be a boy because she knew how much she had wanted a girl; but it seemed that he had won her heart already. 'I'd better go now,' she said after a moment. 'There are hundreds of things I have to do. Besides, you need to rest now after all the hard work you've been doing. I'll come and see you tomorrow at visiting time. Maybe I'll bring the children too, shall I? They'd like to see the baby.'

'Yes, please bring them — I would like to see them too.'

'All right then. Look after yourself and get plenty of rest,' Kavita smiled as she pressed Renu's hand. Renu smiled back a little shyly, and held on to Kavita's hand. She wanted to say something, but didn't quite know how. At one time her situation had seemed hopeless, the future dark and frightening. Even now the future was far from clear, the problems far from solved; the difference was that she was no longer alone; there was at least one person in the world she could turn to and talk to. Without Kavita, she would not have been relaxed enough to enjoy her baby as she was doing now, and these precious moments would have been lost to her for ever, drowned in anxiety and foreboding. All this she wanted to tell Kavita, but the words failed to come. She could only say, 'Thank you for everything,' and hope that she was understood. Kavita affectionately pinched her cheek and smiled again before turning away. Poor girl, she thought, barely more than a child herself and already burdened with the responsibility for another life. She's going to have a hard time. I hope we can work something out for her. It would be such a shame if she became bitter and cynical and started blaming the child for her problems. I wonder?

When Kavita came the next day, Renu's mood had changed completely. Even the sight of the children seemed to have no effect on her gloom and depression. 'What's the matter?' Kavita asked gently, and when there was no reply she proceeded to answer her own question: 'You must be thinking about what will happen when you are discharged tomorrow. Don't worry about that. I told you that you can stay with me as long as you like. And if those people won't take you back as a full-time servant, you can find plenty of part-time work of the same sort. That's better, in fact — you'll be more independent. And I could look after your baby while you are out.'

Still Renu did not reply. She thought, that's all very well for the moment, but I can't live like that for the rest of my life, can I? Your husband won't like it, your children won't like it, even you won't like it after some time. And what about me? What kind of life is it for me, living in someone else's house all the time? What kind of future do I have to look forward to?

Aware of the inadequacy of what she had said, Kavita continued to think aloud. 'What about your family? Should we inform them? They would surely want to help in some way, at least by keeping the baby so that you could work.'

'Out of the question!' Renu burst out violently. 'Inform them? I would rather die! As for their helping me or the baby — they would throw us out of the house and out of the village too, if they could. Don't think of them. It would be better for them to think I am dead.'

It was now Kavita's turn to fall silent. She hadn't seriously expected any other response. In fact she had already been over and over this ground in her mind, each time rejecting these weak alternatives and ending up with the same vague speculation. It seems crazy, she thought, but I can't think of anything else. I suppose there's nothing to be lost by trying. She was interrupted by Asha's urgent voice saying, 'Mummy, Mummy, Sunil is going to make the baby cry! I keep telling him not to do that, but he won't listen to me. He's so naughty, we shouldn't have brought him!' She pulled Sunil back rather roughly, he immediately began to wail, and Kavita turned her attention to the children with a sense of relief. For the rest of the visit she managed to avoid talking to Renu, only saying at the end with a cheerfulness she didn't feel, 'You mustn't worry about anything, just concentrate on looking after yourself and the baby. I'll find something for you, I promise I will. So don't look so gloomy!'

That night, after the children were in bed, Kavita picked her way through the dark web of alleys she could never quite get the hang of and finally ended in front of Laila's hut. When Laila opened the door in response to her voice she entered and began without warning, 'I've come to ask for your help, Laila.' If Kavita had jumped up and slapped her face, Laila could hardly have been more surprised and shocked. Ask for her help? *Her* help! But wasn't she the one most in need of help at present? How could she help anyone? Kavita explained, 'Do you remember I told you about the girl who was working as a servant in the flat next door? Well, she delivered a baby two days ago — a boy. I didn't tell you because you were in such a state. Both she and the baby are fine, but she's very depressed because she has nowhere to go after being discharged tomorrow. She's quite sure her people won't take her in, and our neighbours have refused to employ her after the baby is born. I offered to keep her and the baby in my house, but she's not happy about that and I can understand why. So I was thinking, Laila, would you mind if she came here to stay with you? She would feel much more at home here than with me. And I'm sure you would look after her and the baby as long as they need looking after. And even afterwards, if you find that you get on well with her, wouldn't it be a good idea to keep her here? You could put her baby in the crèche while she went out to work, and she could help with household expenses. It would help both of you. Anyway, you can decide about that later. But for now, will you take her? Shall I bring her tomorrow evening?'

Almost in spite of herself, Laila's interest had been aroused. Now faced with a point-blank request, she shrugged her shoulders and said, 'All right. There's no harm in trying it out.' There was no enthusiasm in her voice, but Kavita left feeling satisfied. There was a chance that it might work.

CHAPTER 39

After fasting for several days, Laila had started eating again because it was less trouble to eat than to resist; at least once she had eaten people would go away and leave her alone, whereas if she refused they would go on and on trying to persuade her until she felt like screaming. Once a day Geeta would bring her food from the kitchen, and that one meal she managed to eat with difficulty. They had given up trying to persuade her to eat another, finding that even if they left more food with her it would still be there, untouched, in the morning. She had also started having baths again. But that was the furthest she would go: beyond that, no more concessions to life. Her hair grew tangled, dirty clothes piled up although Geeta sometimes took some away and washed them. Even the sight of the children, who were now staying with Geeta, didn't have any effect on her — on the contrary, the knowledge that they were being well looked after removed one reason for rousing herself which she might otherwise have had. In the depths of her despair it didn't occur to her that her loss had been theirs too, and she played no part in the process whereby loving friends helped Ishaq and Farida to come to terms with their bereavement. Taking care of her children would have demanded too much involvement with the living at a time when all she wanted to do was to be absorbed in the memory of Shaheed. She couldn't die because they wouldn't let her, but she certainly wasn't going to make an effort to live.

Yet unhappy as Laila was, Renu's plight touched a sympathetic chord in her. Here, clearly, was a being even more unfortunate than herself. At least Laila had known some years of happiness with a husband who loved her; this girl had no such experience, she had simply been exploited and cast off. How terrible! On the morning after Kavita's nocturnal visit Laila started moving around, slowly, as though after a long debilitating illness, trying to put the hut in order. It was dirty and very untidy — not fit for guests to see. Industrious spiders had spun their webs in every corner they could find, and the food she had been keeping for Shaheed on the night he got stabbed was still in the pans, a repulsive mess. When had Kavita said she would bring her? In the evening. That was good, it gave her more time. She needed time, it was taking her so long to do everything.

Suddenly she stopped, her heart beating hard. Evening. Did that mean before the evening meal? The girl would have to be fed! But how? The idea of shopping and cooking seemed impossible; she couldn't face going out of the house, talking to people, explaining everything, and yet, she couldn't let her guest go hungry. The kitchen! Lucky she had thought of it before Geeta brought her meal for the day. She would ask her to bring some more for the night. Explaining everything to Geeta would not be so bad.

Thinking of Geeta and the kitchen made her feel guilty. She had done no work now for... oh, she couldn't even remember how long. Yet she had been fed, her children had been fed. Who was doing that? No one was wealthy enough to afford such an extra burden; she should really make an effort to get back to work. And then there was something else which bothered her, something buried away in her memory. It was from that period which she couldn't bear to recall, yet she must, because it was important. Yes, that was it: they had attacked Shaheed and Anant. But she hadn't even cared to find out what had happened to her friend's husband! Now this thought hurt her so much that she sat down and cried. Geeta had looked after her so well, had kept the children at her house, and yet she might be going through some hell of her own, without any help or support from Laila.

As soon as Geeta came in with the food, Laila astonished her by jumping up and demanding, 'Geeta, what happened to Anant?'

'Anant? Well, we don't really know. He's disappeared completely — we haven't been able to trace him. I've looked in all the hospitals and the men have searched all the places where... where they might have disposed of him. But there's nothing so far. The others think he must be dead, otherwise he would have turned up by now. But I somehow feel that he's still alive, though I've no idea where he could be.'

'Then you've been alone all this time?'

'Yes.'

'Oh dear! And I've been letting you feed me and keep the children how could I do it? You must forgive me, Geeta, I wasn't myself.'

'I know, I know, don't worry about that, everyone has been helping, it's not just me alone.'

'But listen — tonight someone else is coming — you remember that girl

Kavita was telling us about, the one who was expecting a baby? Well, she's delivered, and she's coming to stay at my place from this evening.'

'Will you be able to manage?' Geeta asked doubtfully. 'I could keep her if it's a problem for you.'

'No no, I want to help her, but just for tonight I have a problem with food. Will you bring me some more from the kitchen, please, Geeta? I promise I'll come and start working from tomorrow — I must have a huge debt by now!'

'No, don't be silly, there's no such thing as a debt, this is an emergency situation. Of course I'll bring some food tonight — shall I bring some for you too? She won't like to eat if you don't keep her company.'

'I suppose so. And why not bring Ishaq and Farida home too? She may like them, and they may like the baby.'

'Yes, I'll do that. They will be glad to get back to you, I'm sure.'

Geeta walked away happy. What a change — it was like magic! But back in the hut, Laila was crying again. Shaheed dead... Anant disappeared, probably dead... Renu abandoned... all their children fatherless... what a sad world it was!

CHAPTER 40

Renu lay awake in Laila's hut, running through the events of the previous day in her mind. In the morning she had been discharged from the hospital — she was well and so was the baby, there was no reason to keep them any longer. Kavita had picked them up and taken them home in an auto-rickshaw. Renu didn't like going back to the building where her former employers lived just next door, she would have preferred to go straight to her new home, but Kavita said the place might not be ready for her yet. So she had to spend most of the day in this flat where she felt very awkward and uncomfortable, especially when Kavita's husband came in for a while; only in the evening did Kavita take her to Sheetal Nagar. There had been a bewildering array of new names and faces there, a rather harassed meal during which the baby kept crying, and then, totally exhausted, she finally managed to get to bed.

This morning, however, she felt much better. She had slept well, the baby had taken his feed and gone back to sleep, and she was free to lie in bed as long as she pleased. Looking around, she saw a woman standing near the door. She had evidently just had a bath and was combing out the tangles from her luxuriant hair which hung down well below her waist. You can tell a lot about a person from her back, and Renu imagined that the rather slight, small figure she was looking at conveyed an attitude of tenderness. She tried to recall the woman's face from the night before, but no picture would come to her mind. She got up carefully, so as not to disturb the baby, and stood at the door. 'What lovely hair!' she exclaimed admiringly. 'I wish I could have hair like that.'

Laila turned, startled, and smiled at her. 'Oh no, it's all falling out now,' she said, shy but pleased. 'It used to be much longer and thicker.'

'Well, you're really lucky. Look at my rat's tail,' said Renu ruefully, letting down her own hair.

Laila laughed. 'Are you feeling better this morning? You must have been tired out last night — you fell asleep the minute you lay down.'

'Oh yes, I'm feeling fine today. Where are the children?'

'They've gone to the toilet, they'll be back in a minute. I'll make some tea, then we can all have breakfast. Afterwards they will probably go out to play and I have to go to work, but we'll come back at lunch-time. They have school in the afternoon and I'll have to go back to work, but only for a couple of hours, that's all. Will you be able to manage, all alone with the baby?'

'Yes, of course, why not? He's a good little fellow — sleeps a lot and hardly cries at all.' Renu smiled down at the tiny sleeping form, then looked around the room. 'While you're out, I can put this place in order.'

'Yes, I know it's a mess,' Laila said apologetically. 'I'm sorry... I haven't been quite well lately.'

'I know — Kavita told me about it,' Renu said warmly. 'Those filthy pigs — I know all about them, the people I used to work for are just the same sort. They would commit any crime to make a little more money, they treat people worse than we would treat animals. They didn't consider me to be a person so they used to talk openly in front of me, and the kind of things they used to say! It made me so sick, I often dreamed of putting poison in their food and killing the lot of them. Seriously, it would have given me the greatest pleasure to finish them off.'

Laila was taken aback. In all the time since Shaheed's death, she had never felt this kind of anger and hatred — and yet, when she thought about it now, she had every reason to react in the same way. Renu's anger stirred up her own but she also felt helpless: how could one hit back at them? The night before, while they were having their meal, Geeta had told her that Verma had used the police to smash the sit-in, closed down the factory and disappeared; who could find him and punish him now? These people were so powerful, they could literally commit murder and get away with it.

'It's not so easy,' she said slowly. 'Suppose you had poisoned them you would have been caught and punished. But they can kill us without being punished at all.'

'Oh yes, they've got the police in their pockets. My employers used to talk openly about the bribes they gave the police — it's a regular affair.'

'Then how can people like us do anything?'

'We have to fight the police as well, that's all.'

'Oh no, don't say that! That's exactly how Shaheed and Anant used to talk and,' Laila broke off because she knew she was going to cry. What was wrong with her? She felt like crying all the time. She poured out the tea, blinking to clear away her tears, and distributed chapatis to Renu and the children who had returned and were sitting expectantly on the floor.

Renu silently ate her chapati and drank her tea. At last she said, very softly, 'I understand how you feel. But you mustn't give up. If people like us give up, the world will just go on getting worse and worse. Imagine what a horrible place it'll be by the time our children grow up.' She smiled at Ishaq and Farida, who smiled back.

She was right, Laila thought as she went to work feeling rather bewildered. Renu was not at all what she had been expecting. She had imagined someone quiet and pathetic, crushed and miserable — but this girl was quite a firebrand! Her large eyes could change in seconds from softness to fierce anger and back again, and it was a little frightening to imagine what she might be like in a fight — but no, Laila laughed at herself, why should they quarrel? After all, they hadn't disagreed about anything — Renu had only been angry about things which she herself felt to be injustices. There was no reason why they shouldn't get on well together.

CHAPTER 41

I wonder if this is what it feels like to be a ghost, thought Anant. The familiar streets looked totally strange, yet he could not pinpoint anything which had changed. It must be I who have changed, he mused.

Maybe I am a ghost after all. And indeed, that desperate, shadowy struggle against death, the long stretches of unconsciousness which could have been death itself, were somehow divided from the present by an impassable barrier. They were part of another life altogether, like everything which had gone before.

His legs, which had been carrying him home, suddenly stopped, and he stood still in the middle of the pavement, bewildered and lost. He was going home, but what home? For the first time in the four weeks since he had been stabbed he thought about his home, about Geeta. What could have become of her, poor thing? He had never given her a very good life, but at least he had always provided for her. What did she think when he had disappeared like that? That he was dead? Had run away? More importantly: how would she and Sindhu have managed to survive? She had never gone out to work in her life. The Adarsh sit-in must surely be over by now, settled one way or the other, and the women's self-help scheme would have come to an end. The only thing Geeta could possibly do was go home to her village, tell her parents that her husband was dead and persuade them to take in the child and herself. Or, of course, she could have gone to his parents. That was more likely, since they lived in Bombay and had always disapproved of them living on their own. So where should he go? Home — to find a padlock on the door? Or to his parents' place?

He resumed his former direction, but more slowly and hesitantly this time. He recognised no one he met, and stared straight through two men who were looking fixedly at him. 'For a minute I thought that was Anant,' said one to the other, after he had passed. 'I know,' the other agreed. 'He looks so much like Anant that it gives me a creepy feeling.'

Invisible, intangible, Anant made his way to his own front door. There was no padlock on it; in fact it was open. He stepped inside, and the sudden gloom blinded him for a second. When he could see again, Geeta and Sindhu were seated on the floor with their mid-day meal before them, staring up at him in amazement. And in the moment that it took them to recognise him it occurred to him with a sharp stab of unaccountable pain, 'They're not happy to see me.' The next moment Geeta was getting up with her usual warm smile saying, 'I *knew* you would come back! Everyone else says I'm mad to think that you could be alive, but see, I'm right after all. Come, come, wash your hands and sit down, I'll bring some food for you.'

Geeta hurried out. Although she would hardly admit it even to herself, her first feeling on seeing Anant was one of dismay. It is true she had expected him to come back some time; but never once had she concretely considered how his coming would affect her. She had not uttered a word of complaint to anyone about him, yet she couldn't conceal the fact that she hardly missed him and had been enjoying a varied and interesting life since he disappeared. What would happen to all this, now that he had come back? She found no answer to this question as she ran out to the women's kitchen.

'You'll never believe what's happened!' she burst out as she went in. The women looked up inquiringly. 'My husband's come back!'

'What?'

'Impossible!'

'Didn't I tell you this woman's going mad? All these weeks she refuses to believe that her husband is dead, and now she actually thinks he's come back!'

'But I'm not mad, he *has* come back,' Geeta insisted. 'Come and see for yourselves.'

'You mean he's in your house just now?'

'Yes!' She looked from one to the other, challenging them to disbelieve her. A hush fell on the room. They all looked at her incredulously, but her manner carried conviction. When someone finally asked, 'Are you sure it's him? It's not a demon in the shape of your husband?' the others laughed and told her to keep quiet.

'Geeta — that's marvellous!' said Laila, who had been silent until then. 'What wonderful news!'

'So... what shall I do now?' asked Geeta.

'You should do whatever you feel like doing.'

'What I mean is... shall I carry on working here?'

'Why not? How will it hurt him?'

'On the contrary, he should be glad. Where is his job now, I would like to know? Who will feed the child if you stop working?'

'Yes, in fact now you will have to feed him as well.'

'And don't think you can drop out like that, Geeta. We need you here.'

'All right, all right,' laughed Geeta. 'But give me some food, I'd better run back now. He must be wondering what has happened to me.'

Geeta took the food and went home feeling happier. If she could carry on working, then she was glad Anant had come home. She recalled with pity his changed appearance. He had always been thin, but now he was little more than a skeleton. His ravaged face and the liberal sprinkling of white hair made him look years older. But the greatest change was that lost, pathetic air, so different from his former confident manner. He hadn't died, but he must have been through terrible suffering — the marks of it were on him still. Where had he been all that time? She must find out, but not just yet. Now the main thing was to get back to the kitchen and finish her work for the day. Somehow she felt that this would establish something, after which she could relax.

Left alone with Sindhu, Anant smiled at her uncertainly. 'Come here,' he beckoned. 'Don't you know who I am?' The child neither moved nor smiled, but simply went on staring at him with large, serious eyes. He had hardly noticed her before, hardly taken account of her existence, but now he was forced to realise that this little person was making him feel unbearably nervous. In an effort to escape from those eyes he looked around the room, while the thoughts chasing each other in his head were interspersed with what he saw. The hut was clean and neat as usual; there was even a shiny new metal water drum which hadn't been there before. Surely that must have cost quite a lot? How to account for this unexpected prosperity? Another man, perhaps. Geeta might have thought he was dead. Part of him went hot with rage at the idea while at the same time another part thought, why not, after all I left her without any means of support. But no, it was most unlikely, especially since she had said she was convinced he was alive. Besides — he looked around again, walking to the door to look at the clothes-line outside — there was no sign of any man. But what about the food then? Since when had they been able to afford cooked food? Why had Geeta gone out instead of starting to cook? Why was she gone so long? Was she trying to borrow food from a neighbour? No, it wasn't from a neighbour, he decided as she came back and put it down. It was the same food that she and Sindhu were eating.

'I've brought you plenty,' Geeta said cheerfully as she sat down and resumed her meal. 'I can see that you need it.' He ate in silence for a while before asking, 'Where did you get it from?'

'Oh,' she was a little hesitant, but also proud. 'I got it from the place where I work. In fact...' She stopped, then went on awkwardly, 'actually, I have to go back now. I only came home to have lunch with Sindhu and get her ready for school. But I'll be home again soon. Why don't you have a bath and rest until then? You don't look at all well.' She finished eating, cleared away Sindhu's plate and her own, spread out bedding for him to lie down if he wanted, and finally went out with the little girl. Sindhu, who had scarcely taken her eyes off him for a moment, walked out backwards, still staring.

CHAPTER 42

The minute Geeta stepped through the door, Anant thought of all the questions he wanted to ask and cursed himself for not having had the presence of mind to ask them while he had the chance. What had happened to Shaheed? Had they managed to get the union recognised and win the case for their wage arrears? Or was it still going on? And then questions about her. Where was she working? How had she managed to get the job? But he had missed the opportunity to find out and would have to wait until she returned, however long that would be. Not long, she had said. But every minute seemed like an hour, with all these questions swarming in his mind. He slowly chewed his food, taking pleasure in it despite his preoccupation. After the insipid hospital meals, this was unbelievably good. As he ate, he found his appetite returning; Geeta had brought him a substantial meal and he finished it all. Then he sat for a while looking down at his arms and hands, the bones, the veins, the wasted muscles. He got up to examine his face in the tiny mirror and sat down again with a sigh. I look worse than a ghost, he thought. No wonder Sindhu kept staring at me like that. A dead weight of sadness seemed to fall on him, he hardly knew why, and he sat there without the will to move until Geeta returned.

'You didn't rest?' she asked, looking at him rather anxiously. 'Let's have some tea, shall we?' She started preparing it, then looked up to ask, 'But where have you been? You haven't told me yet.'

'Look,' he said simply, raising his shirt and revealing three long and ugly scars.

She gasped, 'Oh my God,' and turned her head away feeling suddenly sick. 'They were trying to kill you,' she said softly.

'Certainly,' he agreed. 'And they almost succeeded. If I hadn't been so strong, I would have died for sure.'

'That means you've been in hospital all this time?' she asked, puzzled. 'I don't understand. I mean, I searched all the hospitals in the area.'

'That's just what I thought they might do, and come to finish me off. So I went to Sion and got myself admitted there.'

'With those wounds?' she asked incredulously.

He nodded and laughed. 'And I used another name, just in case. You didn't think of that, did you?'

'I did! I even thought you might have lost your memory so I asked to see all the patients. What I didn't think was that you might be crazy enough to go all the way to Sion!'

He laughed again.'I know it was a crazy thing to do. By then I had lost so much blood that no one at the hospital thought I could survive. Look, here too,' indicating smaller scars on his arm when she brought him his cup of tea. She touched one of them and shuddered, imagining what it must have been like when it was open and raw.

'But tell me what happened to Shaheed. I saw him fall but there was nothing I could do with the other guy after me, I had to run.'

Geeta's voice just wouldn't emerge. Or was it the words which wouldn't come? Yet she had to say something, with Anant getting more tense every second. 'He died in hospital,' she whispered finally.

'Died?' He seemed unable to grasp the meaning of that word. He hadn't died, so how could Shaheed? After several minutes he roused himself and asked, 'What about the union? The factory?'

Geeta took a deep breath. She sensed how much this struggle meant to Anant, and if there was any way of concealing the truth from him she would have done so. But it was not possible, he would be sure to find out. It was better to get it over with. 'The next day after the attack,' she began, 'the police invaded the factory, beat up the workers there and chased them out. Most of the machines were smashed in the fight but they removed everything and closed down the factory. No one has seen Verma after that — we don't know where he has disappeared to.'

'The cowardly swine! He's afraid I'll come after him and kill him! And I will too. I'll search every bloody industrial estate in this country till I find him. He's bound to be in one of them — he can't survive without sucking the life-blood out of some poor fools — and God help him when I find him, there won't be enough left of him to...' Anant broke off into harsh sobs interspersed with incoherent mutterings.

Geeta stood where she was, paralysed. If he had suddenly gone into an epileptic fit, she would have had more of an idea about what to do than she had now. And yet it was not in her nature to witness such suffering without trying to help. What could she do, what could she say? She waited until he was a little quieter and plunged in desperately, grasping at sentences and phrases as they occurred to her and trying to make sense of them as she went along. 'It's terrible, I know. You should have seen the state Laila was in. We thought she would die, too. She didn't eat or speak to anyone for nearly a week. Those poor children! I had to take them in and look after them. But... you won't really try to find Verma and kill him, will you? I don't know anything about these things, but I feel sure there must be some other way. You know, in the place where I work, there is a girl who used to work in a small workshop. Their boss used to harass the women and girls to go with him and... he must be doing it still. That's just as bad, isn't it? I mean, just as bad as Verma? And there must be hundreds and thousands more like that. If you kill Verma, they will still be there, won't they? And you can't kill them all — they would get to you first, and finish you off.'

He had stopped crying now, and was looking at her intently. At last he sighed and nodded. 'You're right, of course. But what you don't understand is that I must *do* something, I *must*, otherwise I'll go mad.' How could he explain to her? He had been through countless defeats before; had been victimised, blacklisted, beaten up, charged with criminal offences. Yet this was worse. He had clung to life, survived injuries which would normally have killed a human being, only because he didn't want to leave this struggle halfway. He had come back to complete it — and suddenly, there was nothing. No factory, no employer, no struggle, no... Shaheed. So what was he doing here? He thought he had cheated death, but actually death had cheated him. If only he had died!

Sindhu, coming back from school, put an end to their conversation. But his anguish went on — through the blank, empty days devoid of activity and the dark, lonely nights when bitterness spread through him like poison. This was suffering far, far more acute than anything he had known before, and to bring him through it Geeta needed more skill than all the doctors had at the hospital. Because then he had his own purpose in life; now she had to help him find a new one.

CHAPTER 43

When the news spread that Anant was back, friends and colleagues arrived in batches to meet him, happy that at least he had escaped even if Shaheed hadn't. But they found him strangely distant and uncommunicative; those who had lost their jobs at Adarsh found he was not interested either in joining them in their frustrating search for employment or in listening to their stories of various casual or contract labour jobs they had undertaken. After a while it became awkward, even embarrassing, to try and talk to him. So one by one they dropped away, feeling that something was dreadfully wrong. Anant himself was rather relieved when they stopped coming. He, who had earlier talked to them so easily, now found himself at a loss for words. He simply didn't know what to say.

Yet he wasn't completely silent. Alone with Geeta he would painfully retrace every step of his life, beginning with his first involvement in a strike and ending with the struggle at Adarsh. Again and again he went over it, trying to discover only one thing: where had he gone wrong? He did this so obsessively and each time ended in such despair that Geeta was frightened. 'It's not true that you haven't achieved anything,' she told him. 'You've forced Verma to close down the factory, haven't you? That means he's scared. Even if he starts it again somewhere else, he'll be more careful not to cheat the workers so badly. And... why do you think you must have made a mistake?' she asked more timidly. 'It's not your fault if all your employers have been bad, is it? That's just your luck, your fate. You did what you had to do, but you couldn't succeed because they were too strong.'

He shook his head. 'I know they are strong, but they can be defeated. In fact, sometimes we have defeated them. If we understood the situation correctly, we wouldn't have been smashed like this. If I were clearer in my own mind, I would know what to do now. But I don't.' He stopped at this thought which tormented him most of all. Where to go now, what should he do? He had no idea at all. Whenever he came to this question, his mind remained blank.

Geeta shared his suffering, yet some part of her rejoiced at the change in him. Never before had he talked to her like this and listened to her so seriously. It was the first time she understood the reasons behind his often mysterious actions in the past, and it was like discovering a new world. Strangest of all was the feeling that although he had been married to her for almost seven years, she was getting to know him for the first time. This feeling was so strong that she sometimes even felt rather shy at the close intimacy of her present relationship with this unknown man — especially when he stopped talking and simply watched her as she went about her household tasks, or looked at her while she was talking to him. What was he thinking? What did he feel about her? These questions kept coming into her mind but were quickly pushed out.

One day when she came home she had a surprise. The clothes which she usually washed after work were already washed and wrung out, ready to be hung on the line. Like the other women, she usually did her washing out on the doorstep where there was more light and space — and she had never seen a man do this job — even single men like Ravindran usually paid someone to do it for them or gave their clothes to a dhobi. She imagined what a sensation it would have caused when the neighbours saw Anant scrubbing clothes. But it hadn't happened like that, as she soon found out. 'I did it in here,' he said, indicating the corner where they had their baths. 'You work so hard and I just sit at home all day, so I thought I should do something to help. Now you only have to hang them out, then you can sit and relax while you have your tea.' What a strange experience that was, sitting at home and doing nothing but drinking tea and talking for more than fifteen minutes! It was really too strange to enjoy properly, and Geeta was rather relieved when Sindhu came home and had to be bathed. It was nice to talk at home, but surely one should be working at the same time? Even her hands felt unhappy lying idle in her lap, they kept moving around, looking for something to do. Throughout her adult life, it was only through work that she felt her existence gained any value, and deprived of it she felt useless. Yet Anant seemed to think otherwise, and continued his campaign to turn her away from the work which had been her life. When she started preparing the night meal he asked, 'Can't you bring enough food from the kitchen to last for the night? Why do you have to cook in the evening?'

'Ask this girl,' laughed Geeta, indicating Sindhu who was doing her homework before going out to play. 'She refuses to eat the same thing for two meals running, so I have to cook something different at night. But I don't mind,' she added, 'it doesn't take me long to do this sort of work.'

'I know! It took me more than an hour to wash those clothes, while you take hardly twenty minutes. And if I tried to cut vegetables as fast as that, I would chop off my fingers!'

Geeta laughed again. 'It's the only work I can do, so I should be able to do it well, shouldn't I?' But she knew that even compared with the other women at the kitchen she worked quickly, and took pride in her efficiency.

'But still,' Anant insisted, 'it's a waste of time to do so much cooking. Can't you at least bring chapatis home?'

'I suppose so,' Geeta said doubtfully. What was in doubt was not the possibility of bringing chapatis home but something else. A few months ago she would have kept her thoughts to herself, but now she felt bold enough to voice them. 'Supposing I get more free time... what would I do with it?'

'Anything you like. Even just resting would be better than working continuously from morning till night. Can't you think of anything else you would like to do?'

Geeta's eyes fell on Sindhu's school books lying haphazardly where she had left them. There *was* something she would like to do and had never found time for. But should she mention it? Wouldn't it sound silly? She was silent for so long that Anant prompted her gently. 'So?'

'Well, I don't know. Something I would really like is to be able to read and write properly. I've learned the alphabet and the words we need for accounting, but that's all — soon I won't even be able to follow Sindhu's books. But how can I learn? I find it very difficult to learn by myself, and I can't go to school, can I?'

'I'll teach you! That's no problem at all. I'll tell you what — we'll come to an agreement, shall we? You teach me how to cook, and I'll teach you how to read and write. What do you say to that?' He held out his open palm and she slapped it lightly with her own as she had seen children do when they made a bet or agreed on something. 'That's good,' he said with satisfaction. 'We will both be learning something new.'

CHAPTER 44

Laila need not have worried about how she would get along with her new lodger: Renu found herself strongly attracted to all three of her house-mates, and decided privately that this was where she wanted to settle down. With the meticulous care and sensitivity of an artist, she very soon set about reconstructing Laila's shattered life and building a better home for the children. She shifted everything around so that each of the four of them had a little corner. 'I don't know what we'll do when the baby grows bigger and wants one too,' she told the children. 'Maybe we can make him a little nest on the roof. But for the moment he's not complaining, is he? Let's see how nice you can make your corner — if you can keep it not only clean and tidy but also pretty.' The children were delighted, especially Farida. They had taken to Renu at once, and now more often than not stayed at home in the mornings instead of going out to play. She told them stories and invented games to amuse them, and it was not unusual for Laila to hear peals of laughter coming from her home as she approached it at lunch-time. She herself was slower to recover. There were still times when everything seemed to grow dark around her and neither Renu's skill nor the children's antics could rouse her from her depression. At other times, especially when she had been unusually cheerful, she would unaccountably start crying; she was haunted by the image of Shaheed, stiff and cold, excluded for ever from everything they were enjoying. How short his life had been! He had wanted to do so much and had been struck down so early. Before he died he bitterly regretted having spent so little time with her, but now it was she who ached and longed to be with him again. Where was he? Somewhere, surely. But not where she could reach him — that was the most devastating thought. In those early days, when she was in such a terrible state, she had been too numb to feel very much; now, when she seemed more normal, she actually missed him more acutely. Sometimes she could hardly bear it, and it seemed all the worse because this was a pain which would not go away: it would remain with her for the rest of her life.

Renu was baffled and sometimes hurt by Laila's frequent fits of gloom, but she persisted in her efforts to create a happy home. It was clear to her that Laila's income was not enough to feed them all, so when her own savings were exhausted she went in search of work, leaving her baby at the crèche for an hour or two at a time. Two families took her on as a domestic servant, and this helped a little. She hated the work, but was ready to do it so as to be able to carry out the improvements she dreamed of. She asked whether she could join the kitchen co-operative where she would enjoy the work and earn more at the same time. Laila discussed the question with Kantabai, but they both agreed it was impossible to take on more workers unless they got more work. If they did manage to expand they would certainly take Renu — she needed the income, and it was hard for her to go out to work with such a small baby. It would be much easier in the kitchen with the crèche just at hand, and she would be able to take her turn at childminding, too.

Renu was disappointed but undefeated. Her first target was a proper cement floor. This earth-and-cowdung floor was impossible to keep clean, and besides she suspected that it got very damp during the monsoon. Laila confirmed this and added that Ishaq, whose chest was rather weak, usually had a cough all through the rainy season. 'But that's terrible!' Renu protested. 'A home should be a place where you can be clean and healthy and comfortable.' She would have liked to get the roof done as well, but that was less of a priority. You could ignore a roof and if the water leaked in you could put a vessel below, but you couldn't avoid looking at the floor and there was nothing you could do if the damp came up through it. Renu ran around for several days, enquiring about the price of cement and trying to find any soft-hearted local boys or men who would help to lay the floor free of charge for two lone women and three fatherless children. When she was sure that she had pushed down the estimate as low as it could possibly go, she went off to Kavita's house to enquire about loans.

'What on earth for?' asked Mariam, who happened to be there.

Renu explained her case. 'That makes sense,' commented Kavita, 'but why take a loan? You'll have to pay interest on it.'

'I know that. But I want to get it done before the monsoon, and there's no way Laila and I can save up enough in the next few weeks. There are some people in the basti who give out loans, but they charge huge interest rates. That's why I came to you — I thought you might know of some way I could get a loan on better terms — from a bank or something like that.'

Mariam and Kavita looked at each other, the same thought striking them at the same time. 'Look Renu,' Mariam said, 'suppose we manage to raise the money and lend it to you: would you pay it back to us bit by bit?'

'Yes, of course! With interest.'

'Forget about the interest. If we lend it to you, it'll be without interest. What I can't promise is that we will be able to get the money together. Will you give us a couple of days to see if we can raise it? We'll do our best.'

Renu ran home convinced that in two days she would have the money in her hands. She was so overjoyed that even Laila was infected by her enthusiasm and participated laughingly in the plans to beautify their home.

'Just you wait,' Renu promised. 'One day this place will really be something worth coming home to.'

'But it already is,' smiled Laila, pinching her cheek. 'Laughter and happiness are what make a place worth coming home to, and we've got that ever since you came to stay here.'

This time it was Renu's turn to blink away the sudden tears. She had tried so hard to make Laila happier, putting her whole self into the task, that success when it came overwhelmed her. 'No, it's not good enough,' she shook her head, smiling through her tears. 'We'll make it even better.'

CHAPTER 45

The acquisition of Mariam as a colleague and companion hadn't turned out quite as Ranjan had anticipated. It was not that she failed to fulfil his expectations — not at all. It was as much of a pleasure working with her as it had ever been. It was the side-effects of her presence which were disturbing. Kavita had changed enormously over the past few months, and that change could mainly be attributed to the fact that Mariam was there.

It all started with the idea of her going to that slum. At first Ranjan had been reluctant to agree, but soon he reconciled himself to her absence two afternoons a week. His work hardly suffered since the children slept for most of that period and he didn't have to cook. And even the time when they were awake was not lost. No, it came to be distinctly enjoyable and rewarding after a while. The biggest problem in the beginning was coping with Sunil when he woke up, because he always made two contradictory demands: he insisted on being carried, but he also insisted on being given his milk at exactly the temperature which suited him. Initially Ranjan tried heating the milk at the time he expected Sunil to wake up, but this plan failed. Sunil would either sleep until the milk was too cold and then demand to have it reheated, or he would wake up too early and the same problem would arise. Then Ranjan tried waking him at the moment when the milk was at the right temperature, but soon abandoned this experiment: Sunil awakened before he had slept his fill was a fearsome creature. It was only when he learned how to heat the milk while carrying Sunil that the problem was finally solved. He had known that babies are born dictators, able to make your life hell if you don't satisfy their every wish, but he hadn't quite realised how much careful planning and skill is required to keep them happy and sweet-tempered during the stage when they are too small to listen to reason and understand your difficulties.

That was one achievement. The other was the rapidly improving relations with his daughters. With Shanta it was even spectacular; he couldn't help feeling with a pang of remorse that the little girl had been waiting and longing for him to take notice of her for years. And once he did, it was very easy to get close to her. They often thought along such similar lines that they could almost communicate telepathically; whenever he got stuck at some point in his stories, it was Shanta who suggested how he could carry on. Her singing was amazing, too. He had never realised before how many songs Kavita must have taught her — a patient work of love, surely, but one which had its reward in the result. Ranjan had never had any formal training in music and was not familiar with many of the songs, but each time he asked Shanta to sing he was doubly moved, by the beauty of her singing as well as by her happiness at his appreciation. Asha was much more cautious, yet even with her he made considerable progress in overcoming her initial hostility and establishing a more relaxed, humorous relationship.

It was the change in Kavita towards which he had very mixed feelings. Of course it was a great relief not to have her going around looking like a living reproach to him or breaking out into tears at the slightest excuse, and yet... and yet... It was difficult to define what was disturbing him. Was it that she was getting rather distant from him? Earlier she used to discuss her feelings about him with him, and although at the time he had intensely disliked these sessions, he found himself missing them now that they had stopped. He guessed that she discussed him with Mariam, and for a while anticipated criticism from Mariam. He was dreading such a confrontation, and yet was even more put out when it didn't come. What was happening? He talked about different things with Mariam and Kavita, he never told one what he said to the other, and this seemed quite natural and proper. But the idea that they might talk to each other about things which neither discussed with him, and that he himself might be one of the topics of their conversation — that was galling. He was extremely curious about their work with the women, yet somehow could never bring himself to show the slightest interest or question either of them.

Then one day he had a horrible shock. He was standing at the window carrying Sunil when he saw Kavita return — but not alone! She was accompanied by Ravindran right up to the gate, and they parted in a way which unmistakeably suggested familiarity. Ravindran! What could it mean? How could she have met him and what could she possibly be doing with him? And most important of all, how should he, Ranjan, react? He had to think fast. He couldn't keep completely silent — that was beyond his strength. On the other hand, to betray the agitation he felt would be undignified, out of character — especially if there turned out to be some perfectly ordinary reason for this strange sight. He couldn't imagine what that might be, but one couldn't rule it out. If he pretended he hadn't seen them, then that would make it impossible to raise the question later on. No, he mustn't do that. Instead he asked casually, soon after Kavita came in, 'Was that Ravindran at the gate with you?'

'Yes,' she replied at once. 'Did you want to meet him? I would have asked him to come in if I'd known.' She didn't seem in the least bothered that he had seen them.

'No, I was just wondering why he had come,' he replied, still casually.

'Oh, we're cooking in his place at the moment so he has nowhere to go, poor fellow. He has to roam around waiting for all those women to finish with his hut.'

So, that was the explanation for his involvement with the women's group. But not for why he had accompanied Kavita home. Or was it? Well, maybe. It was just possible. If he were really at a loose end, he might have done it to kill time. But even that was not a very comfortable thought. Especially not if it happened again.

The weeks that followed were pure hell for Ranjan. Because it did happen again — he saw it once, but there could have been more occasions. If only he could talk it over with someone, he might be able to calm himself. But there was no one. With Kavita herself, he shrank from that. The longer he waited, the more afraid he was of what he might discover. With Mariam? No, she would laugh at him, or worse, perhaps castigate him for being a jealous and possessive husband. And her bad opinion was what he dreaded most. So he had no one to talk to or to reassure him. Instead his imagination worked overtime, producing all manner of disastrous outcomes. Because whenever he tried to tell himself there was nothing to worry about since Kavita had been so casual and unconcerned when she answered his question, he would recall their manner at parting, the smiles on their faces, which betrayed far greater intimacy than he could possibly account for.

Then came other disasters which almost crushed him: Shaheed's death and the collapse of the sit-in. On the day that Shaheed died, he came home and wept. It was something he hadn't done for years, probably since adolescence; but the pain and despair were so intense that they dragged out the tears from deep down where they had been hidden. After that nothing seemed to matter much; yet if the occupation of the factory had continued he would at least have been forced to think, to act. But once the factory closed down and Verma disappeared there was nothing; no meetings, nothing. The workers' study circle had become absorbed into the Adarsh struggle and collapsed along with it; and since the vacation had begun he had neither his university discussion groups nor even his teaching to occupy him.

Kavita's love and sympathy sustained him during this time, and in some ways they grew closer to each other than they had ever been before. But she couldn't completely share his feelings; her loss had not been as great as his. She hadn't lost a friend, although she had known and liked Shaheed. And her work continued, even expanded. Mariam too, with a foot in both camps so to speak, escaped the full weight of the blow. He was left more alone than ever. If there was one bright spot in all the gloom, it was learning that the women had apparently shifted from Ravindran's hut to another place. Deprived of an excuse to wander around all evening, Ravindran would presumably fade quietly from the picture.

But he didn't! Almost without realising it, Ranjan had got into the habit of looking out for Kavita's return, and for some time she had been coming back alone. But suddenly, there he was; and he seemed to be so deep in conversation that he couldn't stop even when they reached the gate. They stood there for, how long? At least five minutes; then Kavita said something, they both laughed, and she came in. Ranjan was thrown into such a panic that when he heard her step outside he locked himself in the toilet to try and get a grip on himself. He was trembling. No, this was impossible, he must be calm, but how? What should he do? This time he must have it out with Kavita. He couldn't go on like this, it was like living on the edge of a volcano, fearing that your whole life may be blown to pieces any minute. Better to be blown up at once — then at least you could be sure there was nothing worse to come. But it was impossible to talk about it with the children around. He would somehow have to get through the evening until they had gone to bed. He waited until Kavita was in the kitchen, slipped out and sat down at his desk pretending to be deep in work. At dinner he was preoccupied and silent, but this was not exceptional. There was nothing in his behaviour to indicate even a fraction of the torment he was going through.

CHAPTER 46

When Kavita came out after putting the children to bed, Ranjan was still sitting at his desk and seemed to be hard at work, so she started to rearrange the books which Sunil had pushed right back on the shelves. He would do it again, she knew, so there didn't seem much point in this laborious task, but one couldn't leave the bookshelves like that either. She was startled to hear Ranjan ask without any warning, 'Kavita, what's going on between you and Ravindran?'

'Ravindran?' She half turned towards him in surprise, but then returned to her task smiling to herself. 'What makes you ask that?'

'Well, surely I have a right to know, haven't I? I'm not trying to restrict your freedom or anything, but it does concern me too, doesn't it?'

'What I meant,' she explained calmly, 'was what makes you think anything is going on which might concern you?'

'Look, Kavita, I told you I don't want to restrict your freedom in any way, but if you have a lover I want to know about it. Have you?'

Kavita was silent. She didn't want to lie, but even less did she want to give away her most closely guarded secret. Because she did have a lover — not Ravindran, nor any other man of flesh and blood, but nonetheless someone very real to her. She had not spoken about him to anyone, not even to Mariam. She knew what Mariam would say: dreams are all right if they are a guide to action, but what is the use of a dream if you don't try to make it come true? No one would have been more horrified than Kavita if this particular fantasy had materialised. It was one thing to have a lover who you could call up at will and put away when he was not needed, and quite another to have someone who perhaps wouldn't be around when you wanted him but might walk in at any time, upsetting Ranjan and the children. Besides, she strongly suspected that no real man could measure up to the standard of her fantasy. No, the dream was beautiful but she knew the reality would be sordid. So she had no wish at all to make it come true; yet did that mean it was useless? Surely not. On the contrary, this man was very important to her; in her mind she spoke to him as much as she spoke to Mariam, and gained a similar satisfaction out of the conversations. Even more, the relationship itself was one she had craved from the time she was a young girl, still in school.

To build it had been her ambition for years. Why should she abandon it now? When you live for a dream, you don't give it up just because reality doesn't conform to it. But of course Ranjan was the last person to whom she could tell all this. Not because he wouldn't understand but because he would understand only too well. He would probably be almost as jealous as he would be of an actual lover, and he would harass her to give him up. And she would either have to lie to Ranjan and continue her fantasies, or renounce them altogether. Neither of these alternatives did she want to choose. So she stayed silent. Let him think what he wanted.

Ranjan stood up with a strong impulse to seize her by the shoulders, turn her round to face him and insist that she answer — shake the reply out of her if necessary. But he controlled himself and sat down again instead. 'Don't do this to me, Kavita', he pleaded, 'you know what a bad time I've been through, what a state I'm in now. I still feel crushed by Shaheed's death, and if I were to lose you as well that would finish me off — there would be nothing left for me to live for. Even the thought of it frightens me so much that I can't think straight.'

It was now Kavita's turn to restrain her impulse to put her arms round him. But something told her it was too soon to reassure him — that he would then stop thinking and her chance would be lost. So she continued rearranging the books. 'Oh, but I would never do anything to *hurt* you,' she said, racking her memory to remember some of his phrases. 'Of course I still love you. This is at a completely different *level*.'

It couldn't be true! For a minute Ranjan was too stunned to speak. 'Don't say that!' he cried at last. 'I know I said it, but that's different. You're not the same as me, Kavita. I know that if you started something it would be deadly serious. You said so yourself.'

'But people can change, Ranjan. Or is it that only men are allowed to have casual affairs?'

'No, that's not what I mean! Haven't I told you, so many times, that I know I was wrong, it was a mistake and I'll never do it again? I've promised, haven't I?'

Kavita slowly shook her head. 'I don't want promises, Ranjan. What hurt me was not that you had an affair but that you should have wanted it — can you understand that? If you want to relate to someone else, I don't want you to stop yourself because you are bound by some promise to me. If you stay with me, it should be freely, because you want to. And

I want the same freedom. I don't think people should live together unless they really love each other, and I want to be free to split up if... I know it's difficult in our case because of the children, I don't want to give them up and they shouldn't be taken away from you either, but we could find a way to solve that problem... if it becomes necessary.'

Could this really be Kavita? The same person who would cry hysterically and beg him to stay if ever he threatened to leave? Talking about splitting up as if it didn't much matter to her one way or the other? How could she have changed so much? Only one thing could account for it — she could talk so calmly about leaving him only if she had an alternative in mind. Ranjan wished he could cry hysterically or beat his head against the wall, but he couldn't, that was not how he expressed himself. He had no way of communicating to Kavita the pain which was eating through him.

The silence that followed made Kavita turn round, and this time she came and put her arms around him as he sat. 'Silly man! What are you so worried about?' she asked gently. 'Why do you think I married you if I didn't love you? Why do you think I stay with you if I don't love you still? I don't change so easily. So the only reason we might have for splitting up would be if you didn't love me. Do you think that might happen? Are you so unsure of yourself?'

'Oh no, Kavita!' he said, looking up at her eagerly. 'If it depends on me, I'm quite sure of myself. It's *you* I can't be sure of. You make me feel so insecure. I feel I may lose you from one day to the next.'

'But that's so unfair, Ranjan! What have I ever done to make you feel like that?'

'What about Ravindran?'

'Ravindran!' she laughed. 'Well, what about him?'

'You know what I mean!'

'I like him a lot, if that's what you mean. Don't you?'

'Well, yes, but that's different because I'm a man.'

'And I'm a woman. Does that mean there's something wrong if I like him?'

'Not wrong, but it's more likely to become something more than liking. For example...'

'For example?'

How difficult it was to say all this! Ranjan half wished he hadn't embarked on the conversation, but it was also a relief to be able to talk, so he stumbled on. 'For example, the way you talk to him is very different from the way you talk to me. Why don't you ever talk to me like that?'

'Because every argument with you is such a battle! I'm afraid to say anything in case it leads to an argument because then it just becomes a matter of scoring points. It's not like that with Ravindran — however hotly we argue, neither of us is trying to put the other down.'

'But how do you know I would try to put you down when you never talk to me in the first place? You haven't even told me anything about the work you're doing in the slum.'

'You've never shown any interest! Have you ever asked me about it? Think and tell me truly.'

'I may not have asked, but that doesn't mean I'm not interested. And don't have this image of me as someone who's always trying to score points — it's not true!'

'It's not an image — it's my *experience*. That's what puts me off from trying to talk to you.'

'Well,' he conceded, 'supposing I undertake to listen to you more sympathetically — then would you try to talk to me more?'

'I'll certainly try. I can't promise that I will succeed straight away, because habits are hard to break — especially the habit of silence. But if you are patient, I'm sure it'll gradually become easier. Happy?'

'No,' he said frankly. It was all very indefinite and he still felt insecure. It wouldn't be so easy to fulfil his side of the bargain, and if he failed there was the fear that Kavita would retreat into herself once more. But at least it was better than sitting back helplessly and watching her drift away — any task, however hard, was better than that. So he added, holding her tightly and leaning his head against her, 'I'm not happy, but I don't feel so hopeless.'

Kavita nodded. Maybe Mariam was half-right about dreams; not that you should necessarily try to make them come true, but that they had a life of their own and strove to fulfil themselves. That could be the only reason why she found herself hoping that her fantasy-lover would acquire some of Ranjan's features.

CHAPTER 47

Geeta went home from work each day with a sense of adventure. She was leading a double life and her second, secret life was dark and mysterious, anything could happen in it. The cookery and literacy classes were proceeding satisfactorily, but that was not where the real excitement lay. Or rather, it was mixed up with all that and yet something different, a process of learning which followed no rules at all, neither culinary nor grammatical nor anything else, and which was therefore totally unpredictable. And as she carried her new knowledge with her she was absent-minded and preoccupied at work and her friends might have thought she was worrying about something were it not for the brightness of her face and the readiness of her smile.

Anant was slowly coming back to life, the hollows in his face filling out, the strength returning to his limbs, and it was impossible not to feel that she was largely responsible for the change. Not simply because she was feeding him, although that was part of it, but because of a subtle yet perceptible effect which her presence had on him. When she was in the room, his eyes lit up with an inner light which was otherwise absent; he found it possible to smile, even, occasionally, to laugh. Coming in on him suddenly, she could sometimes see the transformation, as dramatic as an electric current being switched on. And she felt torn between pain for his suffering and joy at her power to rekindle the hope which at times seemed to have been extinguished for ever. To have attained that degree of importance for someone so admirable was no small achievement.

There were some incidents she liked to recall not just the next day but over and over again. Like the time when Anant had said, completely out of the blue, 'You know something, Geeta? I love you.' Geeta was stunned. People said such things in films, but surely not in real life? And what on earth was one supposed to say in reply? She thought frantically for a moment, but then realised that he was not expecting a reply; it was more as if he were reflecting or thinking aloud, but thinking aloud to her. 'It's only now that I realise it,' he continued, 'but I think I've been loving you for a long time. Quite a long time, though I can't remember when I started.'

This was a surprise to her. So far as she could tell, he hadn't even been aware of her as a person before his disappearance. She could remember one occasion when she had completely run out of money and had nothing for the evening meal. Some husbands coming home hungry to an empty kitchen would have created a scene; some would have shown concern; but he did neither, just went out for a meeting, and went out again next morning on an empty stomach. Not a word of complaint, nor a word of sympathy. She might have thought that he hadn't noticed, except that he came back with some money in time to get the rations before the shop closed. Maybe that was before he started loving her? But his behaviour towards her had never changed, not in any noticeable way — until his return. His thoughts seemed to be following the same path because he continued, 'You may not believe me — I know I haven't shown it in any way. But it's true. When I think back, I can remember things about you which I didn't even know I knew: bright memories, times when I felt happy and secure to know that you were at home, that you were my wife. And now, that is the only thing keeping me alive. What else do I have to live for? My work has disintegrated. Even Sindhu. I love her, but I know she can live without me, and I could manage without her too. But you — if I didn't have you I would be nowhere.' He looked at her and smiled. 'You haven't changed at all. You're just as young and lovely as you were when we first got married. Whereas I... I'm only a broken old man. Not nearly good enough for you. That makes me feel very sad.'

'Don't say that!' she made a movement as though to stop him from going on. 'It's not true. You've been through a bad time, but already you're much better. And... and... anyway, that's not what is most important. Looks and things like that, I mean. It's much more important what kind of person you are — whether you're a good person or not.'

He was smiling again. 'So what about me? Do you think I'm a good person?'

'Yes of course,' she said earnestly, 'Of course.' These were the only words which would come to her, though what she really wanted to say was that she loved him now, whatever she had or hadn't felt about him earlier. Had he understood her? She often wondered afterwards. At least he kept on smiling.

Then there was the time when, at her reading lesson, he presented her with a notebook opened at the first page instead of the usual children's story-book. 'What's this?' she asked in surprise, turning over the handwritten sheets. 'I can't read this!'

'Why not?' he protested. 'It took me ages to write in my best hand.'

'You wrote all that?' she was even more astonished.

'Yes — and I'll be miserable if you don't read it. Please try.'

It was a little story about Anant and Geeta, written so simply that Sindhu could have read it with ease, but expressing so much that halfway through it Geeta's voice faltered and stopped. 'What's the matter?' Anant asked gently. 'Shall I read the rest?' He took her hand in his hand which had been pointing out the words one by one, and carried on reading. His voice sounded good at meetings, she had always thought, but it was even more beautiful now, soft and full of feeling, She listened, enchanted, and at the end shyly put her other hand over his, holding it in her lap between her own, as if capturing the moment for eternity.

When Geeta started working at the kitchen, she had thought that life couldn't possibly get any better. But she had been wrong, she realised; she hadn't even known what happiness was, at that time.

CHAPTER 48

Returning home from work one day, Laila saw a woman with a baby standing in front of the locked door of her neighbours' hut. She looked exhausted, and Laila could hear the distress in her voice when she turned round and asked, 'Doesn't Muktabai live here?'

'Yes, this is where she lives, but I saw her going to the market a few minutes ago. Have you come from far?'

'All the way across Bombay...the furthest I've ever been on my own. In the last fifteen minutes I've had to ask my way at least ten times.'

'You must be really tired,' Laila said sympathetically. 'Why not come in to my place and wait in comfort until she comes back?'

But it was too late. The woman was standing there shaking her head with the tears streaming down her face, and no matter what Laila said she couldn't persuade her to come in. A crowd had started to gather with the usual questions and comments:

'What's happening?'

'Someone had an accident?'

'I don't know, I think she's looking for Muktabai.'

'Poor thing, she looks worn out — must have come a long way.'

'I saw Muktabai going to the market just now.'

'Let her wait in someone's house.'

'No, she won't come in.'

'Why not?'

A chair appeared from somewhere, a glass of water from somewhere else, and someone took the baby from the woman's arms.

'Oh, she's hot! Has she got fever?'

'That's why I came,' replied the woman, now seated and more in control of herself. 'Two days we've been out in this burning sun — who wouldn't get fever? Two days ago they came with their vans and their lathis, and smashed up everything. Everything. Our houses, the tubs in which we wash clothes, even our pots and pans.' She started crying again. 'Why do they do this to us? Aren't we human beings too?'

There were murmurs of pity and sympathy. Laila went in to her hut and came out with a damp towel which she used to cool the baby's hot face and neck. Someone asked, 'Where did this happen?'

'Dhobi Basti, near Malabar Hill,' she replied.

'Malabar Hill! I thought only rich people live there.'

'They do. But you don't think they wash their own clothes, do you? Or clean their own houses? We've been living there for years and years doing their work, but now it seems some builder wants the land and suddenly the municipal vans come and start, without any warning, they wouldn't even give us time to remove our belongings. But we won't let them drive us out! A slum-dwellers' organisation helped us to get a stay order and the judge actually said they had no right to break up our hutment. But who bothers about rights? If you're strong enough to do something, do it, and never mind about rights. That's how they think.'

'So what is happening now?'

'We've camped out there — we're going to fight it out in court, we're not going to move. My husband is there still. I wanted to stay, but this child got ill so he told me to bring her to his brother's place. Can you imagine being out in this heat all day without any shelter over your head?'

Someone extended a cup of tea and the woman accepted it gratefully. She had stopped crying and was much calmer. 'I wonder how long the court will take. And after all that is over, how many years will it take to replace our homes and utensils? We can't even work and earn properly because they've broken our tubs.'

'I don't understand the municipal workers who do such things!' commented a man. 'It was the same in my sister's basti — they came and smashed up everything. Why do they need to do that? It's one thing to do their job, but they seem to enjoy making people miserable.'

'They're all goondas — that's why they get recruited in the first place. You think you would get one of those jobs if you applied for it? No chance! They would take one look at you and say, "Not qualified".'

'That's right. You don't need any S.S.C. or H.S.C. for those jobs. You just need to know how to beat up people.'

'No one is safe these days. Evictions are going on all over the place. What shall we do if they come here? We should also get in touch with that organisation.'

'I wonder what will come of that case. Do you think they will get back their basti?'

'Why not? If the judge says the Municipal Corporation had no right to smash their houses, he should actually make them pay to repair them.'

'That's not likely. The judge may be honest, but still they'll do something and get their way. People like us can never get justice.'

'Why do you say that? Isn't it our city too? I think this lady and her husband have the right attitude. If you don't stand up for yourself, naturally you'll get pushed around.'

'Please come inside now,' Laila pleaded again. 'It looks so bad, sitting out here as if no one has invited you in.'

This time the woman agreed, and as she got up to take her baby there was a general cry of 'Here's Muktabai, here's Muktabai!' The whole story had to be told once again, inside the hut and over another cup of tea. When she heard all about it, Muktabai sighed quietly and proceeded to prepare their evening meal.

Talking to her the next day at the water-tap, Laila learned that she was finding it difficult to accommodate her husband's sister-in-law, who was called Kamal. Muktabai's family was large and their income was small; she would just have to divide the same amount of food so that it would stretch to another portion. She was used to eating so little that it wouldn't make much difference to her; it was her children she was worried about.

But they would have to manage somehow; in cases like this there was no alternative. It was not Kamal's fault; she had not wanted to come, and was willing to work in order to contribute to the household as well as save up for the time when she could rebuild her own home. But jobs were scarce, especially jobs which could be done with a small baby.

At work later that day, Laila kept thinking about Kamal and her baby, and ultimately spoke to Kantabai. 'Isn't there any way we can help?' she asked. 'She'll need money even to get a new tub and start doing her dhobi-work again.'

'I know what you're thinking,' said Kantabai. 'I also know one or two women with similar problems, and I keep wishing we could do something for them. But how? We're barely surviving ourselves — how can we help them?'

Laila had no answer to that, and after a while gave up worrying about it. If Kantabai couldn't think of a solution perhaps nothing could be done after all.

CHAPTER 49

Lakshmi was happy. She had only begun to worry about her mounting debts when this job turned up, and it was wonderful — there was no other word for it. Right at the beginning she had had a bad week because of that girl Preeti — she really thought too much of herself, just because she could read and write so well, and Lakshmi wasn't prepared to take orders from a chit of a girl. But then they had a series of meetings and sorted it out and although some ill feeling remained, they managed to work together without fighting. Today she had paid off the last of her debts, and she felt like celebrating. So even though it wasn't a festival, even though she didn't have much money left, she decided to make some sweets — Chandran's favourites, because he, too, deserved a treat.

While stirring the mixture over the fire, she was troubled by an idea which often occurred to her. What happened to people after they died? Lakshmi was not sure, but she thought there was a good chance Vasanta might be angry with her if she were still around. She had never got to know Vasanta or made friends with her, in fact had latterly felt so hostile and bitter towards her that mightn't she be held partly responsible for the girl's horrible death? And if so, wouldn't Vasanta, from wherever she was, be justified in taking revenge? This was a disturbing idea. Better to pacify her, Lakshmi thought; and therefore when the sweets were ready she kept some aside for Vasanta, saying to her, 'Please forgive me for hoping he would catch you. I was too desperate to think straight, otherwise I would have realised you were not to blame for my beatings, only his own cruelty was to blame. I should have hoped he would get run over by a bus, not that he would find you. You never did me any harm. When you came, he didn't beat me so much, and later you helped the police to catch him so that now I can live in peace with my children. I am grateful for that, and hope you're not angry with me.' It was not much, but Lakshmi felt a little better after that. The sweets later disappeared, though she never found out whether it was Vasanta who took them or Sanjeevani.

The other person to whom she took a plateful, as usual, was her neighbour Salma. But Salma, usually busy assembling hairclips at this time, was sitting idle and crying. She didn't look up when Lakshmi entered. 'What's the matter?' Lakshmi asked anxiously. Could she have quarrelled with her husband? No, that was not likely, Salma and her husband never fought.

'The second week running he said there was no work for me,' sobbed Salma, pointing to her empty sack. 'What can I do? My husband has to go looking for work every day and if he finds any he brings home sixty to seventy rupees, but half the month he doesn't find anything. What's the use of being skilled if you don't have work? I have no skill, but at least I used to get a regular salary through this. I've become quite fast at it and we counted on that income. Now it has stopped for the moment — maybe it has stopped permanently, how do I know? And if my husband doesn't get work for three days running, we don't eat. How can I let my children starve like that? Today I went from house to house with Shahnaz and found her a job in one of the apartments — twice a day she has to go, she does the floors and washes the utensils and clothes. I feel so terrible, Lakshmi-behen, I just can't tell you. It's not that I mind so much taking her out of school — if only she could do something at home. But if I don't have work to do at home, how can I give her any?'

'I know, I understand how you feel,' sympathised Lakshmi. 'It was the same when I had to take my boy out of school because even with this job of mine we couldn't manage to pay off our debts and make ends meet. Now the debts have been paid, but we sold so many things from the house that we still need the extra money to replace them. I wanted to get another job, work in these buildings as well or something, but he wouldn't let me. He said, "Amma, you've had such a hard life all these years, now you must rest and get better. See how thin you've become — your sari blouses hang on you like empty sacks." That's how he talks to me — can you imagine? He's only eleven years old but he looks after me like an elder brother!'

'But he's working in the same place as you, isn't he? In this basti itself?'

'No, in Sheetal Nagar. But it's true, we're working in the same place and the others are all very nice to him, so it's all right.'

'Ah, that's different. I wouldn't mind so much if Shahnaz were working with me. But sending her out all alone... and she being a girl too.'

'Can't you go out instead and leave her at home to look after the little ones?'

'That's what I thought at first, but this one,' indicating the baby, 'won't let go of me. Any time he gets up he wants to be fed, and if I'm not there he screams the place down. I've tried and tried to make him sleep and get up at regular times but it's no use. And these apartment people are so strict that if you miss a day or come a bit late they may dismiss you. So at least while he's so small, Shahnaz will have to go,' she finished gloomily, feeling she had sacrificed her daughter to a cruel deity.

Lakshmi was silent for a while. 'I was thinking,' she said at last, 'wouldn't it be nice if you and Shahnaz could come and work at the place where I'm working? The problem is that there may not be enough work for more people to be able to join. But shall I ask in any case?'

Salma remained downcast. 'It'll be the same as this factory work — too many people and not enough work,' she predicted. 'But there's no harm in asking, I suppose. Isn't it strange — only a short while ago I was earning while you were crying because you didn't have a job, and now it's the other way round?'

Lakshmi sighed. 'That's how life is, Salma-behen. That time I needed your help, and now you need mine. Tomorrow I may need your help again. Poor people like us can't survive without helping each other.'

'That's true,' Salma agreed. 'What's this you've brought for me? Is it some festival today?'

'No, but I felt like making them. They're Chandran's favourites — poor boy, he works so hard and never gets any fun. My girl is just the opposite — never serious for a second, laughing and playing all the time. If she had been bigger, I would have taken her to work and let him go to school instead. But she's too small.'

'Mm... They're good,' said Salma, referring to the sweets. 'I don't know how to make this kind, you must teach me some time. Thank you, Lakshmi-behen, it was nice of you to bring them.'

When Lakshmi left, she went straight to Kantabai's hut. She didn't have very much hope but it was worth trying.

CHAPTER 50

Chandran had heard from his mother that Shahnaz had left school, and when he saw her walking ahead of him to the toilet-ground in her faded brown salwar-kameez he called out and hurried to catch up with her. 'Is it true that you had to leave school and start working?' he asked as they walked together along the stony path, now dry and dusty.

Shahnaz nodded. 'See that building over there?' pointing to one of the new, expensive-looking apartment blocks. 'It's on the sixth floor of that one. I have to go up in a lift. I was so frightened at first that I used to climb up the stairs, but once or twice I went up with some other people and now I'm not frightened at all. Well, only a little.'

'But it's terrible that you have had to leave school,' said Chandran. He was partly concerned for himself, because he had been in the same class as Shahnaz and after leaving school had managed to study a little on his own by looking through her lessons. But mostly his concern was for Shahnaz herself. 'Without an education it's impossible to get a good job, even in a factory.'

'What job do you think I'm going to get?' asked Shahnaz. 'I'll be getting married, and if I work it will be at home, like my mother.'

'But isn't this work very boring?'

'It is boring, but not as bad as doing my lessons. And the people scold me but I don't get beaten as I did at school. So I'm quite happy.'

'But even if you get beaten you're learning something in school,' objected Chandran.

'What do you learn? I think you learn more by doing a job. It's one thing to read about Kubera and all his wealth, but that's nothing compared to what you see when you go into one of those places.' Her eyes grew wide and mysterious. 'Have you ever been in one of these rich houses?'

'No.' Chandran was fascinated in spite of himself.

'Bap ri! The things they have — you would never believe it. All kinds of different chairs and tables and beds, and so much space, and such big windows, I would be afraid to stay in a place like that! Then they have television, and video-sets — do you know what they are?'

'No.' Chandran had seen television sets in shop windows, but video was something new.

'It looks like television, but you can put on any film you like. And they have music sets like that, too, you can put on any song you like. And rugs on the floor, and things in the kitchen. It's like another world. Where do you think they get so much money from?'

'I don't know,' said Chandran, expecting Shahnaz to come up with an answer.

'I don't know either,' she admitted. 'But I'd like to know, wouldn't you?'

'That's why you need an education — to find out things like that!' said Chandran triumphantly. 'It's true there are some things you can find out by looking, but there are other things you can only find out from books. I like my work — the people are very nice, they never scold me, and I can learn something there just as you do in your job. But I would like to go to school as well, and I would go if I could, but I can't, it's at the same time as my job.'

They had reached the toilet-ground, a dirty patch of wasteland adorned by a few dusty bushes and piles of rubble from the building sites, and dotted with excrement. Chandran hesitated. His tin can was filled to the brim with water, and there was something he had to do before going to the toilet, but could he trust Shahnaz? 'Will you keep a secret if I show you something?' he asked, looking mysterious.

'Yes, of course!' Shahnaz was bursting with curiosity.

'But I mean really secret — not even tell your mother?'

'I never tell my mother anything, why should I tell her a secret?'

'Come with me then,' said Chandran, leading her by a complicated route to a part of the ground which was seldom used. There, concealed from casual observation by a pile of broken bricks and other rubbish, was a little patch of brilliant green.

'It's a garden!' exclaimed Shahnaz in delight. 'A tiny little garden! How did you find it?'

'I didn't find it,' said Chandran, smiling at her pleasure, 'I grew it.'

'You mean it's yours?'

He nodded. 'I come and water it every day. No one knows about it except you and me.'

'It's a wonderful idea! You're really clever, Chandran-bhai. You don't even go to school and you can grow such lovely plants.'

Chandran laughed. 'But if I went to school I would be able to grow better plants! See, I think these are buds, they'll soon grow into flowers. Do you want to see what they look like when they come out?'

'Oh yes! Look, I can see buds on these as well. They're different, aren't they? How pretty your garden will look when they all come out!'

'Well, you can come with me every day to see them, but we must be careful not to be seen. I don't want anyone coming and spoiling my garden — it's not so easy to grow plants in this hot weather, some days I have to water them twice so that they don't die.'

'I'll help you, shall I? Because now it's getting hotter all the time and they may need water twice a day every day. So you can do it once and I can do it once. Otherwise your mother may think you have a stomach upset if you keep running to the toilet!'

They both laughed, and then carefully worked out a scheme to keep the plants irrigated. As they walked home later, Shahnaz hugged her new found knowledge while Chandran thought that a secret becomes even more exciting when it is shared.

CHAPTER 51

The weekly meetings of the co-operative kitchen had become rather routine affairs recently. This was both a good thing and a bad thing, Kantabai reflected. Good, because it showed that everything was running smoothly. Bad, because the women no longer felt the need to think about things or take any initiative. And they began to resent any new suggestion as a disruption of their well-ordered schedule. Still, it had to be done. The responsibility had been weighing heavily on her for weeks, and it was too much to bear all alone. She sighed. The meeting was already beginning to break up on the assumption that there would be no other business when she forced herself to speak.

'Just a minute, friends! I've still got something to say.'

They turned towards her but remained standing as though expecting nothing more than an announcement.

'No, sit down,' she insisted. 'The meeting isn't over yet.'

There were muttered grumbles: 'How long is this going on?' 'I've got piles of work to do at home,' and so on. But they sat down all the same, and waited. Now that they were looking at her, Kantabai didn't know how to begin. But she had to say something soon, otherwise they would get restless again.

'Listen,' she began, 'our co-operative has been running very well, and that is something to be proud of. But is it enough? We started it mainly to help women who are desperately in need of an income, and it's true it has been a great help to us. But how many are we? Very few. In the past few weeks I've come to know about at least four or five women who want to join. They are as badly in need of an income as we are — why should we be here and not they? Isn't there something wrong with our group if we only look after our own needs and forget about everyone else?'

She had hardly stopped speaking when the protests broke out.

'But you yourself said that there isn't enough work for any more women!'

'If anyone else joins, our income will go down, and it's low enough already.'

'What's the point of doing this work if we can't support our children with it?'

'We started this to help ourselves, not to help all the poor women in Bombay.'

'That's a job for the government, not for people like us.'

'All right!' Kantabai had to shout to make herself heard, but now she was angry. 'If that's how you feel, you had better tell them so yourselves. They come to me because I'm the oldest here, even *you* come and tell me when you come across such women, but why should it be my responsibility to tell them that we can't help? I'll call them here one by one. Next week I'm going to call Kamal-bai. Some of you know her — she's been thrown out of her home in Dhobi Basti, her house has been smashed and her husband can't work because their washing-tub is broken. She has to earn to support the two of them and their baby, as well as put their home together again. But you tell her to her face, "Sorry, we can't help you, you'll have to go somewhere else. The government!" That's a good joke. It was the government that threw her out on the streets in the first place. You think they're going to help her?!'

There was silence as Kantabai looked around triumphantly. She knew very well it was one thing to refuse help to an anonymous mass of faceless women, quite another to turn away someone whose story you knew. Her battle was already won.

'Don't get so angry, Kantabai,' said Laila pacifyingly. 'You know that we, too, want to help other women. It's just that we don't know how.'

'The trouble is,' Preeti went on, 'the amount we earn is really only enough for a woman to support herself and maybe one child. That means if we take on more people, we have to find more work.'

'The other thing we could do is help them to start their own group,' contributed Geeta. 'But that means thinking of another product, selling it, finding out so many things. No, that's more complicated.'

'I have to go now,' said Lakshmi decisively, 'my daughter must have come home from school already. What I suggest is that each of us tries to think of ways to involve these women, either by expanding our co-operative or by starting another. We'll make any necessary enquiries and come back next week with our ideas.'

'All right, but you had better really think about it,' warned Kantabai. 'Then you don't want to call Kamal next week?'

'No!' they all chorused as they went out.

Geeta walked home despondently. She had been so contented, so happy, that she had completely forgotten about the misfortunes of others, and this made her feel guilty. She felt worse because however hard she tried she could think of no way in which more women could be involved without affecting the income of the others — and that was something she couldn't afford. As it was she was finding it very difficult to manage.

Anant noticed her change of mood at once and asked what was troubling her. She related the problem, but he didn't seem to think it was as insurmountable as she did. 'There are a lot of possibilities. For example, there isn't a single canteen in the entire industrial estate, and even some of the big factories nearby don't supply meals. Workers bring lunch-boxes, but I know for a fact that many of them would prefer hot food if it were cheaper than what you could get in a restaurant. They would certainly grab the chance of getting the kind of meals you provide. Do you want me to get a rough estimate of how many might want to take them? I know people there who could find out.'

'What a good idea!' Geeta exclaimed gratefully. 'None of us thought of that. Yes, that would be a wonderful way to solve our problem. Can you find out who's interested in time for our meeting next week?'

'Easily. I'll go tomorrow morning, catch my friends as they are going in and ask each of them to find out from his own factory. Those that I miss in the morning I'll catch at the end of the shift and ask them to find out the next day.'

Geeta was silent as a doubt entered her mind. She didn't know who the other women who had approached Kantabai were, but they would probably not be very different from the women who already worked at the kitchen. And somehow, Geeta found it very hard to imagine any of them going into that industrial area and selling lunches to crowds and crowds of men. Suppose she herself were asked to do it? No, it was out of the question!

'Now what's your problem?' asked Anant, looking at her troubled face.

'Who will sell the food? It's quite a long way to the industrial area — almost twenty minutes on foot. And even if someone were willing to take it there, it's not very nice for a woman to have to sell to all those men. Even if two women went together, I don't think they would like it.'

'Don't worry about that. I'll do it for you if no one else wants to go. I can take it on my bicycle in no time at all. Satisfied?'

'All right,' Geeta smiled, feeling lucky to have such a helpful and supportive husband. The other women would surely be pleased with the solution he had found to their problem.

At the next meeting, the response to Anant's proposal was not at all what Geeta was expecting. Far from being pleased, some of the women were suspicious, even hostile.

'No chance! Once we start taking in men, that'll be the end of our collective.'

'In no time at all they'll be running it and we'll be taking orders.'

'In any case this is a women's group, isn't it? We can't have men in it, can we?'

'Well, Chandran works for us.'

'That's different. He's only a child. He doesn't even come to meetings.' But you're wrong about Anant, Geeta wanted to say. He won't try to dominate us, he won't be a threat to our group. But she said nothing, just sat there looking downcast. At the height of the debate, Nirmala and Mariam walked in. 'What's the matter?' 'What's the argument about?' they asked at the same time.

All the women, including Geeta, turned to them with explanations, and that it was some time before they could understand anything. Finally, when they were fairly clear about the situation, Nirmala said, 'Now, let's be sensible about this. How can any man take over this group and start running it unless you allow him to do it? What is to prevent you from keeping him in his place?'

'Nirmala-tai, have you ever heard these men give speeches? Of course you must have! Words flow from them more easily than water flows from our taps. Even if afterwards you think about what they have said and find that it was all nonsense, at the time it sounds so good that you just have to nod and applaud. Whereas we women, we're the opposite. What we have to say may be absolutely right, but when we speak, it sounds all wrong. We stammer and stumble, and anyone who's listening thinks, what a fool, she doesn't know what she's talking about, she ought to keep her mouth shut.' Everyone was laughing by now, but Kantabai continued, 'It's true, isn't it? And it's not just the fault of the men, it's our fault, too, we're also ready to agree with a speech because it's well delivered or reject another one because someone is too shy or timid to speak out boldly. So naturally in a mixed group men always carry the day. We don't stand a chance.'

'I haven't noticed *you* having much trouble expressing yourself, Kantabai,' smiled Mariam. 'But if that's what you're worried about, there's a simple solution. We'll ask Anant not to speak at meetings.'

'It's not so simple. Some women feel inhibited to speak if a man is present at all. I know this is something we must overcome, but in the meantime...'

'All right, then we'll ask him not to come to meetings at all.' But Mariam felt this to be unjust so she corrected herself, 'What I mean is, we'll invite him to participate in meetings only if the discussion is concerned with something he is doing, and we will also give him a chance to request attendance at meetings if he wants to say anything. Is that all right?'

There was a doubtful silence, and Mariam waited tensely. She desperately hoped that the suggestion would be accepted because that would mean a larger co-operative with the possibility of a greater variety of activities, including some non-traditional ones.

'If the rest of you don't have anything better to suggest, I think we have to accept this proposal,' Kantabai said finally. 'After all, it does give us a chance to involve more women.' She shared Mariam's dream of a large co-operative which would give many more women a chance not only to earn a living but to gain the confidence that they could do something worthwhile collectively. She had asked herself many times whether she could have done anything to prevent Mangal's death, and always concluded that alone she could have done nothing more for a woman who was victimised by so many people — both her husbands, the women in the basti, the rapists. But if there had been a collective at that time, maybe they could have helped her. Maybe.

'Will Geeta's husband be paid for selling the packets?' someone asked.

'He's not asking for any money,' said Geeta hurriedly.

'I don't think that's right,' Laila said warmly. She had been feeling dreadful about the negative response to Geeta's suggestion, and wanted to support her in some way. 'Everyone who works for us gets paid, so why shouldn't he? We can't ask people to spend time and effort without giving them anything in return.'

'That's true,' agreed Lakshmi. 'He'll have quite a difficult job. Maybe

Chandran should go along with him — then one of them can handle the food while the other looks after the money.'

'Is that agreed then?' asked Nirmala. 'Because if you have transport, I know of a few other places you could try.'

'That'll mean more than double our present output, won't it?' asked Preeti.

'If we're going to have more women working with us that won't be a problem,' responded Lakshmi.

'Maybe we could all earn a bit more too,' suggested Laila. 'Most of us have to support two or three people out of our earnings, and they aren't really enough for that.'

'Yes, and Kantabai has to save up so that she doesn't have to go on working for ever,' Geeta added.

The meeting went on far beyond the accustomed time as they tried to plan their work on a larger scale. Some women went home, fetched their children and continued the discussion. But it was impossible to finish everything. 'Let's carry on at the next meeting,' suggested Nirmala. 'Meanwhile I'll contact the people I thought of and find out whether they would like to have meals supplied. As far as possible we should have a precise estimate of how much extra we are going to produce.'

'Kantabai, why don't you bring along the women you mentioned? They should also be involved since they're going to be working with us.'

'And shouldn't we call Geeta's husband as well?'

'Yes, let's call all these people. We have a lot of work to do!'

CHAPTER 52

When you have been forced to grow up too fast, to look after others and take responsibility for them before you are ready for it, you have a tendency to be attracted to people who you feel will, on the contrary, look after you. Long after the strike was over Suzie still clung to Nirmala — not obtrusively but in small ways, mainly doing her little services like bringing her cups of tea, carrying things, or holding a place for her in the bus. She told herself that this was the only way she could express her gratitude to the woman who had saved her life and her mother's, but Nirmala could see that it was not just gratitude, she needed something more although it wasn't clear what. So she kept the girl with her as much as possible, involving her bit by bit in her own work, and Suzie was happy to find that she could help. It was a pleasant surprise to discover that trade union work was not simply a matter of attending meetings and making speeches, there were also things that a very shy person could do; and in any case shyness grew less important as you came to understand and share the vision which inspired the work. There were also other interesting things that Nirmala was involved in, like her work with the group of slum women. It was through this that Suzie first met Mariam, and later Kavita — two friendships which became increasingly important in her life.

After weeks of agonising, she finally decided to talk to Kavita about the problem which tormented her most — her secret love for Dr Mehta. Kavita was all sympathy, thinking that Suzie simply wanted to pour out her unhappiness and hoping that she feel better by talking about it. She thought to herself, poor girl, she's desperately miserable now, but she's young enough to recover; however she didn't actually say this, knowing that in her present state Suzie would not be likely to believe her. In fact there was not much she could say at all, nor did she feel it to be necessary, believing her role to be primarily one of listening and sympathizing. But Suzie was clearly dissatisfied with this, and for a long time Kavita couldn't understand what it was she wanted until she burst out despairingly, 'Isn't there *anything* I can do to stop myself from loving him? It makes me feel so wretchedly guilty, I know it's wrong and still I go on doing it — what's the matter with me?'

'But why?' Kavita asked, astonished. 'Why do you feel there's something the matter with you? Why do you feel guilty?'

'Because he's a married man, he belongs to someone else. It was all right so long as I didn't know, but once I knew I should have stopped thinking about him like that, shouldn't I? But I *can't*.'

'That's no reason to feel guilty,' said Kavita gently. 'What have you done wrong? Have you hurt anyone? Have you told him about it?'

'No!' Suzie was horrified at the thought. 'I haven't told anyone in the world until now. You're the first.'

'Well then, you haven't done anything to hurt anyone, so why should you feel guilty?'

'It's my thoughts, my feelings, which are bad. I've tried and tried, but it's no use.'

'I know — it's difficult to control our thoughts and feelings, isn't it? I think you should try, for your own sake, because you're getting hurt so much. Maybe it'll help if you make other friends, get involved in other activities which keep your mind away from him. But you certainly mustn't feel guilty, because that only hurts you without helping anyone else.'

Suzie thought about these words afterwards. Was Kavita right? She couldn't be sure. What did comfort her a little was the thought that she hadn't hurt anyone else — that was certainly true. And maybe it was a good idea to get involved in other things. She had already begun to do that, and would take it more seriously; maybe she should visit her old chawl and revive her friendships there. It was not easy to get away, but she could try at the weekends and during the daytime when her mother, heavily sedated and generally asleep most of the time, could do without her.

Seeing more people did help, but Kavita was right to think that Suzie's obsession would persist so long as she continued to meet Dr Mehta regularly and to be so dependent on him to mitigate her mother's terrible suffering. In fact, Suzie's mother was in such pain towards the end that in a way it was a relief when she finally died. She had refused to be taken to hospital; 'I don't want to die among strangers,' she said. 'Let me die in my own home with my own daughter beside me.' She remained lucid to the last although the injections made her drowsy, and with dogged persistence tried to achieve just one thing: to convey to Suzie how much she appreciated her tireless care. Her last words, whispered with lips which refused to smile despite all her efforts, were, 'Good girl. Good girl.' Over and over again Suzie felt grateful that her own patience had held out as long as there was need of it. It was true she had felt angry and resentful at times; but she had never expressed these feelings to her mother, she had never hit back at her in any way. If she had, how bad she would have felt now! As it was, she sat crying quietly while relatives and friends came and went, but there was no self-reproach or bitterness in her sorrow because she knew she had done all she could for her mother and that her mother had acknowledged it.

Her father didn't come for the funeral in response to her telegram. Instead he wrote her a long, emotional letter, treating her for the first time as an adult, trying to explain his behaviour over the past few years, begging forgiveness for leaving her to carry the burden of her sick mother alone. He announced his forthcoming marriage and wrote that he was sending a ticket for her to come and join him. Arriving less than two weeks after her mother's death, this letter once more sent Suzie's feelings into turmoil. To begin with, she had to adjust to her father's changed attitude to her and digest his confidences. It was clear he had suffered and was still suffering from guilt for what he had made her go through; perhaps in his mind he even exaggerated the wrong he had done, because he wrote as if the entire experience had been a negative one for her whereas this was not actually the case, there had been many rewarding moments. He pleaded that he wanted a chance to make up for this now, that he would give her a really good time once she came over, that she could continue her education or do whatever else she liked. It moved Suzie to discover that he was so afraid of losing her, and she found that on her own side she still loved him as much as ever. She couldn't bear to hurt him by refusing to go; yet her whole life was here, in Bombay — in Kuwait there was no one who knew or loved her except her father, even he would have a new wife by then, and who could tell what she would be like? 'What shall I do?' she asked Nirmala, unable to come to any decision.

'Don't decide immediately,' advised Nirmala. 'You haven't yet taken your annual leave, have you? Well, take it and go. See what the place is like, whether you would like to live there or not. If you like it there, write a letter of resignation; if not, you can come back.'

Mariam and Kavita had more decided opinions. 'Oh no!' exclaimed Mariam. 'Those Gulf countries are terrible for women. I don't think you should go.'

'Another thing which worries me is what will happen to Joe,' explained Suzie. 'He's much better now and doesn't want to stay with my uncle — in fact, I think the only reason he went on to drugs and left home was that he couldn't stand seeing what had happened to my mother. Now he wants to come back, but I don't know what he would do if I went away.'

'It would be nice if your brother came to stay with you,' remarked Kavita. 'I was thinking you must be rather lonely all on your own.'

'He's a very nice boy really, it's just that he got mixed up with a useless crowd and there was no one to prevent him. Now I think he'll be all right with me, but what will happen to him if I go? My father hasn't even thought of calling him.'

'Well, why don't you treat it as a holiday — go for a while and then come back?' suggested Kavita. 'Your father won't force you to stay if you don't want to, will he?'

'Oh no, he's only trying to be nice to me, he'll do anything I want. He's afraid I'm angry with him because he left me alone to look after my mother and didn't send money regularly.'

'He *should* be afraid!' exclaimed Mariam. 'Nirmala told me that you and your mother were starving during the strike. It would have been on his head if you had died.'

'Oh, you mustn't think he's a bad man,' said Suzie, not wanting her father to be judged so harshly. 'He really loves us a lot and he was very good to us until my mother fell ill.'

'If he really cares for you,' Kavita intervened hastily, 'I think he will realise that you'll be much happier here. You can go there to show him you're not angry, that's all right, but convince him that you want to come back.'

Yet two weeks later, at Sahar Airport, Suzie still hadn't quite made up her mind. Nirmala, Mariam and Kavita as well as Joe had come to see her off, and their presence made her all the more reluctant to leave. 'I'm going to miss you badly,' said Nirmala with real regret. 'So will the others. It's not often we get young people taking such an interest in union work, especially girls.'

'We'll miss you too, so mind you come back,' smiled Mariam.

Joe was feeling dreadfully awkward and shy with so many strange women, and sat silent and morose while Suzie went to check in her luggage. The immigration call for her flight had already been announced when she came back to say her final good-byes. Joe jumped up and hugged her tightly whispering, 'I can't last out more than a few weeks longer with Uncle, Suze, so you'd better come back soon!'

The others kissed her and watched as she walked away from them. Just as she was about to pass out of sight she turned to wave and saw the four smiling faces blurred through her tears. Without warning, she turned and ran back at top speed, and they gathered round her in concern as she shot out through the barrier again. 'What's wrong?' 'Forgotten something?'

'I'm coming back,' she panted. 'I'll return before my leave expires.'

'Of course!'

'Good girl!'

'We'll come to meet you.'

The women kissed her once again and Joe, smiling, gave her the thumbs-up sign. 'You be a good boy,' she said, patting him on the head, 'otherwise I may change my mind.'

This time when she turned back, the faces were not quite so blurred. She waved and walked on, wondering what it would be like to meet her father after all that time.

CHAPTER 53

Anant had felt strange when he first went to contact his former comrades and find out about orders for meals; that ghostly feeling came upon him again, and he couldn't help noticing that they looked at him oddly, as at someone who was already dead. Of course, they had every reason to do so, he reflected; they were out in the world, battling against the daily harassment and injustice of work in small-scale industry, while he had withdrawn from everything, living the life of a recluse. Almost everyone who had lost a job at Adarsh had by now found employment of some sort. As far as they were concerned, he was indeed dead.

Now, however, it seemed that he had been reincarnated and had come back to life in a new role. Standing outside the entrance of the industrial estate every working day from eleven o'clock to one-thirty, he met all those who could rarely meet one another because their lunch breaks were staggered. His lunch stall, ostensibly popular because of the quality of the food, also drew workers for a very different reason. He had become a kind of living newsletter, and the crowd round his stall seemed to overcome, if only symbolically, the dreadful sense of isolation which was their greatest weakness. He could not claim to be active, couldn't even imagine in the present circumstances what *being active* would mean; but he hoped he wasn't being dishonest with himself when he felt that he was, in some marginal way, useful.

That was one attraction of his new job, but not the only one. An unexpected bonus was that the women had insisted he should be paid for his work. At first he had refused, fearing they might think he had suggested the idea only in order to make money out of it; but once he had been persuaded otherwise he was grateful for the chance of contributing to the household income and lightening the burden on Geeta. An even more unexpected benefit was his steadily developing friendship with his little assistant Chandran. It had really started with an incident which never failed to make Anant smile when he thought of it. One day when he came to pick up the food on his bicycle he met Chandran on the pathway in great distress on the verge of tears. 'What's wrong?' he asked. Chandran pointed. 'It's those boys,' he replied. 'Look what they're doing. They've tied that pigeon's feet together with a piece of string, and they keep frightening it to make it try and fly. If it gets off the ground at all, they pull it down with the string. I asked them, how would *you* like it if someone tied your legs together and chased and pulled you, but they wouldn't listen, they only laughed. How can I fight them? I'm not strong enough. Look! they are doing it again! Oh, I'm sure it will die if they keep doing that,' and he started to cry in earnest. Anant walked up to see what was going on. 'You ought to be ashamed of yourselves,' he said with all the sternness he could muster, 'two big boys like you persecuting a little pigeon. Leave it alone!' The boys drew back and he caught hold of the string. This was the most difficult part because the bird was so terrified that it kept thrashing about madly and he was afraid it would be seriously injured. But he finally managed to undo the knot and stood watching until it had recovered its strength sufficiently to fly away.

Chandran had been watching the whole scene, but it was only later that Anant realised what an impact it had on him. As he was taking the containers into the kitchen to be washed, he overheard the child giving his mother a graphic account of the incident, and found to his amusement that in the story he had gained heroic proportions and become a model of courage, goodness and compassion. On his own he laughed rather ruefully at the transformation of Anant the militant into a rescuer of pigeons in distress, but this single action had more significance for his future than he could possibly have guessed. Previously, Chandran had been shy and silent with him, a willing helper but nothing more. He was still shy, but he slowly began to talk to Anant, confiding to him thoughts and experiences which astonished and sometimes shocked him. These confidences touched Anant all the more because he had never succeeded in building up any such intimacy with his own daughter, so that the world of children had until then been remote and unknown to him. There was still much that puzzled him. For example, Chandran was an intelligent listener to all the conversations which went on around the food stall, and often asked questions which indicated a good grasp of what went on in the factories they were talking about; yet at other times he would say things which seemed to come straight from some region of fantasy miles away from the world which Anant knew. Was the child strange? Or were all children like this? He had no idea. But little by little, imperceptibly, he came to cherish as something infinitely precious the short bicycle rides during which the little boy rode the bar in front of him.

One day, on the way back, Chandran stopped him and got off. 'You want to go to the bathroom?' asked Anant, because they were passing the waste land which was used by people from both slums as a communal toilet.

'No, I want to show you something,' replied Chandran. Mystified, Anant followed him to a rather inaccessible corner. 'Look,' he pointed. There in front of them was a tiny plot of green plants, some flowering, some with the flowers already turning into pods. 'What are they?' asked Anant smiling, because the sight was a pleasant one.

'Different kinds of dals. Look, I think those are chana, and I know these are moong because I planted some here. My friend and I water them twice a day and I wash the leaves when they get dusty.' Chandran was smiling with pride and pleasure, but suddenly his smile vanished and he looked apprehensive. 'I didn't steal them,' he said, looking anxiously at Anant. 'I only took the ones which spilled out while they were being washed. You know, some always fall out, and it's so sad that they just go into the drain and rot away. It's much nicer for them to be in the earth where they can grow.'

Anant squatted down, put his arm round the boy and drew him closer, but said nothing because there was an awkward tension in his throat. There was something miraculous about this bright patch of green shining out amidst the dirt, rubble and excrement. But it was even more miraculous, surely, that amidst the sordid violence of Patthar Basti a consciousness could have been born full of such tenderness towards all living things?

Chandran shyly and timidly put his hand on Anant's shoulder and looked down wonderingly at the greying head which was now lower than his own. This was a miracle for him, too. Most of his life he had been surrounded by women, and until Anant came into it he had never been physically so close to a man without feeling sick with terror.

'It's a lovely garden,' Anant said at last, 'and I think you'll be able to take in your harvest before the rains. It's good that you have planted different kinds of dals — a mixture of dals makes a better diet than just one kind.'

'Why?'

'Well, you see, whatever you eat has to be broken down inside you and burned up to give you energy or put together in a different way to build up your body. Dals have protein which you need to build up your body, but no single dal has all the different bits which are necessary. Different dals have different bits, and if you mix them they all fit together.'

Chandran, who had been listening intently, sighed. 'I wish I could learn about such things,' he said sadly. 'But I don't get a chance to go to school at all now because I have to work.'

'I can tell you about them,' said Anant, confident from his experience with Geeta that he could be a good teacher. 'If you really want to learn, nothing should stop you. But I'll have to get you some books...' He broke off, musing. A vague, fantastic idea was entering his mind. The vision was still the one he had shared with Shaheed, but mightn't there be other ways of working towards it? That idea... was it just a fantasy or a real possibility? He should discuss it with Ranjan — perhaps Ranjan would be able to tell him.

CHAPTER 54

It must have been nearly ten o'clock at night, but S.T. Road was still full of life as Renu, who had already been walking for more than fifteen minutes, turned into the far end of it on her way home. She was returning from a long discussion with Mohan, a friend of one of their neighbours in Sheetal Nagar. He must have noticed her on his visits to the basti and made enquiries about her, because one day, completely unexpectedly, their neighbour had conveyed a proposal of marriage from him. Renu was flattered and amused, her sense of adventure stirred; she found out his address and one evening took the bus to his place to talk about the proposition. She left promising to give him a definite reply within a week, but she knew that for her own peace of mind it would be necessary to make a decision much sooner than that.

The prospect was attractive, certainly: a normal life, a husband who was devoted to her, children who had a father — all this was within her reach, she had only to say one word to possess it. And yet, when she had all but made up her mind, the horror of her memories gripped and paralysed her. Hadn't Sunder been devoted to her too, sworn to love her for the rest of his life? And she had known such happiness in surrendering herself to him that it seemed no cloud could touch her future. What had happened to it all? What had she done to lose his love? True, she had become pregnant; yet ignorant as she was, she knew that was something they were both responsible for, not she alone. But she had wanted to keep the baby — that was the decision she made on her own which had dealt a death-blow to her happiness. She had gone with him to a woman whom he seemed to know already, watched while he haggled over the price — the price of her baby, the baby she wanted so much — when suddenly in a blinding flash it was clear to her that this was something she would never agree to. She was already halfway down the road before he noticed her absence and came running after her, furious.

Yes, that was when her life had begun falling to pieces. Why had she done it, why was she so stubborn even when her happiness itself was at stake? After he left her for the last time, once she had given up hope of ever seeing him again, she kept tormenting herself with the thought that it was all her fault. If only she had listened to him, had given in to his pleading, his threats, everything would have been all right. She would have lost her baby, but he would have continued to love her and life would have gone on as before. Or would it? Looking back, she couldn't find it in her heart to regret what she had done, in spite of all the trouble it had landed her in. She had wanted the baby so much, and yet her feelings didn't seem to count for him at all. What did his love for her mean, then? In fact did she, as a person, figure in his mind at all? Apparently not, since the first time — the only time — she had expressed a desire which was not directed towards him, he had been incredulous at first and then recoiled from her with such revulsion that she in her turn was stunned. He hadn't loved her at all, then; he only loved her love for him, her devotion to him. Through her, he had loved himself. Maybe he hadn't known it, maybe he genuinely thought that he loved her; even now, after all she had been through, Renu couldn't bring herself to believe that he had consciously, cold-bloodedly deceived her, taken advantage of her innocence and inexperience. But did it matter anyway? The end result was the same: he didn't really love her. It would have made no difference if she had gone through with the abortion — in fact, things would have been much worse; she would have had to cope with his withdrawal from her without any baby to look forward to, and at a time when she was suffering from the terrible depression of an unwanted abortion. She would have committed suicide for sure! No, she had been quite right to be stubborn, some instinct for survival must have directed her.

She had never been out alone so late before, and there was still a fairly long way to go. She should have accepted Mohan's offer to accompany her home after all. But then she would have had to talk to him, whereas she desperately needed to be alone to think things over by herself — that, after all, was why she had chosen to walk rather than take the bus: it was easy to think while you were walking, whereas there was perpetual distraction in waiting for a bus, pushing your way on to it, watching for a seat, watching out for your stop so you didn't get carried past it. No chance to think with all that going on. Besides, there was no danger here; the streets were relatively well-lit and crowded until late at night, women walked about alone without attracting undue attention. That slight spasm of fear had been an irrational reflex, a hangover from her village days when they had dinned it into her head that she should never be out alone after dark. They had tried so hard to protect her from life, but they still hadn't managed to save her from getting hurt. Well, it was a good thing Mohan wasn't with her; he would have spoiled everything. It's nice to be alone in the dark on a crowded street; you can let your mind roam where it will without paying attention to anyone, and yet you are safe, You don't have to be on the alert for shadowy figures or menacing footsteps.

Mohan, now, he was a different sort from Sunder's type. A steady man, with a steady job. Never got drunk, never got violent. You couldn't imagine him getting a girl pregnant and then leaving her in the lurch. Not quite conventional either: few men would have agreed to marry a girl with an illegitimate child and adopt the child as his own. You could have a quiet, decent life with a man like that. You would not need to struggle all the time, constantly protect yourself from the innuendos, the attacks on your personality which hurt so much although you knew they were absurd.

Renu took a good look at the imaginary future ahead of her, and was surprised to find herself completely unmoved. When she left Mohan she had thought the offer tempting, and it was only her habit of caution which prompted her to postpone the decision until she had thought it over a little longer. But now, when she surveyed this future, it seemed to stretch out before her, dreary and monotonous. Mohan was very clear about what he wanted: a good wife, a good mother to his children, a good housewife. Of course she could go out to work if she wanted to; he wouldn't even prevent her from seeing her friends so long as she didn't neglect her domestic duties. A peaceful, well-ordered life with a measured amount of freedom — much better than most women had, much better than she could have dared to hope for after the disastrous turn her life had taken. So what was holding her back?

She walked on for a while, trying to puzzle it out. Not far to go now — within five minutes she would be back with Laila. Her pace quickened in anticipation. Laila... Laila had spoiled her, that's what was holding her back! Laila asked nothing of her, just accepted her as she was. In Laila's home she had no conventional role to play — indeed, according to convention Renu had no business to be there at all. But she could feel absolute security in the relationship because she knew that Laila loved her not for what she did or did not do, not for this or that quality imaginary or real, but simply because she was herself, Renu. In the short time they had stayed together they had developed an intimacy which a lifetime with

Mohan could never develop. They could talk together, cry together, share each other's deepest feelings without any sense of inhibition or fear of being hurt. Best of all they could enjoy themselves, laugh together until they were speechless and limp. Renu smiled involuntarily as she thought of the fun they had had — which they could go on having. She must have been mad to think of giving all this up. Of course other people, who always saw things upside down, would say that she was mad to refuse Mohan's offer. But her mind was made up: she already had what she wanted and she was going to hang on to it.

Renu felt like celebrating — she bought some cheap sweets at the corner stall which was still open with the bus fare she had saved, and walked up to the hut feeling euphoric. She knocked.

'Renu?' through the closed door.

'Yes, it's me, open up fast!'

Laila felt her heart sink, sensing the elation in Renu's voice. That could mean only one thing — she must have accepted his offer. She took a long time unbolting the door, struggling to control herself and to look normal. It was useless. Laila could never manage to hide the fact that she had been crying. Not only her eyes — which she could conceal by looking downwards — but also the tip of her nose, that embarrassingly conspicuous part of her face, would grow bright red at the slightest hint of tears, and remain red after she had stopped crying. Renu immediately saw that something was wrong, and her face changed at once. 'You've been crying! What's the matter?' she asked anxiously. 'One of the children... had an accident? Sick?'

Laila made an effort and gave a weak smile. 'No, no, the children are fine. Just give me some time — tell me your news first and then afterwards I'll tell you. Let's eat, I was waiting for you.' Renu was still worried, but decided not to press Laila. Give her time, she thought, she's sure to tell me later of her own accord, she isn't capable of hiding anything from me. So she sat down to her meal and began to describe in detail her meeting with Mohan while Laila tried to concentrate on her food in order to hide her impatience and anxiety. When Renu came to the point where she parted from him saying that she would think it over, Laila broke in, 'Then you didn't accept? Why not?' She broke off in confusion; she hadn't intended to speak at all, and the voice which emerged scarcely sounded like hers. But Renu didn't seem to have noticed anything. She paused a few moments before replying.

'I don't know exactly what prevented me from accepting there and then. Some feeling of uneasiness, I suppose. But on the way I thought hard about it, and I'm glad I didn't commit myself.'

'Meaning?' This time Laila was almost as startled as if a third person had unexpectedly joined the conversation. She really ought to control herself a little better! But Renu continued serenely, thoughtfully.

'Meaning, I decided I didn't particularly want to get married to him. I would have to give up this life which I enjoy so much, and wouldn't be getting anything in return. It would be different if I had no children. Maybe then I would have decided to get married. But as it is, I have children. I even have a daughter.' She smiled at Laila. 'Besides, all he wants is a wife. Any number of other women could play that part as well as I could, or better. I don't want to be like that. I mean, I want to be someone special, someone without a substitute. No, that's not what I mean, that sounds as if I'm terribly conceited. What I mean is... you know what I mean, don't you, Laila?'

Laila suddenly smiled and nodded, a wave of joy going through her. 'I know,' she said softly, 'I know exactly what you mean. It's not conceit. You *are* different from everyone else, and you want to have at least one person in the world who appreciates that. Someone who would not be able to replace you if ever you were lost to... to that person.' She hesitated, and continued still more softly, 'That's why I was crying when you came. Because I thought I had lost you. I would never have been able to replace you if I had. I didn't want to tell you in case it made you feel bad about leaving me.'

Of course! Now that she had said it, it sounded so obvious. Yet it hadn't occurred to Renu until now. 'How silly you are!' she laughed, but her voice was gentle and so was her gesture. 'What made you so sure that I would accept? Though it's true,' she added thoughtfully, 'it never entered my head that you would be so upset. Still, it was the thought of you which ultimately tipped the balance. Not the thought of what you would be losing, but the thought of what I would be losing.'

'Well, if you thought a bit longer you'd realise that you wouldn't be losing anything unless I, too, had something to lose. It's only because you mean so much to me that you would be losing something by leaving. But that doesn't matter now. The only important thing is that you are staying.'

The whole room seemed to have filled with a warm glow of happiness. Both of them sat in silence for a while, unwilling to break the spell. Finally Renu got up saying, 'I don't feel like going to sleep at once, do you? Let's have some tea instead — look, I brought some sweets to go with it.'

'You and your sweets!' laughed Laila. 'When will you ever grow up?' But she ate her share all the same — and enjoyed it too.

CHAPTER 55

A sudden heavy shower of rain forced Anant and Chandran to take shelter on their way back from the industrial estate. It was only the last day of May, not yet time for the monsoon, but this was unusually heavy for a pre-monsoon shower. Lucky it's after the lunch break, thought Anant, now there's no hurry, we can wait here until it stops. The unending drops of water were conducive to dreaming, and he had a lot to dream about. The day before, he had had a long talk with Ranjan, and he went through it in his mind. How strange that had been! His only thought at first was to discuss his idea, find out whether Ranjan would think it mad and impossible or something worth trying to do: the idea of starting a school for children like Chandran and Shahnaz and so many others, working children who could not afford to give up their jobs. It could not, of course, be a conventional school with conventional hours. The children would have to be encouraged to do as much as possible on their own, but he would be there to help them.

Ranjan responded with an enthusiasm which was beyond his wildest expectations. It was a marvellous idea, he said; he would do everything he could to help, from raising money and looking for a place to working out the curriculum and a method of teaching. His wife would help, too — she was very good with children and had been wanting to write for them; she would certainly collaborate in the venture. In fact he would like his own children to attend such a school.

Rather bewildered, Anant pointed out that they would then find it difficult to fit back into the normal system and go on to a higher education; this was meant to be a substitute for normal school, not an alternative — although an alternative was of course necessary and should be worked out.

'You're absolutely right,' Ranjan agreed. 'My daughters are always complaining about the ridiculous things they are taught in school. Working out an alternative is certainly a much bigger task, but even in your experiment we can try to do that, can't we? We can try to give your little working children a better education than they would get in a conventional school!'

Then had followed, through a transition which he couldn't quite remember, that incredible conversation. Up to now Ranjan had been a rather remote figure to Anant — a university professor or whatever he was, after all, was not the sort of person you would expect to be intimate with. So it came as a shock to him to find that Ranjan had been just as shattered by Shaheed's death, and if possible even more demoralized and depressed in the subsequent period. It seemed unbelievable that someone like Ranjan should have such feelings and, moreover, that he should communicate them to Anant. Strangest of all to Anant was to find himself reflecting aloud on how difficult he had found it to think at all when he came back and found Shaheed dead; they had got so used to discussing everything, their thought-processes were so closely interlinked, that without Shaheed Anant felt mentally paralysed, only half a person. And, he added shyly, his wife had helped him a lot. 'Yes yes,' Ranjan had said eagerly, 'I understand exactly what you mean. We don't realise how much we depend on our wives, how important they are to us, until something like that happens.' Amazing! Anant went away with his thoughts in a whirl. However much he told himself that the idea was absurd, he couldn't escape the conclusion that this man was asking for his friendship. It was difficult to identify Ranjan as that self-sufficient, invulnerable person who had earlier run their study circles. What had changed? Who had changed? It was impossible to understand it all. But it was pleasant, all the same, to think about it. Especially since he had pledged his full support to the idea of the school, so that Anant could count on his active collaboration in making it a concrete reality.

Chandran brought Anant back to the present by persistently pulling at his hand. 'Let's go,' he said. 'The rain has stopped.' It was not quite true:

the drops were still falling, but they were rapidly thinning and the sun was shining again. Anant deeply breathed in the fresh smell of earth after the first rain. Everything looked cleaner and brighter after the shower, but Chandran was too anxious about something to appreciate any of this. 'Oh please let's go soon,' he said. 'I want to see my garden.' Anant was surprised but rode off with Chandran and parked the bicycle in the usual place.

'What's the matter?' he asked as they made their way to the plot.

'I'm so worried that the rain may have spoiled my pods,' explained Chandran. 'I didn't pick them because they're not quite ripe yet, and I wasn't expecting it to rain for at least another week.'

'Oh no, there's no need to worry about that,' said Anant as they reached the little plot, the drops of water on the leaves now sparkling in the bright sunlight. 'Look, the rain has done them good, they're looking finer than ever, and the sun will dry out the pods in no time.'

'Then you don't think they'll get mouldy?'

'Not at all. Just leave them a few more days, then they'll be ready to pick. You're a first class farmer, my son, you should have the whole of this ground to grow your crops.'

Chandran looked up at him and laughed. 'Where would we go to the toilet then?' he asked.

'We could build proper toilets for ourselves,' replied Anant. 'Better still, we could build proper houses with toilets in each one.'

'That would be great!' said Chandran. 'Just think what I could do if I had this whole ground — I would grow creepers and trees, fruit and flowers and vegetables and food-grains — every single plant in the world!'

Anant smiled. He found it hard to imagine this wasteland in the midst of brick and concrete being converted into a jungle full of exotic plants, but if Chandran could see it so clearly, why not?

GLOSSARY

agarbatti	incense-stick
amma	mother
ari	exclamation
bai	woman, lady
bap ri	exclamation
basti	shanty-town
behen	sister
bhabi	sister-in-law
bhai	brother
bhaji	vegetable dish
chapati	flat round cake of unleavened bread
chappals	Indian sandals or slippers
churidar-kameez	matching suit of tunic and trousers which are close-fitting round the calves
D.A.	Dearness Allowance, an allowance linked to the cost of living
dada	leader of a lumpen gang
dal	pulses (lentils, chick-peas, etc.)
dharna	a sit-down protest
dhobi	person who washes clothes for a living
E.S.I.S.	State Insurance Scheme
G.B.M.	General Body Meeting
gherao	militant form of action where workers physically surround employers or managers and press for their demands
goonda	thug
H.S.C.	Higher School Certificate — a public exam taken at the age of 17-18 years
ji	suffix denoting respect
kurta	tunic-like shirt
lathi	long truncheon or baton
maoshi	aunt
murdabad	down with or death to
paisa	one hundredth of a rupee
pallu	the end of a sari which is left loose
Parsi	a community of Zoroastrians

Ramayana	a classical epic
salwar-kameez	matching suit of tunic and baggy trousers
S.S.C.	Senior School Certificate — a public exam taken at the age of 15-16 years
tai	elder sister
teeka	spot painted on forehead
U.P.	Uttar Pradesh, a state in the north of India

CHARACTERS (in alphabetical order)

Anant	lives in Sheetal Nagar, works in Adarsh Garments. Husband of Geeta, father of Sindhu
Arvind	lives in Sheetal Nagar. Self-employed carpenter. Father of Lalita
Asha	eldest daughter of Kavita and Ranjan
Ashok	works in Adarsh Garments
Chandran	son of Lakshmi and Shetty
Farida	daughter of Laila and Shaheed
Ganesh	works in Adarsh Garments. Husband of Shobha
Geeta	lives in Sheetal Nagar. Wife of Anant. Mother of Sindhu
Gopal	victimised worker who becomes a trade union activist
Ishaq	son of Laila and Shaheed
Jayshree	works at Jackson Pharmaceuticals
Joe	brother of Suzie
Jyoti	works at Jackson Pharmaceuticals
Kamal	evicted from Dhobi Basti. Sister-in-law of Muktabai's husband
Kantabai	lives in Patthar Basti. Works as a domestic servant
Kavita	lives in a flat next to the one where Renu works. Wife of Ranjan, mother of Asha, Shanta and Sunil
Kelkar	a professional unionist
Laila	lives in Sheetal Nagar. Wife of Shaheed, mother of Ishaq and Farida
Lakshmi	lives in Patthar Basti. Wife of Shetty, mother of Chandran and Sanjeevani

Lalita	lives in Sheetal Nagar, works in the same workshop as Preeti. Daughter of Arvind
Mangal	lives in Patthar Basti with Ramesh
Mariam	activist among slum women and trade unions
Dr Mehta	Suzie's mother's doctor
Mohan	wants to marry Renu
Muktabai	lives in Sheetal Nagar. Wife of Kamal's brother-in-law
Nirmala	trade unionist at Jackson Pharmaceuticals
Pauline	works at Jackson Pharmaceuticals
Pillai	general secretary of union at Jackson Pharmaceuticals
Preeti	lives in Patthar Basti. Works in the same workshop as Lalita
Ramesh	lives in Patthar Basti with Mangal. Works as a truck driver
Ranjan	university lecturer and political activist. Husband of Kavita, father of Asha, Shanta and Sunil
Renu	works as a domestic servant in the flat next to Kavita's. Cousin-sister of Shyam
Salma	lives in Patthar Basti. Mother of Shahnaz
Sanjeevani	daughter of Lakshmi and Shetty
Sarita	works at the same workshop as Lalita and Preeti
Seema	works at the same workshop as Lalita and Preeti
Shaheed	lives in Sheetal Nagar, works in Adarsh Garments. Husband of Laila, father of Ishaq and Farida
Shahnaz	daughter of Salma
Shanta	second daughter of Kavita and Ranjan
Shetty	lives in Patthar Basti, local dada. Husband of Lakshmi, father of Chandran and Sanjeevani
Shobha	wife of Ganesh
Shyam	keeps a vegetable stall. Cousin-brother of Renu
Sindhu	daughter of Geeta and Anant
Sunder	friend of Shyam, boy-friend of Renu
Sunil	baby son of Kavita and Ranjan
Suzie	works at Jackson Pharmaceuticals. Sister of Joe
Teresa	works at Jackson Pharmaceuticals
Vasanta	second wife of Shetty
Verma	owner of Adarsh Garments
Yasmine	works at the same workshop as Lalita and Preeti